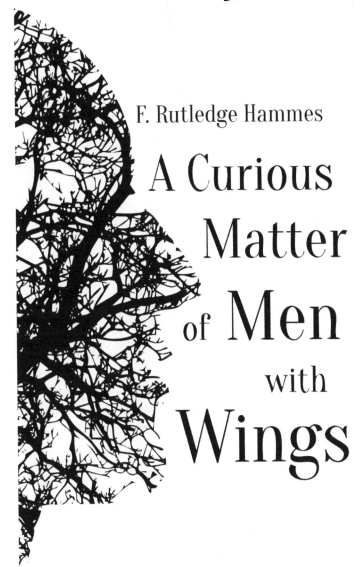

F. Rutledge Hammes

A Curious Matter of Men with Wings

Praise

"A Curious Matter of Men with Wings *is where magic comes to life in a bold story that celebrates the Gullah world of the South Carolina Sea Islands. With lyrical prose, the novel takes us into a hidden realm where life is still enchanted, and storytelling abounds. In these pages, the transfixing Walpole family grapples with loss, the madness of grief, and ultimately healing, while surrounded by a community whose only salvation lies in the ties that bind them."*
— *Sue Monk Kidd,* **New York Times** *bestselling author of* **The Secret Life of Bees** *and* **The Invention of Wings**

"*Atmospheric, penetrating and imaginative,* A Curious Matter of Men with Wings *is a story that takes us on a journey to both the rich lands of the Sea Islands and the richer lands of the heart. With a story layered in mythology, fairy tales, and Gullah folklore, Hammes enchants. As the mystery of the Flying People unfolds, two cultures come together and show us what we can be at our very best."*
— *Patti Callahan Henry,* **New York Times** *bestselling author of* **Becoming Mrs. Lewis** *and* **The Bookshop at Water's End**

"*Hammes flat-out dropped this northern boy into the mud, in with the bugs, the birds, the sweat, the salt, the booze, and, for sure, the water of coastal South Carolina. This sweaty, lovely novel is set only a couple of hundred miles*

from where I now sit, but it may as well be another world. Or some kind of dream. Because this is a book that's as real as a burning tree in the woods but also somehow a timeless, gauzy mystery, too, in which men fly and women can be owls. I put down this book only to wipe my brow, drink a glass of something cold, and dream about a family and a secret little town as American and as real as any I've read in a long time. This is a book of secrets, mystery, water, and loss, and I'll be thinking of these people, and their ways, until the tides stop."
—Seth Sawyers, editor at **The Baltimore Review**

"Part Southern Gothic, part magical realism, part folklore, A Curious Matter of Men with Wings is a dazzling literary debut. F. Rutledge Hammes joins the ranks of contemporaries Jennifer Egan and Daniel Wallace with his original coming of age story. Set on an isolated South Carolina barrier island, it reminds us what we all miss living indoors, disconnected from the natural world. Thank you, F. Rutledge Hammes, for describing the things that matter most."
—Marjory Wentworth, **South Carolina Poet Laureate**

"A Curious Matter of Men with Wings is a deeply felt and masterfully crafted novel about one family's coming to terms with a sudden loss—steeped in mystery—amidst the wounds and the secret wonders of the South Carolina Sea Islands. It's been a long time since a novel has lifted me off the ground like this one did. Congratulations to F. Rutledge Hammes, who has written a debut that is nothing short of stunning."
—Beth Webb Hart, **bestselling author of Moon Over Edisto**

"F. Rutledge Hammes is that rare new voice you run across once or maybe twice in a lifetime. His spectacular debut novel, A Curious Matter of Men with Wings, soars! It is a coming of age cautionary tale about power. It's a mystery and a love story wrapped up in humidity and pluff mud, and it is as fascinating as it is addicting. In the Lowcountry, things are never quite what they seem, and what if all those old Gullah superstitions were true? Don't miss this one. I cannot wait to see what he comes up with next. Congratulations, Mr. Hammes! Bravo!"
—Dorothea Benton Frank, New York Times bestselling author of By Invitation Only and Same Beach, Next Year

"World, meet F. Rutledge Hammes with his astonishing debut A Curious Matter of Men with Wings. In a potpourri of Southern Gothic fused with the magical, levitating elements of something Marquezian, Hammes writes in prose beautiful like Conroy, quirky like Irving as he offers up the heartrending story of the Walpole family. As eccentric as they are heartbreaking, children tell the tale, and Hammes strings his plots taut across the valley of the novel's central mystery — the Flying Men. Gullah tradition, the aching beauty of South Carolina's Lowcountry, a narrative voice thick as sea island humidity, this novel is unlike any I've ever read. I couldn't put it down. Hammes writes like the angels he describes."
—Sean Scapellato, Novello Literary Award finalist, and contributing writer in Our Prince of Scribes: Writers Remember Pat Conroy

"With all the pleasures of old-fashioned storytelling, F. Rutledge Hammes's A Curious Matter of Men with Wings *is a novel by a writer who knows much about the Lowcountry, and much about love."*
—*Janet Peery, National Book Award finalist, and* **author of The River Beyond the World**

"*If you truly want to know the Lowcountry, A Curious Matter of Men with Wings is a uniquely wondrous must-read. Here we experience the loves, the losses, the day-to-day lives of the Gullah-Geechee folk on a barrier island off Charleston through the eyes, ears, noses, through the hearts, minds and imaginations of a family. It reminds me of Julie Dash's* Daughters of the Dust *... that's how good he is, and how good this book is. The language, the characters, it's all magically evocative. Hammes is so good that readers will inhabit the minds and imaginations of these characters just as he did."*
—*Bernie Schein, author of* **Famous All Over Town** *and* **If Holden Caulfield Were in My Classroom**

"*I love the wise old storyteller voice, and Hammes's attention to place and detail is nothing short of magical."*
—*Sheri Reynolds,* **New York Times** *bestselling author of* **Rapture of Canaan**

"A Curious Matter of Men with Wings *is a passionate first novel by a writer who knows well the coastal waters of South Carolina, a writer who understands the ebb and flow of daily life on those islands and the moon glow of Gullah myth. The Walpole family, like the Dead clan in Toni Morrison's* Song of Solomon, *struggles to find a way to*

soar above heartache and grief without leaving everything they love behind. The novel imparts an important lesson — that 'love enters through the door it exits'. A Curious Matter of Men with Wings *tracks the road that leads from curiosity to faith and, ultimately, to love.*"
—Michael Pearson, *author of* Dreaming of Columbus *and* Shohola Falls

"*A book to devour, and a Lowcountry must-read.* A Curious Matter of Men with Wings *is a brilliant and compelling debut, an enticing lure into the lush culture of Lowcountry storytelling. With richly drawn characters and a magical island setting, this book will make you a believer in the veracity of Gullah folklore passed down for centuries. Hammes skillfully whisks the reader along the tale's swift and shifting air currents—of love and of loss—as if on wings.*"
—Nicole Seitz, *author of* The Cage-maker *and* The Spirit of Sweetgrass, *and co-editor of* Our Prince of Scribes: Writers Remember Pat Conroy

"*If Gabriel Garcia Marquez and Pat Conroy met in a bar and drank their way to dawn, the barkeep would have overheard a story that went something like this. Part family saga, part historical mythology,* A Curious Matter of Men with Wings *brings the magic of the Lowcountry to life. F. Rutledge Hammes has written an utterly readable and charming debut that will carry you away.*"
—*Danielle DeTiberus, SC Academy of Authors Poetry Fellow*

"This wonderful debut novel is a paean to the beauty, mystery, and mysticism of the South Carolina Lowcountry. Drawing on Gullah legends and set among the thousands of uninhabited islands off the South Carolina coast, A Curious Matter of Men with Wings is part love story, part fable, and part saga that chronicles the lives, legends, and customs of the people who live on those little-known islands."
—J. E. Thompson, author of The Girl from Felony Bay

"What a singular, weird, fascinating and satisfying book this is. A Curious Matter of Men with Wings satisfies my taste for a truly unique experience. You've never read anything like this before, I promise. It's a story that paints unexpected, but vivid, photos. Is it science fiction? Fantasy? Long-form poetry? You'll have to read to find out. The book is also impressive in its distinct portrait of the Lowcountry and lure of Gullah culture."
—Marcus Amaker, Poet Laureate of Charleston, SC

"A mysterious disappearance sets A Curious Matter of Men with Wings in motion, but the novel takes flight in so many ways, throwing a bright light upon sibling relationships, family secrets, first romances, and the sometimes strange and inexplicable ways we deal with loss, that it is all you can do to hang on and see where the next gorgeously-written page will take you. With more sympathy and warmth than seems fashionable in contemporary fiction, this is a book that will stay with you for a long, long time. Memorable and inventive, with energy to spare."
—Anthony Varallo, author of Everyone Was There

SFK
PRESS

STK
PRESS

Published by
Southern Fried Karma, LLC
Atlanta, GA
www.sfkpress.com

Books are available in quantity for promotional or premium use. For information, email pr@sfkmultimedia.com.

ISBN: 978-1-7325398-2-2
eISBN: 978-1-7325398-3-9
Library of Congress Control Number: 2018950832

Cover design by Olivia M. Croom.
Cover art: sunset image by pixabay.com/12019; man made of branches by pixabay.com/GDJ.
Printed in the United States of America.

To my mother, Ruth-Anne G. Hammes, my father, Burke Hammes, and my grandmother, Ruth Champion Glover, each of whom instilled in me a love of story, a lifelong passion for all the tales of magic and beauty and suffering that is at the heart of my home, the South Carolina Lowcountry.

Chapter One

NEARLY SIX MONTHS IN NOW, AND THE INVESTIGATIONS WERE still ongoing, though not a one of them was any closer to uncovering the truth. And that was how it happened that a certain number of eyewitnesses with a certain kind of story to tell started to come forward and, at town hall hearings, swore—hand to God—to seeing flocks of winged men in the sky. And it didn't take long for the vast majority of those privy to these accounts to find it suspect that these "Flying Men," as they came to be called, were only spotted along the coast when someone had drowned. The headlines in the papers only got more and more ominous with each passing day, issuing their generally vague warnings to the public at large, like The Flying Men Strike Again! and Death from Above. And so it was that all those who resided in Charleston clear down to the Georgia coast reverted to whispering about what someone or another swore they had seen flying in the sky.

Both Bohicket Walpole and his little brother Ley had grown up hearing similar stories told in their home. Similar in that their father told them the stories like they were true, like he himself had seen such things, and he swore they were true. Their father spoke always of the strange goings-on he'd witnessed while living on those coastal South Carolina islands, islands so remote they were yet unnamed, islands so isolated neither Bohicket nor Ley had ever even seen a road, much less a car, seeing as no one—save for their own family and the people of the small Gullah village just inland across the narrow strait—had ever dared to venture out so far. And while their father would've gladly crossed his heart and hoped to die, if only to convince them what he had told them was true, neither Bohicket nor Ley (now eighteen and sixteen years old respectively) ever actually believed that he had met a man with wings, as he so adamantly claimed he had. That is, until late one evening, when their little sister was carried away into the sky.

It was the weekend, and it was summertime, which meant the recreational boaters were out in droves, exploring the endless waterways up and down the Lowcountry, tossing back cases of beers and casting out nets or just looking for the perfect spot to jump in and cool off. Just like they did every weekend, right around dusk, Bohicket and Ley were headed down to the johnboat, readying themselves for another evening of hunting down boaters and pillaging their wares.

By the time the Walpole boys were eight and ten, they knew the waterways. And before they were teenagers, they were almost wholly responsible for feeding their family from what they dragged up from the sea. Their little johnboat was as permanent a fixture out on the water as the sun and the moon and the breathing lungs of the tides. Most mornings, the boys would be up and out on the water, even before all the shrimpers and fishermen from the neighboring village. The trawlers, heading out to sea around the same time each day, would bellow their loud horns hello to them, as they passed by. And having witnessed the luminous lanterns of night-time fishermen, returning to shore just after dusk, this gifted the boys with a sense of a world they were entitled to, a world ripe for the taking.

Bohicket was busy loading his shotgun, so he didn't hear his sister sneaking up behind them, but Ley did. It was all she could do to catch up to them, much less to keep from being noticed, especially since their mother in her booming voice was shouting after her from the house.

"Sister Dew!" their mother yelled. "Sister Dew, get your

butt back here, this instant!"

Their mother seemed always to be angered by something, like a flower with seeds that won't grow in winter, and it seemed it was always winter in the Walpole home. It was as if she was angered by even the touch of her own skin, its very presence refusing her the growth of her bones. Her children just assumed she was made that way. Angry. Angry perhaps for the sake of being angry. Made that way. What they didn't know, however, was that she was never really comfortable with her life on those islands, with the fact that her husband had dragged her out there eons ago. What her children did not know was that she—whether she could admit it to herself or anyone else—was really just angry with their father still, and with no other recourse, she had, long ago, reverted to sneering at him, until theirs was a marriage made up almost entirely of her sneers and snide remarks, which only grew more and more cruel as the years went by. "See there, kids?" she was fond of saying. "See that father of yours? Way I got it figured, he ain't worth the skin he was born in. See him there? Just look at him."

Their father, on the other hand, was a kind and steady man who seemed to just go on loving his woman endlessly. He tried his darnedest to keep the peace and would stroke his dark unkempt beard whenever his unyielding fondness for his wife called on his patience or a turn at his moonshine still. And whenever there was a shortage of patience itself, he would call upon the bottle. It seemed, everything he did upset her. And that day was no exception since he had decided that that day was as good a day as any to patch up the siding on their house. It was all the hammering that finally got to his wife, ringing as it did in the alcove of her skull.

"Good God, you buffoon, would you please stop with all the noise already?!" she yelled out the kitchen window at him. "Ya hear me, Sweetie? Honey cakes? Dear? Don't make me murder you in your sleep. Don't make me do it 'cause

I will. I'm a kind woman, so I'll make it quick and painless. But I swear to God, I'll bleed you out like a pig. So help me God, I will! Just try me; I will! That is, if you don't bring the whole house down on our heads first!"

She was exaggerating, of course. Maybe not about the whole murdering-him-in-his-sleep thing. But she knew as well as anyone that, if the roof were to come down on their heads, it would not be because of him, seeing as their father, if he was good with anything, he was good with his hands, and he had built her that house, decades earlier, by way of those same two hands. So no, no amount of hammering was going to bring it down, not then, not in a million years, despite the fact that the house did, from time to time, go rocking back and forth atop the fifteen or so twenty-foot pylons it had been erected on in a way that made it feel like it could collapse.

"No!" Ley shouted, having spotted his little sister racing up behind them. "No, Lil Dew, no! How many times do we have to tell you? You're too young, and this here is way too dangerous for the likes of you. So don't even think about it. Don't go getting your hopes up either. Don't you dare even ask."

Ley's abruptness stopped their sister dead in her tracks. She sort of slumped passively where she stood about twenty yards away and began kicking at the sand. "But I'm almost eight," she argued, holding up as many fingers then pausing to double-check her math. "Yep! Eight!" she proclaimed, like she was never more proud of that fact. "Mama says I got the eagle eyes of the family. Mama says I can see farther than most anybody, farther even than my own two brothers, she says. Mama says I got her bested by at least a mile. I got the good eyes," she said. "Most all the time, I can read off the names of the cargo ships before Mama can even spot them." Dew then peered out over the ocean, as if this was, in fact, her superpower and she was ready and hoping to prove it to them.

And she was right about one thing: she did have the sight, as her mother put it, a rare gift indeed. She could see things that most others could not, things that were either there or not. Always, she was carrying on with these things, invisible people she had met, invisible worlds only she could see, which of course, had her family scared to death at first, before they came gradually to acknowledge and accept it as a present from God.

"But you're still a girl," was Ley's response. "And the high seas ain't no place for a girl."

It was all Dew could do to keep from crying in front of her brothers. She didn't want to be a girl. In fact, she hated it. And she knew crying is what girls did, so she didn't. She didn't cry and instead tried with all of her might to fight back the tears, as she continued to plead with them. "Please? Oh please? Just this once? Pretty please? Please?" She was cupping her hands prayerfully now. "I'll be your lookout, and I won't say a word except 'Land Ho!' when land is ho. I promise. Promise. Please?"

Neither Bohicket nor Ley could tell you now why they agreed to her terms even, as it were, against their better judgment. She had been begging them for years to take her along with them, and they had always—always—said no. Maybe it was the way she had asked them this time, sort of resigned to the certainty of their rejection but still persistent. Maybe they just figured one trip, and it'd be out of her system for good. Maybe they could still hear their mother yelling for her to come home. Maybe it was the insinuations of anger they could hear in the pitch of their mother's voice, the same shocks of anger that had, long ago, bloodstained her eyes. Maybe they understood what it was to return to a mother so full of rage, or maybe they just loved their sister the way good brothers do—with that unspoken desire to protect her from anything and everything and, most especially, from all the cruelty in this world.

"I don't know, Ley," replied Bohicket. "What do you think?"

"Ah hell," Ley said. "Maybe just this once, okay? But. Just. This. Once."

Ley hadn't even finished what he was saying before Dew had bounded past him and into the boat. "I won't let you down," she said, perching her tiny self at the bow. "I won't. I promise."

"No talking," Bohicket said. "Remember? No talking."

"Right!" she said with a firm salute. "Got it. No talking. Aye, aye, Captain! Not a peep."

With that, Bohicket, as the oldest and therefore the captain of the vessel, took up his rightful place at the stern of the boat. He pumped at the gas line a time or two then jerked at the cord to rev the engine, all while Ley made busy attending to his job as first mate, hauling up the anchor and walking the boat away from dry land.

"Wind's good," Bohicket half-mentioned, having tested its direction with a wet finger. "So today, we head north and stay downwind to keep 'em off our scent," to which Ley promptly replied, "Right, right, Cap'n sir! We're as good as invisible that way. They'll never see us coming." And in no time at all, Bohicket was steering them masterfully through the labyrinth of oyster beds and sandbars that endangered their route through the side-creeks and out onto the riverways, which led out eventually to the channel.

The engine growled when Bohicket opened her up full-throttle.

And Dew, unable to contain herself any longer, let out a big, loud growl of her own.

And before long, all three of them were growling. They were growling like pirates.

"Look out, here they come! The Black Marauders are on the prowl!" Bohicket exclaimed.

Now, the long stretch of coastline, known to most as the Lowcountry, is made up of thousands of islands. And life out there meant living alongside all those islands' inexplicable mysteries and the inhabitants who were far too accustomed to superstition and rumors. Sometimes at night, if you took care to listen, you might even hear a drumbeat or two, followed then by chanting or singing and dancing around some distant bonfire that seems to have appeared out of nowhere on a nearby coast. Given enough time out there, folks tend to believe in the strangest of things. The Spanish moss is to blame, quilting together the whole wide coastal landscape the way it does and lending a sort of believability to it all, a sort of lovely geometry to even the tallest of tales. The world, as it goes out there, gets its shape in how the moss sways, and seeing it move with the conviction of its lies, it is said that folks too are moved to suspend their disbelief. And so it was not hard for the Walpoles to believe themselves pirates.

"Looks like a yacht, three clicks off the port bow!" Dew yelled over her shoulder a few minutes later.

"Where?"

"There!" she said, pointing down a ways toward a bend in the channel. "Three clicks!"

Ley leaned into the turn sharply, shielded his eyes from the setting sun, noticed something far off in the distance and then nodded in the direction they should be headed. "I see her now!" he yelled up to his sister excitedly. "Yessir! She sure is a beaut'! And I'll be damned, Lil Dew. Gotta hand it to ya. Keep it up, and we might just find some use for ya, after all!"

It's hard to say what this comment meant to their sister. Neither of the boys could see her face when it was said, but if they had, they might have likened her expression to that of a believer being baptized, to that single moment when the believer emerges from the water, eyes wide and mouth agape, gasping with a sort of panicked delight for whatever cleanliness there was to be had in a lungful of air. It was the look of someone struck suddenly by the locale of their own heart, the look of the sun breaking across the water in so vivid a reflection of itself its very presence is validated in replication. And yet Dew did not turn around or say a word in response. She only nodded to acknowledge she heard him, choosing instead to keep her gaze fixed on the task at hand, looking out into a world closing in on the dangers of the night.

There were two gods in the sky that evening, and they partitioned their reign over that channel equally. The sun in full retreat over the ocean to the right, and the moon rising over the tree-line to their left. And yet it turns out what they would really need, come nightfall, was a third and merciful god, a god of redemption and salvation, the same god they had met by way of the New Testament scriptures their parents raised them on.

Unfortunately, that god was too busy.

Already night was upon them by the time they reached the other boat and Dew hollered over her shoulder to them, "We're nearly on top of them! Hurrah! We got 'em now!"

"And lookie there, they're none the wiser!" Ley shouted.

Bohicket swung the johnboat hard along the portside of the yacht, cut the engine and ordered Dew down in the well of the boat. "And stay down, okay?!" he shouted to her. "Whatever you do, stay down, okay?! It's for your own protection!"

Dew did exactly as she was told. She laid her tiny body along the bottom of the boat and then covered her eyes, frightened now by whatever dangers lay ahead. She whimpered a little, but only to herself, as Ley cast the heavy anchor over the side of the yacht and—with one good Heave! followed by a Ho!—pulled them up alongside the other boat.

Bohicket snatched up his shotgun and let out a barbaric roar, as he leapt across to the adjacent boat. He had found, after a good many years at this sort of thing, that the scarier his threats sounded, the more cooperative people were, and so he unleashed every last expletive he had in his arsenal and waved his gun wildly over his head. "If any of you fucking motherfuckers so much as think of moving, I'll fucking postmark you right where you stand, and hand to God, I'll fucking mail you directly to Him!"

(Turns out, Bohicket only really knew one cuss word. Good thing he knew how to use it.)

Bohicket ordered the whole family face-down in the boat and, there, stood watch over their every move. And once he felt he had the situation sufficiently under control, he called for his brother to come aboard and start plundering their possessions.

Ley vanished below deck for a while, and before long, came up shouting, "Gold watch!" He held it up for his brother to see. "Been wanting myself one of these little numbers for a while now! And by the looks of it, this one here's a nice one." Ley's hands were full, so full, in fact, he could barely carry it all. "Got us a wallet and a purse here too! And money, I'd imagine. Lots of it. I think we're all set here, brother," he said, tossing all the loot into the johnboat and then leaping in himself and shouting, "Sure made out like bandits, this time around, brother! Now let's get outta here!"

After more than a few narrow escapes, the boys had learned that it was best if their victims couldn't recover their wits in time to start up their engines and give chase. So Bohicket went about crippling the yacht, throwing all the gas tanks overboard and cutting a hole in the gas line. He then fired off a warning shot, and just to be safe, he took their keys.

Turns out, it was the sound of the gunshot that startled Dew to her feet and had her glancing around frantically to see how she could help. The tide was high and receding fast, and so the current was swift. The two boats had drifted so far apart that Bohicket was left stranded, and Lil Dew panicked, as would any worried sister, and she reached out over the side to offer him her hand.

And the third god was nowhere to be found.

The little johnboat tipped just enough with her added weight on one side that, before Ley or Bohicket could even think to save her, Dew went careening over the side and into the water.

Bohicket just assumed he'd see her head and hands come bobbing back up to the surface any moment now. So rather than go in after her, he left that to his younger brother and decided instead to keep a watchful eye on the family behind him just in case any one of them decided to get all brave and try something stupid.

It was Ley who went in after her, almost on instinct. He dove in and then came back up, caught his breath and then dove back down. Ley was a strong swimmer with strong lungs and an even stronger feel for the tides and the currents in those waters, so Bohicket had little doubt that his brother would rescue her. Only after the sixth or seventh time that his brother resurfaced did the gravity of the situation set in. And caring little now for his own well-being or the angry insurrection that might ensue, Bohicket went in after her as well.

They were a hundred or so yards away, dragged there unwittingly by the heavy currents, before Bohicket resurfaced a final time. Ley appeared about the same time. And that was when they locked eyes and recognized a similar helplessness on the other one's face, the look of attrition before the surrender, before any one person is willing to admit that all was lost.

"No," Ley said, before vanishing once again under the water.

"No," he said when he came back up.

"No."

"No."

"No," he said.

But the night proved otherwise. The night said Yes.

Ley was still searching for her when Bohicket finally reached him.

"No," Ley said.

"Yes, Ley. Yes," Bohicket said, grabbing his brother up in both his arms.

Ley struggled to get free of him, but Bohicket would not let go. "Yes. Yes. Yes," Bohicket kept telling him, until the ocean too was repeating Yes into the shell of his ear, each Yes an echo, an answer that went on and on answering itself. "Yes," he whispered, "Yes."

Ley was weeping now in the nape of his brother's neck.

And Bohicket knew there was nothing more to say.

They did not swim back to their boat. They did not think to. They instead relinquished their bodies to the surface of the water and floated there a while, gazing up into the night and considering what other terrible things may lie beneath a sky full of stars.

Neither one could say how far they drifted. Miles perhaps? They were far enough away from where they'd started that neither of the boats nor the people left onboard were visible any more. And as it were, that is when the inexplicable happened; that is when they saw the Flying Men for themselves, appearing in the skies above their heads, as if emerging directly out of their father's stories. And that is when seeing what they saw finally made believers out of them.

They were just rounding a crook in the channel, where the water began its final mad dash to the sea when two shadows appeared suddenly from nowhere. Dark shadows. Human shadows. Only not, seeing as these shadows, they had wings. They were carrying something, and by the looks of it, it must have been a body. Though the body appeared small and limp and sort of upside down, the way the head was left to barely skim the surface of the water. They held the body up by the legs then, slowly but surely, began their ascent to some place high in the heavens.

And to them, it seemed only right somehow to wave goodbye.

Chapter Two

NOTHING COULD'VE PREPARED THE PEOPLE OF THE LOWCOUNTRY for the inexplicable tide of dead bodies that had come washing ashore since early that year, all the blued and bloated cadavers of somebody or another's dearest loved ones, only now returned from the sea. But news of such things did not travel fast to remote places like these. The Sea Islands, particularly their island out near the Ashepoo River, were another world, you see.

And yet back on the mainland, between the city newspapers' seemingly endless conjectures as to the possible reasons for what had killed these people, together with the rash of panic and terror it seemed to incite in anyone and everyone who lived in those cities, one might reasonably assume that the locals were off drowning by the thousands. But in reality, the coroner's report that came out early that summer had the count hovering around a dozen or so. And while the whole phenomenon was undoubtedly strange, even disturbing, what made it all the more frightening was the inability of anyone—including the police—to offer so much as one plausible explanation as to how they died, leaving so many to be haunted by their own worst-case scenarios. Were they killed? Who will be next? Is it safe to go in the water? Was there something sinister at play here, some rhyme or reason, some prehistoric squid perhaps or some waterlogged fisherman with a vendetta? And what about—Oh God!—what about the children? All anybody had at that point were questions, and the only thing scarier than the questions they had were the answers left to their imaginations.

One after another, witnesses stepped forward claiming to

have seen flying men in the sky, and always, always with a body nearby. This became the story, the plausible link. The skeptics that peopled the nearby cities, though, were a different story entirely. The skeptics simply dismissed any eyewitness accounts of the Flying Men outright, convinced that the real answer for what they saw was far more scientific than "all that hullaballoo you gone and talked all these poor folks into." In their minds, the answer would prove to be far more logical than all that, something readily explained by numbers and statistics, evolution or birds. "Albeit, strange birds," the skeptics would admit, "But birds nonetheless."

Of course, at the time, the Walpoles hadn't caught wind of any of this, hadn't heard the rumors, no not a whisper. So much of the Walpoles' life, you see, was spent merely surviving; an inevitable byproduct of having been born on an island so far from civilization, where merely carving out a life for oneself, finding food to eat and fresh water to drink, meant living by their wits. As proof, Bohicket, the oldest son, wore the sun like a bronze tattoo, like some permanent reminder of how harsh the reality of his life could be. Always on the air out there was the omnipresent scent of sweat and saltwater, ocean air and the sentient intrusions of pluff mud in his nostrils, which is why, as a boy, Bohicket came to understand these, the hardest of truths, by way of his senses, and why, even now, fearing he'd forget, Bohicket would simply press his face to his father's shirt from time to time and steal one long sniff of the truth that clung to his skin. And yet Bohicket had remained a dreamer through it all because, if Bohicket was anything, Bohicket truly was a dreamer. And it seemed he walked around mostly with his head in the clouds, which his mother never tired of pointing out, and though she most assuredly meant to demean him, Bohicket would inevitably reply, "Where better for your head to be?" arguing for the vantage point of clouds.

It all started when Bohicket was five and his father

returned home from the mainland with a June 1985 edition of National Geographic. Thing was, they had little-to-no access to reading materials of any sort (aside from the occasional newspaper their father bought in the market of the Gullah village, a small collection of books, and an ancient set of encyclopedias their mother brought with her when she first followed her husband out to that island). And living as they did without a bookstore or library nearby, their father would only occasionally happen upon the idea that some light reading might do his children some good. And so it was that the boys learned to read by way of that magazine mostly, same as Bohicket learned to love the very notion that someone out there had taken all those photographs inside the pages; everything from those blue Caribbean seascapes to the weary war-torn faces of the Afghan people. The pictures, yes, the pictures were what enthralled him. So much so, he spent years just scouring them over, imagining himself as that unknown factor settled in behind the lens.

Unfortunately for him, his younger brother also developed his own aspirations, aspirations of becoming a pilot one day, and having witnessed his first airplane pass overhead, Ley went and tore out nearly every page of that magazine to fold into paper airplanes and go flying them around the island, propeller sounds and all. This, of course, infuriated Bohicket at the time, though it turned out to be good for him, as the loss of those photos drove him to practice decidedly at his craft: wandering around the island day after day, framing shots with his thumb and index finger then snapping closed his eyelids, like makeshift shutters, to capture a photo. What Bohicket wanted more than anything, though, was a camera. A real one. And by his tenth birthday, he was already plotting his escape to the city to buy himself one, a plan he never saw through nor entirely regretted having abandoned, until some eight years later when he found he wanted a camera more than ever, as he watched his sister carried away into the sky.

And so it was that Bohicket, absent a photograph as proof, carried on for days with only the sneaking suspicion that whatever happened that night in the channel was nothing more than a dream, a really awful and awfully real dream. He and his brother had abandoned their boat in the river that night and walked all the way home, deciding instead to retrieve the boat at first light. And upon returning home well after midnight, the boys struggled to tell their parents the terrible news, struggled even to ration the truth from what they had seen. Had she drowned? They couldn't say. Or had she been kidnapped by those, uh . . . creatures in the sky? They certainly hoped it was the latter.

Upon hearing the news, their mother was understandably upset, rending her hair hysterically and tearing off her clothes and carrying on like that, until their father was forced to save her from drowning herself in the ocean. Even her grief managed somehow to be mean.

Their father did not show it, but he was equally saddened by the news. In private, he would drink himself into bed that night and cry himself to sleep but put on a brave face the next morning for the sake of his family. Someone, he reasoned, had to be strong. So he took to busying himself instead with all matters of upkeep, mending his cast nets and the holes in their roof, patching up the rain-catchers he'd built in the treetops to gather their drinking water and carry it to their house through an intricate system of wooden aqueducts that ran like veins around the island.

Ley was always the more brazen of the brothers, more pragmatic than Bohicket in some ways and yet far less practical, and so he took to the odd practice of carrying his pillow and sheets up on the roof and there making a bed for himself, night after night, lying awake for the most part and searching the horizon for any sign of the Flying Men, any sign that it was not as he feared and his sister was still alive and well out there. Ley's unpredictable behavior could seem, at times, bigger-than-life in this way, remaining as he did largely unfazed, only to then act out rashly and often on a whim. This whole business of sleeping on the roof, however, was especially concerning to his family because, as it were, Ley had never concerned himself much with serious matters, matters like church or God or hurting somebody's feelings. Always, Ley was more the sarcastic one, the one with the witty retort forever on the ready, guarded as ever by his way with humor, which he turned to now more than ever. "Are you okay?" his mother would ask him, revealing a side of her rarely on display. "No ma'am," he'd tell her. "My name is Ley, not Okay." And he would laughingly blame how troubled he looked on an uncanny bout of hemorrhoids. And yet it was precisely that—Ley's stubborn insistence that he was indeed okay and in perpetually good spirits—that gave him away. It was precisely that that had them all concerned, especially when you account for all the many dangers a boy, in such silent desperation, will hazard in curing whatever it is that troubles him.

Unlike his little brother, Bohicket found he was more and more at peace with his sister's disappearance as the days went on, having found a strange peace in both the idea that she was alive and the idea that she might be dead. He couldn't say why this was, but it was. Perhaps his sister's eternally frail body and her mind plagued so by visions meant she was never long for this world, or perhaps he just found a certain justice to a soul as good and other-worldly as his sister's finding a suitable home in heaven. Way he had it figured, our time here on earth depends solely on how long our souls needed to be here, how long it took to come clean of all the body's restrictions. Way he had it figured, the time allotted to each of us here on earth was a sort of Rumspringa for the soul that lasted just long enough for the soul to be tried and tested, purified and refined, before at last being returned anew to the presence of God. And that, for a soul like his sister's, wouldn't have taken long.

As for their mother, she was never the same after her only daughter did not return home. And she seemed to devolve, with each passing day, into her former self, a form perhaps of her childhood self. Reverting back perhaps to a time when no one ever really dies and anything is possible, even her once-firm girlhood conviction that, if she wanted to bad enough, she could change herself into a bird and she could fly. The change in her was so slow and so gradual that it was hardly noticeable in the days that followed. It started first at the edges with a sort of softening of her permanent scowl, followed then by the slow letting go of that certain definable anger she was known for, which at last, gave way to kindness—or else a fraud resembling kindness—that was neither expected nor becoming of a woman so proud and so practiced at being and remaining forever angry. Her softer, kinder side made its appearance first by way of her actions, in cooking them all their favorite meals and in actually folding their laundry for them instead of just pitching it at their beds. Though in the end, her mouth would give her away. There she is, the boys would think, whenever she got to opening it and speaking to them in the same demeaning ways. There she is. There's Mama. But so taken were they by her gradual change in temperament, it would be some time before any one of them noticed what was really going on, before any one of them realized that she had been, for some time now, secretly fashioning herself wings from the feathers she found, and only after fashioning those wings into a costume of sorts and trying it on did they find her squawking about on the porch outside. "Squawk!" she cried. "Squawk! This old bird was meant for flying!" And then she leapt up on the railing before anyone could stop her, flapped her wings wildly and then jumped.

Between the height of the pylons and the velocity of

her jump, to say nothing of the distance the porch railing added, it was quite a long way down. All things considered, she was just lucky to walk away with only one broken leg. And all things considered, she should've learned her lesson the first time around. But she didn't. Instead, the fall only served to harden her resolve, and from that day on, she set about spending all of her time, while her leg was healing, figuring out where exactly her plan had gone wrong and readying herself for her next attempt.

Their mother would need plenty of looking after in the days to come, of course. But having lived so long out there on those islands, so far from any doctors or a hospital, their mother had learned a trick or two about healing up naturally. So she gave the boys a list of berries and herbs she would need them to gather and told them where they could find them growing in the wild as well as how to extract the ingredients she would need. "Now, can the two of you remember all that? Or should I write it all out on a big square of paper and paste it to your foreheads?" she asked when she finished with her instructions.

There she is, they thought. There she is.

The boys did as she asked them to do. And in no time at all, her leg was healing right up.

The closer she got to being mobile again, the more they felt they needed to watch her. And by the time she was well enough to get around on a cane, their father saw fit to task the boys with keeping an eye on her, while he was away fishing for their dinner. And genuinely concerned for their mother's safety, now more than ever, the boys took the task seriously. However, in the end, it mattered very little. Whether they were watching her or not, she was going to do what she was going to do, now that all she wished for were hollow bones.

The seed had already been planted long, long ago, back when she was a child and, longing to be a fish, spent hours upon hours swimming at the beach near her home and fancying herself a shark, deciding life was better at the top of the food chain. Of course, being a shark meant she had to be hungry. As a child, she would spend whole afternoons, stalking the sunbathers among the sand castles and carefully selecting her prey, based on whatever attributes she found the most detestable, whether it be a man too fat for the Speedo he was wearing or a woman picking knuckle-deep in her nose. She would then wait for her unwitting prey to wander out into the surf and strap a homemade shark fin to her back and go swimming around them in wide circles. There's really no way of telling how many people she scared the ever-living bejesus out of, before the whole matter was done, or how many times she cleared the oceanfront after inciting a panic, but she would smile a little to herself whenever she heard someone cry out, "Shark! Shark!" Yeah, she'd think to herself. Yeah. I'm a shark. And when it dawned on her one day that a real fish needs gills, she went and cut slits into both of her cheeks and peeled them back into flaps, which, of course, made her the laughing stock of her school, but she didn't care because she had her own school; she was a fish.

Her desire to be a fish did die out eventually with the passing of her father. For solace, she fled to the beach and retreated to the dunes where she found she could swim in the sand in peace. It was there one day that a bird caught her eye—a seagull to be precise—caught almost stationary in the cross-currents of wind above her head. The bird was so close she imagined she could touch it. Flying is a bit like swimming, she realized. So maybe instead I should be a flying fish. And that was when her desire to be a fish became her desire to be a bird, which came less from her actual notions of flying and more from a desire to be closer to her father, after his soul, having the same bright idea, had sprouted wings and taken flight.

She was too old now to keep on trying. She knew that as well as anybody. Still, she was an angry woman, and anger breeds unhealthy resolve. So no sooner had her leg healed up than she was out and about, preparing herself to try it once again. She bounded out of bed that very morning with a laundry list of tweaks to her plan and busied herself with preparations for yet another attempt. How anyone actually believed they could fly is difficult to imagine, especially when that anyone is a grown woman. And yet something or other had her convinced that she could and, worse, was destined to. Always, it seemed, the aerodynamics of drag and thrust were on her mind. Why? Maybe, now more than ever, she just needed a little levity in her life. That at least would make sense, given the weight of her daughter's absence. Maybe what she was always after was a means of escape, fearing as she did, that she would be bound to that island forever. Or maybe she just needed, as do we all, a little more soul in her shoes. Chances are, no one, not even her, could explain her strange behavior. She did try to, once or twice. She did assure them that she had a plan and she would see it through. She swore she was going to off and fly one of these days—Just you wait, just you see—because, as she put it plainly, to find her daughter, a mother needs wings.

As a girl, she had tried nearly everything to fly. Nearly, she kept reminding herself. But not everything. She had a long way to go, and there was still progress to be made. She started again with the basics: just some feathers and a beak and a high spot to leap from, which only amounted to one clumsy flutter in mid-air, followed thankfully this time by a safer landing. When the feathers alone couldn't do the trick, her plan was to simply add more feathers. And in less than a week, she had culled together a whole costume of the brightest feathers she could find. She gathered what she could, here and there, and chased birds around the island to pluck out the rest. And despite her family having watched her like a hawk, she still managed to sneak away somehow when no one was looking, and proceeded to jump from their dock, only to land with a splash in the water without incident.

Eventually Bohicket did catch on to her methods of escape, along with all the many ways she tried to distract them so she could. Like letting a T-shirt burn in the oven until it filled the house with smoke, or leaving the battery-powered radio on in her bathroom to fool them into thinking she was singing in the tub. And the one time she did slip past them, Bohicket found her in the attic just in time to talk her down off the window ledge, which was really quite fortunate for her, seeing as the fall from there would've resulted in at least a dozen broken bones, bones that, at her age, may not have healed up so quickly, or at all, for that matter.

"What in God's name are you doing up here?!" Bohicket scolded her.

"Don't be so dense," she replied. "Any fool, any fool like, say . . . your father, can see what I'm doing up here. I am her mother, and she needs me."

Not long after that came the brilliant realization that what she really needed was more wind. Yes, she thought, more wind should do the trick. And so she checked the weather every day before breakfast, and sensing the stirrings of a tropical storm on the air early one cloudy morning, she climbed out a window and up to the roof, and there she waited for the winds to pick up. All she needed was a good strong gust and a long running start, she reasoned. So when the time came, she spread her wings, ran full sprint and dove headlong from their roof. That she survived at all was a testament to God's mercy or some higher being looking after her, because it just so happened that, this time around, there came in off the ocean just enough wind to carry her clear over the yard and out into the water.

With the assistance of its gale-force winds, she did manage to fly quite a long way in the storm. Though for her, even that was not far enough. So she decided it was time she re-envision her plan and settled, at last, on a lighter approach. Inspired by the mosquito, she made goggles out of yarn and a few shards of sea glass. She fashioned four translucent wings out of wire hangers and a thin tulle-like fabric that had washed ashore. She even went as far as to stop eating altogether, or for as long as she could bear it. Weight, she decided, was the enemy now. Gravity too. She measured her progress religiously, checking the scale in her bathroom eight and nine times a day, until she had lost no less than ten pounds in just under a week.

"What are you, Gandhi or somethin'?" her husband had asked her. "You're already a string bean, girlie. Pretty soon, you'll be a shadow." He meant to scare her into eating more. "We Southern boys like a little meat on our bones, you know," he added, sipping again at his drink. But that he'd noticed her losing weight at all only encouraged her further. In the mirror at night, she would suck in her tummy and count her ribs. "Getting there," she would tell herself. "You'll be a no-see-um in no time, ol' girl. You'll be buzzing around, all invisible-like, and sucking people's blood like it's nobody's business 'fore long. Bzzz, bzzz," she said to herself. "Bzzzzz."

There was this one tree on the far side of the island that stood head-and-shoulders above the rest. They had nick-named it The Castle Spire because of its resemblance to one. And she was in full mosquito garb, complete with a TV antenna strapped to her head, when she jumped from the top of it late one night. And for the single momentary instant she was suspended in air, she almost thought she had finally done it; she almost thought she could fly. Of course, her husband was not the least bit amused when he found her the next day, still unconscious in the woods with little more than a scratch or two from when the tree branches had broken her fall.

"Jesus, Mae! What on earth are you doing?!" their father cried out, pitching his drink to the ground the moment he found her. There was a genuine horror in his voice, a kind she had never heard before, a kind that scared her to her core. "Well I, for one, will not stand by, while you go around trying to off yourself," he told her, scooping her up in his arms and carrying her deeper into the woods.

"Where are we going, dear? You brain-dead or something? Home is the other way."

He did not answer her. Instead, he continued on quietly through the woods and out to the beach, where he laid her down beneath an umbrella of leaves, beneath a tree that seemed far less interested in where it was than where it was growing. "You wanna fly, my flower?" he asked her. "Well do ya? Then come on, let's fly." And with that, he scooped her up once more in his arms, and he carried her out beyond the breaker-line to where the water was calm and reflective.

And they swam together in the ocean that day, splashing around and gathering up clouds, until the reflection of the sky felt akin to being in it. To her, it felt somehow like swimming and flying at the same exact time, a sort of beautiful hybrid of bird-meets-fish, and she confessed she liked that. A flying fish, she told herself. That's what I am. A flying fish.

Chapter Three

THE WALPOLES WERE THE ONLY WHITE FAMILY FOR MILES AND so were already a rarity out on those islands. And yet their strangeness was only compounded by the fact that the three Walpole children had been named for the places they were conceived. Bohicket was named for the tidal creek where his parents first made love, and for short, they tried to call him Bo, but he wouldn't hear of it. "Bohicket's my name," he had insisted from an early age. "Bohicket, not Bo." Pawley was named after an old hammock that used to hang on the porch of their mother's childhood home, but they chose to call him Ley instead of the far more likely nickname, Pawl. As their mother put it, "There can only be one Paul, and he was a saint. You, dear boy, are no saint. Every woman ever has been in danger of an unsaintly Paul and his unspeakable intentions, of all the Pauls who touch where they shouldn't touch." Their sister was named Clara after her mother's mother, but rather than go by her first name, she went by her middle name, Dewee, for the island where their father's boat had run aground in a storm, and late that night on the beach somewhere, she had been conceived. Of course, she too went by her nicknames, and there were more than a few. To her mother, she was Sister Dew, while to her father, she was Dewdrop or Morning Dew. It was her two older brothers who liked to tease by calling her names like Dew-dew and Peeeee-Yew! "Dewdew, Dewdew!" they would call out to her. "Well dew ya, Dew-dew? Dew ya like our stinky socks?"

Ley had always been the better-looking brother, with eyes that would widen like the parting Red Sea when he laughed and inspirited an immediate fondness in anyone who witnessed it. In shape and stature, they were very much the same, but Ley carried himself with a certain qualifying assurance that his older brother never had, resulting in a sort of gravity to his person that left those around him feeling like a moon in orbit. Bohicket and his brother did share their mother's long skinny nose and slight hide-and-seek lips, but their tall stature and wiry frames were like replicas of their father.

Even so, Bohicket saw little else of his father in himself. For one, their father bequeathed to Ley his middle name, Parker, almost foreseeing the near-unbreakable bond they would share in their life. What they shared, however, went far beyond a name. What they shared was a long and almost alphabetical list of common interests that Bohicket envied but took little part in. Even as a toddler, Ley would follow his father around wherever he went, tracking his every step, as if Ley was the caboose and his father the locomotive. They both enjoyed fishing and crabbing and shrimping with their father, but it was Ley's love of airplanes and his dream of someday flying one that made his bond with their father unique. And so it just made sense that their father would turn to their shared love of planes while attempting to coax Ley down off the roof.

It took him weeks of convincing, but their father had always possessed an uncanny gift for spotting an airplane on the horizon, noting its type and capacity as well as where it had probably flown in from. And so night after night, he joined his son up there on the roof and made a sort of game of it, disarming him slowly by how much he knew.

"Yep, that one there's a 747. Boeing, by the look of it," their father said. "Maximum load: 400 or so passengers, including luggage and crew. Likely stopping off from Newark or Philly before ending up in Dulles or Chicago."

"How do you know that, Pops?" Ley would ask skeptically.

"I don't," their father would answer. "Well not for sure."

"Come on, Pops. You had me going for a second there. Surely, you aren't just yankin' my chain now are you? Come on, Pops. Maybe if I was younger. But I'm older now, and I've got you all figured out."

"No honestly, son," their father would say, sipping at his glass. "I just count the lights. See 'em there? See? Six . . . eight . . . nine . . . nine lights. So that one there's a 747. And typically, a plane that large ain't flying regionally. A plane like that's headed someplace else. Ya see? Just a bit of deduction is all it takes. The rest is just good ol' common sense."

Ley appeared skeptical still. "Common sense, huh?"

"Common. Sense," their father would respond, throw one arm over his son's shoulder and say something like, "Ain't nothing harder to come by in this here world. And son, there ain't a soul who can teach it. Yep. Seems the only thing common about common sense is how uncommon it actually is." He nodded at a few more lights vanishing down the coast, and added, "Thing is, son. As hard as it is to believe, your father just so happens to know a thing or two about a thing or two. And planes most especially."

And that was how their father eventually convinced Ley to come down off that roof, with promises that he would teach him everything he knew about airplanes and the trick of distinguishing the ones that they saw. Their father, of course, being a man of his word, kept his end of the bargain, and the two of them would set aside an hour or two every day combing the skies for visible planes.

The rest of their days were dedicated to their responsibilities. And Bohicket would work beside his father from sun up to sun down, feeling it was his duty, as the oldest, to help his father out. Especially now that their mother was still preoccupied and the responsibility of doing all the chores had fallen, almost exclusively, to his father. The sheer volume of work it took to keep their day-to-day lives out there running was far too much for any one man to bear, and so Bohicket took it upon himself to ease some of the burden, and every day, he set about assisting his father however he could.

For a boy his age to consider his father at all was no small miracle. But to act on it too? And with such conviction? Well, that took a considerable amount of maturity on Bohicket's part. Then again, it wasn't so much that he was especially mature for his age either. Far from it, in fact. Bohicket was simply brought up to believe, from an early age, that preserving their way of life out there was of absolute importance. Of course, it also helped that Bohicket saw his father as a kind of drunken visionary, if only for the foresight he had shown in building this life for them from scratch, in hauling that double-wide trailer of his across the riverway by way of a barge he had made out of palmetto trunks. Bohicket saw too a kind of manifest destiny in how long and how much they had survived out there, relying almost solely on their father's sage-like wisdom to see to essential matters like propping that house of theirs up on pylons to evade the occasional blue-moon tides that would come in, like a prophecy, and give rise to floodwaters. Having outlasted so much and for so long, the decades of rising seas and storm surges, brought on by dozens of hurricanes and tropical storms, having survived the ocean's many attempts to reclaim their land, Bohicket approached his work like it was his calling.

And according to their father, it most certainly was. This was their calling. He had been telling them as much since before they could walk, much less understand what he was saying. And yet it seemed they did understand even then. Perhaps a father can speak conviction into his sons without a need for words. "Come hell or high water," he used to tell them, time and again, "Ain't nothing—save God's own hand—can pry us from this land. Nothing. Not hell. Not water."

Though honestly, even he would admit it was a miracle

that they had lasted that long. And it was a miracle alright, a miracle that his wife had even followed him there in the first place, a miracle that she had stayed for as long as she had. Their father could not, for the life of him, imagine why his wife hadn't just up and left him long, long ago and moved to Savannah or someplace else. Though he could not, for the life of him, imagine why she or anyone else would even consider leaving, after witnessing the God in that place, with all its living mysteries and all its waterways that, like pathways, seemed always to be paved in light. Charleston maybe, he might have conceded. *I could see Charleston, just not Savannah.* She treated him always with her dreams of that city. Charleston had always held a special place in his heart, which he permitted quietly for how it had clothed itself in rivers. Either way, a city was a city was a city. And in his book, there was something wholly unforgivable about a city. Still, he was no longer frightened by his wife's dreams of the city. No, in those days, what frightened him more was the prospect of what a mother like her must abandon, escape and finally yield to in coming to terms with the loss of her only daughter.

Living out there meant facing down hardships. He knew that, and so did his wife. Surviving at all meant struggling to survive, gathering what little sustenance there was to be gathered, whether by working the land or trolling the sea. But they did what they had to do to get by. Their father, for one, bartered at the market for eggs and bread, gas, tools and other essentials. Their mother and Dew had been tasked with gathering up driftwood every day, which they would use to mend the house or build furniture. Their father would, on occasion, return from the village with a week-old newspaper to read, which amounted to the only real glimpse they ever got of the outside world. Bohicket, of course, preferred the lifestyle section for the pictures, while Ley liked the comics, a matter that was typically settled between them after fighting it out. What clothes their mother didn't sew for them, their father would have to barter for, or if they were lucky, they'd find a shirt or a pair of shorts washed up on the shore. For shoes, they had to place special orders with a guy in the village who would take monthly trips into the city to purchase a grocery list of requested items. But what little they had to barter with was not limitless, and so they would typically have to wear those shoes until their toes poked through. The oven and the lights in their house ran off two large gas-powered generators. And they ate mostly whatever the world offered up to them: crabs, squirrel, raccoons, deer, fish, oysters, shrimp or the occasional seaweed stew. Fortunately for them though, their mother could never really stomach plain food and had learned to season their meals with a wide assortment of herbs and spices from her garden. When they bathed, they bathed in saltwater hauled up from the ocean because, as their mother claimed, saltwater was best for their skin. Soap was a rarity, but vinegar wasn't since their mother would make jars and jars of it from leftover fruit rinds, sugar and alcohol fresh from the still. Whatever they needed beyond that was left to piracy.

And with living coming as hard as it did out there, it stood to reason that, to forget his worries, their father poured himself a drink and then poured himself into his work. He had done his darnedest to teach his children how to make good on a life worth living, so it wasn't surprising when Ley, taking a cue from his brother's persistence, eventually joined in and helped out. And together the three of them spent every waking minute of every waking day tending to all matters of the island, including dredging up the riverway that divided them from the mainland, encouraged by their father's reminders of the good in their continued separation, that the division from the mainland alone kept them unique.

Day after day, they set about tending to this matter and that. That's what it took to go on fending for themselves, sometimes barely succeeding. And perhaps that is why a sort of bending of the rules, a tick in an otherwise precise moral compass, saw the boys doing their part by pirating for clothes and gas and fishing equipment as well. They stole mostly to get by. And sometimes to make the isolation slightly more bearable. They stole and got really good at it.

But if they could get it honestly, they did. They took axes to trees and chopped a few down then stacked the firewood neatly on the porch, so they could heat the stove and the furnace. They scaled nine or ten of the taller trees scattered around the island, and there at the top, they mended all the rain-catchers and patched up the leaky aqueducts that brought the drinking water down to their house.

"See there?" their father would say, scooping a fistful of rain into this mouth. "Water is freshest when it comes from God." He would say, "Go ask Moses, if ya don't believe me. He will tell you. Manna tastes best when it falls from the sky." And every afternoon on into evening, they would wade out into the water to cast nets for their lunch and fish for their dinner. If ever they got a hankering for a snack between meals, they'd simply go on their hands and knees and rifle through the pluff mud for a handful of fiddler crabs to eat.

Their father was glad for their company because he could use the help, but also because he used the time, as he often did, to impart a little wisdom on what it means to be a well-mannered Southern gentleman. He would show them how to repair whatever needed fixing, from a leak in the roof to a sputtering motor. As promised, Ley did learn a thing or two about airplanes in the process. And in passing, almost as collateral to their daily conversations, both Bohicket and Ley picked up a few interesting tidbits of knowledge on everything from history to science to literature and arithmetic. Though perhaps far more importantly, they got to know a few new secrets of their island, the inner workings, the natural mechanics, along with all the good that comes with discovering such things for yourself.

"And this is the heart blood. This is the magic," their father told them one day at a clearing in the thick of the woods. "Only you and I know where they grow. You and I and no one else. It's important it stays that way, okay? You see these little berries? We need them to survive." And with that, he sifted his fingers through the grass and produced a palm full of bright purple berries. "See this here? This here is the magic."

"They're berries," Ley said.

"No, son. They're not. Well, they are. But they're not." And their father went on to explain that these particular berries could only be found growing in this one place, which is why he used them to barter with the villagers for the essentials they needed. It's how, around those parts, he got the nickname Berry Man. "No one can explain why they only grow here," he said. "It's what some people call a phenomenon. Then again, there are a lot of other islands out there. A. Lot. So many, in fact, even us locals have lost count."

And truth is, their father was right. There were hundreds upon hundreds of similarly isolated, similarly forgotten islands out there along the Carolina coast. "I seem to recall somebody or another—I forget his name—had taken on the rather daunting task, a good century or two ago, of charting every last one of these islands and, no doubt, naming them all too. So it stands to reason that there would be a map somewhere with every island on it, complete with all the fool-ass names no one bothered to remember. Names like Ricketts Island or Breach's Spit, I'd imagine, each named all right and proper after English royalty. Isle of Wakefield," he guessed. "Duke Norwich's Perch. Or one to honor some highfalutin earl whose shit, it was said, don't stink. More than a few of them islands have Indian names too. The word for, say, *Welcome*, which in turn, got bastardized in translation, as it inevitably does, somewhere down the line.

One way or another, there sure as hell are a lot of them islands out there, son. Thousands. So, yeah sure, chances are, I could be wrong. Wouldn't be the first time. Still, I have this sneaking suspicion I am right, that these here berries only grow in this here soil, and that makes them special, which is why they must remain our little secret."

Their father glanced over his shoulder, as if there could be others around who were listening, and something in how he furrowed his brow made the boys think this was a cause for concern.

"Our neighbors," he leaned in and whispered, referring to the villagers across the way. "Our neighbors pay top dollar for these here berries. They crush them up and use them as dye. That or to flavor their tea. They'll trade next to anything for these here berries, even the clothes off their backs. One time, a man even offered to work a full two months for me in return for a single crate. I mean, to think! So just imagine what they would give to find out where they grow. They'd sell their souls on the cheap probably. Probably? Hell, definitely." Their father paused for a moment and looked them each in their eyes. "Have I made myself clear? Do we have an understanding? This secret stays here, right here, between us. Understand?"

They nodded.

"I want to hear you promise," he said.

"Promise," they said.

THE DAYS WERE LONG AND THE WORK WAS HARD, AND SO THEIR father soon decided they were long overdue for a distraction and made a game of joining the boys at night up on the roof, sitting cross-legged and gazing out across the aqueous horizon. Only when the moment felt right would he place a finger to his lips and tell them to "Hush," to ask them to listen. He would start the game by imitating a sound he heard—the roof giving way gradually to the weight of their bodies, a heron making a splash in the vanishing distance, an affixture of wind waving a distinguishable current through the marsh. There was always a winner, and there was always a loser. There had to be. It was a game, and those are the rules. The real winner, though, was Bohicket, who suggested one night in the midst of their game that there was no equal in this world to the sound of water at night.

What prompted Ley to speak up then must've been the approachable security he recognized in hearing that sound. "The Flying Men," he started, like he was feeling out the options. "They killed my sister. They did. They killed Dew. Or maybe they didn't. Maybe she's out there, maybe she's alive. But one way or another," he swore to them. "I intend to find out." And he would not rest until he did.

No one in their right mind would have believed him. No one, that is, except the sea island Gullah folk who, as it happened, would've needed no convincing of the winged men's presence among them. They had, after all, been telling their story for centuries now, having carried the dawnings of the tale with them from West Africa, sharing it ever since with their children and their children's children. To hear their village elders tell it, to be born in Africa was to be born with wings, and yet misfortune would have it that there was no room for their wings aboard the slave ships, so their ancestors were forced to part ways with them en route to the Americas. "But some of us," they would whisper, almost afraid that somebody might hear them, "Were sly enough to tuck them in along our backs, and sneak them over." And that is how the Flying Men were still explained in certain Gullah circles out among those Sea Islands where age-old beliefs, tied fast to a common history, were still practiced sometimes. Practices like walking backwards out of cemeteries in case a spirit decided to hitch a ride home on their backs, like sleeping with a sulfur match behind their ears and growing bottle trees in every yard, all of which had evolved naturally from West African beliefs, after the slaveholders forced them to bury their dead too soon and without proper rites.

But lucky for Ley, their father was one such believer as well, having seen for himself what could've been birds, except they were not like birds at all. For one, they did not fly like birds. What he claimed to have seen were instead almost human in shape, complete with two arms and two legs and two giant wings that expanded to flap once, maybe twice, before gravity again took hold and the weight of their bodies pivoted towards earth, feet-first, the way a person ceases to float and sinks into water. Then, just like that, with but a flap of their wings, those very same men would again be gliding effortlessly through the air. "Like a kite," he had said. "Yeah, like a kite. A kite with no string."

And yet neither Bohicket nor their father knew how to respond when Ley had mentioned Dew by name, seeing as this was the first time any one of them had dared speak her name. Dew, the name itself was still striking with the pain it could cause. It even took Ley a moment to gather himself and continue what he was saying.

"I've been taking our boat out, every night," Ley confessed. "They are out there still. I know it. They are," he said. "And she might be too. I will find them." He spoke of wanting to hunt them down, of rescuing her and of exacting his revenge, as if it were both his right and his duty.

And their father could not bring himself to blame Ley for feeling this way, recalling his own secretive sadness and where he went when he couldn't bear to miss his daughter any longer. And he could not blame him because of the countless times he himself had retreated to the playroom he had built for her between the pylons underneath their house, because even he needed a place to excuse his own sadness. He found he liked it down there because, despite taking his own boat out to look for her day after day from sun up to sun down, and despite having failed her each and every day, he was reminded, down there, that he was still a good father, if only for having built her that ladder and cutting her that hole up through the floorboards to her room, so that she could come and go as she pleased. "It's like your very own tree fort," he had told her. "All girls," he told her, "Should have a tree fort. Just remember, my dear: no boys allowed." He would just sit there in her sandbox for a good long while among all the toys he had carved out of driftwood for her and all her dolls he had fashioned out of marsh reeds. Down there was the space he had given her, a space that was hers and hers alone. He liked to play with the two tin cans he had given her for Christmas one year, running one from the house down through the floor and connected to the other one by a single piece of string. "One for you, and one for me," he'd explained. "Call if you need me. Call to say hi." And still sometimes, he would find himself picking up the receiver and listening for her voice on the other line.

Ley went on to say he had yet to find them. "But," he said, "There will be justice."

"Really? How?" Bohicket asked. "Justice how?"

"Since it appears we could use a little help to find her right about now, I've decided to go and report this to the proper authorities. See if they can't help," Ley explained. "I mean, that is what they do, am I right? That is their job. Bringing criminals to justice? Finding missing persons? I don't know how to find them exactly, but the way I got it figured, surely someone in the village can point me in the right direction."

Ley's desire to leave their island at all, much less to venture off on such a search, was unprecedented. To that point, aside from the boys' occasional pirating excursions, their exploratory adventures into the woods and the whole family's bi-annual trips to the village on market day, only their father really ever went over to the mainland. And so it is impossible to overstate how troubling Ley's plan actually was to his father and brother.

Their island had always had lungs. Their father knew that better than anyone because, whenever he listened, he could hear the island breathing. And yet that night, its breath was so slow and so steady it was nearly revealing, revealing like an unpacking of suitcases and moving boxes is revealing, like the ready-made calm that presents itself once you're all settled in to a new home in a new city. But what its breathing revealed to him about his son, that night on their roof, took him completely by surprise. It was as if, all of a sudden, he was acutely aware of his own naivety. To think he actually believed that the mainland would never come calling for his children out of necessity or something akin to desire or desperation.

Even the tall necks of marsh grass, it seemed to him, were all occupied with snails and such, as if they too had grown ears to better listen in. He could hear an alligator hissing out along the riverbank. But was it an alligator really, or was it instead charades in the wind? Their father had always known in his heart of hearts that he could not protect his children from the mainland's intrusions, once the four walls of the outside world came closing in around them. He considered this a moment, and he thought of the dangers. He thought that he too was in danger. Loving them this way felt, to him, like being in the clutches, and only now could he feel the jaws tightening at his neck, the teeth bearing down. He knew the alligator too would be grinning.

The look of decisiveness on Ley's face said he had yet to see the horrors of life on the mainland. That out there, the language of the living could be a lesson in didactics, of those who own and those who are owned. Ley did not know, as his father did, that the only thing connecting them to the mainland was but a thin piece of Velcro, that on one side—the side with the bristles—it could all go wrong, while on the other softer side, they would be alright. Ley did not know this. Then again, how could he have known?

Once his boys were old enough to venture off on their own, their father had planned to tell them about the boat he had sunk with a hull full of cinder blocks off the far side of the island where it had remained for years and years now in case of an emergency. But his boys, it appeared, had grown up far quicker than he had wanted, and soon enough, they too would come to know the unruly arbitrations of love and loss that existed out there, and soon, they too would know that even the feast sometimes is a famine out there, and to survive love at all, they too must eat the fallen. So their father did his best to caution Ley against his plan to alert the authorities or breathe so much as a single word of it to anyone in the village because, as he explained, "Nothing is more sacred to them than their secrets, and those men you saw, those men with wings, the fact that they exist at all is one such secret. Mind you, they will do anything, and I mean anything," he warned them, "To keep their secrets a secret."

Then he told them the whereabouts of the boat he had sunk long, long ago, said, "Just know that it's there if you need it. And mark my words: you will, if you don't heed my warning."

Chapter Four

TYPICALLY THE ONLY TIME THEIR FATHER WOULD VENTURE OVER to the mainland was to barter and trade with the villagers for those certain supplies they couldn't do without. The Fourth of July was the one exception. It was his favorite holiday, and so once a year in late June, their father always made a special trip to buy the family a box of fireworks so they could celebrate. What made that particular holiday so special to him was anyone's guess, but the boys liked to think the occasion took on a whole new meaning, once he witnessed the excitement it brought to his children's faces. If they were to guess—and they often did—the peculiar affinity their father had for their nation's birthday began the moment he first laid eyes on a yard filled with sparklers, all three of his children dancing off into the night with a sparkler in both hands, giggling with delight at the flares of color and the pops of sound, as they raced around and around the yard, signing their names in a calligraphy of smoke trails. One can only assume the Walpole children were right, seeing all the wonder they discovered in those jet streams of light and the small fires it ignited in the confines of their heart. One can only assume that it was the hope their father found in their child-like curiosity, the belief it rekindled in him of their chance of making it out there.

It became more and more likely as the days went on that their father might need to make one more exception and venture off to the village in search of help. You see, their mother's condition had only worsened with time, as she took up odder and odder habits in returning to her grief, the most disconcerting of which was the people she began conversing with, people—it should be noted—that only she could see. "The sight" is what she called it. "Sister Dew, she was lucky. She was born with it. And now, it appears, she's left it to me." The whole notion just sort of dawned on her one day, and the next she claimed to see visions in the sky, in the clouds and on the beach—the very same visions, it turns out, that her daughter used to have.

She couldn't say when her daughter got "the sight" exactly, but they couldn't recall a time when Dew could tell you the difference between what she saw and what was actually there. Seeing a flying chariot pulled by a troop of white horses was as ordinary an occurrence in Dew's everyday life as looking up and seeing clouds. Everywhere she turned, the trees had faces, hands and a mouth that spoke to her. The sunset over the water could appear to her like Moses parting the Red Sea. Fish could bubble up to the surface, sprout wings and fly away, while the marsh reeds twisted and turned in an origami of fingers that then became heads and torsos and finally people or ships with tall masts like disciples en route from the Nile to the Promised Land. And so it stood to reason that, even from an early age, Dew had always felt a certain kinship with the John of Revelation, though not so much for the reason you might think. The reality was, her visions came with a sort of lonely isolation, like she too had been exiled to an island alone.

Their mother started to see shadows where before there were none, dark silhouettes and ghostly figures of people she'd never met before and yet felt somehow she knew. And in time, she too began to understand the isolating feeling in having seen such things. What, at first, she believed to be an enviable gift, their mother now saw as a curse she was forced to endure.

She said as much, the evening her husband found her stranded alone, like some debris washed up on the beach, conversing with a scarecrow she'd fashioned out of driftwood.

"Remember the baby seagull she took as a pet?" she said, referring to her daughter. "Bless her heart. I mean, it worried her sick that the world was so cold. Warmed it up in the oven, one day, she did. Bless her heart. And she couldn't have been six when she fed Sparkles to those gators." Sparkles was the stray dog he brought home for his daughter one Christmas morning. Dew loved that dog more than anything else, which is what made the whole thing so tragic when she mistook that nest of hungry alligators for Sparkles' long-lost family and walked the poor dog right out to them, unclasped the leash and said, "There they are, ol' girl. How exciting! We found your family. Go to them, Sparkles, go!"

"And you wanna hear what's even sadder?" their mother continued. "I don't think she ever realized what she had done. She came skipping into the house that day, so happy and so certain that Sparkles had found her family."

Their father shrugged haplessly for he knew that ignorance too was concurrent with love. A fact that was more apparent now than ever. Of course he remembered the fate that befell their beloved Sparkles, but in his mind, he hadn't quite gotten past the sight of his wife conversing with those sticks. He was wholly petrified except for his eyes, which looked her over as if to find something in the way of an explanation. He found none.

"The only thing she loved more than that half-wit dog of hers was her two older brothers," she told him. "So I suppose, everything that she loved could've very well killed her."

He needed a moment to gather himself. "I'm headed off to gather some driftwood, my flower," he told her. "Will you be okay while I'm gone?"

She nodded.

He was not so sure.

He was a good mile or so up the shoreline when he heard

the sound she made when she cried. So he followed the sound back down the beach, and she was hiding her face when he found her again, kneeling ruefully into the shadow of her scarecrow. There were miles and miles in every direction, and yet his wife had the look of someone who herself had been cornered.

"Say, what on earth are you going on about?" he asked, sure he didn't want her answer.

She was quiet.

"You look like a leaf you're shaking so," he said, kneeling down beside her. He was afraid for her. But finding he was devoid of any means of addressing such a strange and terrible happenstance, he just assumed a bit of levity would do her some good. "It's just a scarecrow, my dear," he said. "No need to go on blubbering about it."

She peeked through her fingers at the scarecrow. "It's just, he looks so scary."

"Scary comes with the job, especially in his line of work."

"I wish I never made him," she said, tossing the scarecrow to the ground.

"Why?" he asked, though he secretly wished the same.

"Because," she said, "If he scares off all the birds, there'll be nothing left for me here. Where will I find my feathers? And what then? What about my wings?"

"You mean him?" he said, chuckling. "Aw, he's not the least bit concerned with your birds, my dear. He's a scarecrow, ya see. He's only concerned with scaring off crows."

"Wait!" she said, interrupting him. "Shush! I think you're right. Shush for a moment. Listen. I think he's trying to tell us something. He says . . . He says . . . yes! He says you're right. Thank God, you're right. He says he's only here for the crows."

"Ha! Well ain't that a trip?" he replied and swallowed hard. "Seems your friend here's shit out of luck then. Only seagulls and pelicans 'round these parts." And with that, he retrieved the scarecrow from the sand where she had thrown it and examined it more closely. Only thing to do now was go with it. "Yep . . . Yep . . . Yessir. Seems what we got here is indeed a scarecrow, but not a very good one. Fact, I'd say, by the looks of him, it wouldn't surprise me at all if he was afraid of his own shadow. Here, I'll show you." Then he reached into his pocket and removed the marker he always kept on his person to measure the tides and track tree growth around the island. "Let me just . . . Yep, one squiggle here . . . and another there . . . and presto!" With two quick strokes of that marker at the corners of its lips, he made that scarecrow smile. "There," he said. "How's that? Now tell me honestly, my flower, who could he scare with a smile like that?"

"But now he looks scared."

"Scared? Huh, really? How so? He looks rather happy to me."

"The nights do get dark out here," she said, struggling visibly with the thought. Then she leaned her body back into him and whispered something in the direction of his ear. "I think he might like a little company for a while. You know, till he gets used to the dark."

And their father understood what had to be done. She was nearing the point of no-return, and nothing he said or did seemed to help. If he was going to save her, he would need some help. And yet he did not tell her he was concerned about her, did not even act like he was. He simply took her hand in his and sat there together with her, until the sun went down and the shadows came lurking in from the nearby trees and they were surrounded. At some point, he did ask her what the moon was saying, as if hoping to share in something rarely shared by two people. Love, it seemed, grew easier then and simply lived out its days as a sort of unspoken presence between them, known quietly in the unknown quantities of the evening they shared.

Before their father headed off in his boat the next morning to pay the villagers a visit, he woke his wife up with a voice he made from under the bed. "Top of the mornin' to ya, sleepy head. Rise and shine, rise and shine." He had poked the scarecrow's head up from under the bed and animated its movements, as if it was the one speaking.

"Hello?" she said, half asleep and a little confused. "Hello? Who is that? Who's there?"

"It's me . . . Mister Crow. You know me. It's me."

"Mister Crow? Could it be?"

"Indeed it is. I'm back, and I must say I'm a little bit hungry."

She sat up in her bed. "Yes . . . but oh no, Mister Crow, ya can't eat me!"

"I've come for your fingers, but I'll settle for your toes."

She was giggling now. "Oh no! Oh no, Mister Crow! Not my toes!"

And he couldn't help but laugh a little too.

"Honey, is that your fool ass foolin' around under there?"

"None other, my dear."

"How . . . what . . . what are you doing down there?"

"Hey, look, don't blame me. This was all the scarecrow's idea."

She chuckled again.

And he found he missed that chuckle.

"Come out from under there," she said.

"Well I would. Really I would. The thing is, now that Mister Crow here has quit the whole scaring-the-crows business, the tables have turned in their favor. Turns out, he's more frightened of them now than they ever were of him. Sort of ironic, don't ya think?" Again, he peeked the scarecrow's head out from under the bed and gave it a terrified shake. "Is it safe to come out yet? You don't see any crows around, do ya? Huh, well do ya?"

"Hard to say," she answered. "But I think, for now, the coast is clear."

He was laughing when he climbed back up in bed beside her. "You know, come to think of it," he said, "Mister Crow is right to be afraid of the dark. I mean, it can get pretty darn lonely in the dark. And lonely has me scared."

She was quiet for a moment.

They both were.

He wasn't sure if she understood what he was trying to say or how hard it was for him to say it. He was not a man who opened up willingly. His own father was hard and steady, a vault of a man with an unbreakable lock and no key, and so he was not raised to be like that, to just up and confess his feelings carelessly. But he had run out of options, and this was his last Hail Mary attempt at reaching her before heading off to the village in search of a solution, anyone really with a better idea. So there was a tinge of desperation in how he said it, and he wanted so badly for her to hear it. But she did not, and proposed instead that he "open the curtains, and let in some light if the darkness was bothering him so." And that is precisely what he did. He left her for the windows, opened all the curtains and let in some light. Dawn was a mere whisper of itself by then, but he opened those curtains and let the light wash in and through him and over all the tiny shores of their quiet bedroom.

"Close your eyes," he told her. "It's okay. Close your eyes. Tell me what you see."

She was silent for a while, and then she began to describe the tractor lumbering across the south field of her childhood home. "The tractor is crawling now. It's been a tough year. It's been brought to its knees." She went on to describe the papery shapes of sailboats rising slowly from the marsh line. "The sea is opening up to them," she said. She smiled a little to herself. "And yep, I can see her too. Yep, there she is. There is Sparkles, and she is with her family." She told him she could see the darkness Mister Crow was so afraid of when she closed her eyes, along with dozens of tiny sunspots being relieved of their light.

And that is how he left her that day, with her eyes shut tight. And after a shot or two of liquid courage, he went venturing across the narrow strait between their island and the village in desperate need of help.

Chapter Five

T HE VILLAGE ACROSS THE WAY WAS ESTABLISHED BY A GROUP OF freed people who were left to their own devices after they, with a battalion of Union soldiers, ran off all the plantation owners from the surrounding islands. And to that day, the village remained a place where centuries-old beliefs and local superstitions still abounded in a sort of tangible presence that could still be felt, if not seen. The blue and green bottles that decorated the trees must have numbered in the hundreds and just seemed to go on and on as far as you could see. There were no leaves. There were branches, but no leaves, just bottles and bottles and more and more bottles, all means of entrapping unwanted spirits, for the village itself was a place where all the various island tales came to live among the living, having circulated in those parts for centuries now, primarily in whispers.

Every house was older and bright with colors. Reds, purples, yellows and especially blues. Every house was arranged with a porch, a kitchen, a living room and one or three bedrooms, depending on who all lived there. Were you to step inside any one of those houses at any given time, you would find a certain similarity to their decor as well, for above every hearth were the same three photos, the Holy Triumvirate of Martin Luther King, John F. Kennedy and their Blessed Lord Jesus Christ. Approaching the houses from the fishing docks was an open-air market, complete with booths and sales pitches and a circle of benches, known fondly to the locals as the "Hush Harbor," a gathering place of sorts named nostalgically for the secret meeting places of their ancestors who were said to congregate in the woods by cover of night and there sing songs and share stories in keeping with their African heritage. In the middle of that square was a certain tree that was widely believed to be a healing tree, and this particular tree was so large and so expansive it nearly blocked out the whole wide view of the sky. And as always, there were women sitting around its trunk, handwashing clothes, snapping peas or selling their wares. Mama Hawa's house was just a few doors down from that tree, and that, as it happens, is where he was headed.

Mama Hawa was the village matriarch, in both name and practice, having earned her distinction honestly: by outliving them all. When anyone had an issue, she was the one to solve it. If there was a disagreement, she was the one to settle it. She held court twice a week on her front porch steps where she was the acting judge, the jury, the bailiff and the executioner. In nearly all respects, she was, as the origins of her name would suggest, the mother of the living, or in the literal Arabic translation of her name, the one in possession of Adam's heart, because, as far as daily life went around there, it all ended and began right there on her doorstep.

Unfortunately for him, the two of them had had a long and rocky history that was only appeased by a tenuous trade agreement between him and the village, due to nothing more than their mutual reliance on one another. Everyone in the village knew as much, so when they saw him coming, court was adjourned, and all the occupants of the porch immediately scattered.

"Aw now see, if it ain't the devil himself come to my doorstep with his hat in hand. The famous Berry Man," Mama Hawa said. "To what do I owe the honor or grave misfortune?"

He didn't know how to respond. Typically, they would have bantered a while, trading jab for jab until it settled into laughter. Typically, he would have offered her a lighthearted reply in exchange. But not today. Today, he stayed quiet and just took a seat across from her.

"What, cat got your tongue? Out with it already. What's on your mind? It's only just past day-clean," she said, referencing dawn. "And already I'm hours behind. I'm a busy woman, ya know?"

Still, he did not respond.

She must've realized then that something was seriously wrong because she leaned across the table and touched his hand. "You okay, Berry Man? Sure don't seem so. I've never seen you in such a state. Never thought I would. Neither of us are strangers to the secrets we keep. I: yours. And you: mine. You know I keep my lips sealed. Have for a long time now. I still haven't told no one your real name. Not no one. Not the one you go by nor your real and Christian name. Even when the law came a askin' about you, I said I ain't know nothin' about nobody. Especially no pilot," she said. "I mean I sure ain't no hush harbor, but you know, good and damn well, I can keep my mouth shut. Otherwise, you'd be rottin' in a cell right about now, and ya know that's right."

He was staring off blankly now at the sky through the trees.

"Can't say? Fine, I'll wait." And she rocked back in her chair and began humming a tune. "Wade in the water. Wade in the water," she sang, and her voice was beautiful and clear in the way any woman's voice is, having spent a whole lifetime singing in church. "Wade in the water— You know what?" she said. "We got ways of saying things in code, if and when ya can't find the words. Back in the day, back when we folks were still enslaved by you folks, we would sing this very song to warn the runaways when the dogs came a sniffin'. Wade in the water," she sang. "That's howcome we still sing that hymn in church. To ward off the dogs and get us free."

"Mama Hawa?" he said barely.

"Yes, honey?"

"Think we can put aside our differences just this once and

make like we are friends?"

"Sure, honey."

"It's my wife," he said, like the words themselves were painful. "She's sick."

"Sick? How so? There's all kinds of sick, you know? There's sick in the tonsils and sick in the bones. There's sick to your stomach, and there's worried sick."

"She's sick in the head," he said flatly.

"Oh," she said. "Now that's another matter."

He went on to explain what had happened to his daughter the night she went out on the johnboat with her two brothers. And he had been around a long, long time. Long enough, that is, to know better than to mention the Flying Men the boys swore they saw, and he instead blamed it all on a terribly unlucky shift in the currents, a freak accident coupled with an unnaturally strong rip tide that ended up carrying his daughter out and away from the shore. "Now, my boys have been looking all over for her, and for quite some time," he said. "We're all still hoping she might still be alive. And she very well could be, for all we know, marooned on some island somewhere and unable to get home. She could," he said. "She could also be gone."

"Good Lord Jesus, not Little Dew," Mama Hawa said and clutched at her chest, as if the news had really pained her. "If there's anything, anything I can do to help, you just name it, and it is done. Now, why don't we start with what we can fix and leave the rest, for now, to God? Come now. Why don't you start with her symptoms? Your wife, I mean."

And he told Mama Hawa everything, right down to the details of every last event that had transpired since the day his daughter went missing. He listed off all the many times his wife had tried and failed to fly, all the feathers she had gathered up to make her wings, all the many places she had jumped from and how nothing—not the bumps or the bruises or the bone she broke—had successfully deterred her from her conviction that she could fly.

"A woman with conviction," Mama Hawa said almost to herself. "Gotta admire that."

Then he told her about all the visions and how conversant she was with invisible worlds.

Mama Hawa was never one to consider the advice she gave lightly. In fact, she was known to be methodical and even calculated with it, careful always with the burden of responsibility that came in giving it, and so she took great pains to consider the enormity of what she had just been told before she responded. She thought for a moment, as she looked him over. She scratched her head and looked away, looked away and then back at him.

"Well, first thing's first, I'm guessin'," she began. "If and when she falls and hurts herself again, just find a cobweb and stick it in the wound. That'll do the trick. That'll have her healed up in no time." She allowed herself another moment to consider her response then added, "Which brings us to the far more difficult matter of fixing what actually ails her. The mind," she said, "is a curious thing. But I don't think it's her mind that needs the fixin'. No, I think her mind is the follower here. The mind, after all, is merely a disciple of the heart. We women are like that, you know? Not at all like you men. We think with our hearts, not with our minds. And that goes for all women too, but most especially mothers. And it seems that your wife . . . well, her heart . . . her heart is what's broken."

This made a good deal of sense to him. He had been alive on this planet long enough to understand the vast distinctions between women and men, the modes by which they each seem to operate. He had known quite a few women in his life, and every last one of them almost without exception, acted upon the same strangely alien set of impulses that was wholly and irrefutably different—even bafflingly so—than any of the men he knew. And he had more than a few stories he could have used to illustrate this point, some of them sad, only a few of them true, and the rest would be lies and laughable at best.

"When it comes right down to it, I suppose we women are the mystery in it all," she told him. "And you men would do well to remember that. The heart, not the mind, that's what guides us. Your wife is a woman, and so we must assume that her issues are issued by the heart. Lucky for us, she is a mother as well, so her heart is strong, just as a mother's heart must be. But then again, even the strongest of hearts can still be broken when a piece the size of your only daughter goes missing. But if I'm right—and indeed I am—what we need to remedy is a broken heart."

Mama Hawa suggested that what they were faced with were only two real possibilities: that their daughter was alive or that she was dead, the latter being the far more likely of outcomes. "I mean, the whole rotten thing smells of a haunting to me," she said. "All the same telltale signs of one too." So Mama Hawa offered him the use of a few of her remedies, were this indeed the case. "First," she said, "We must try and rid her of the spirit. And I should warn you, in all fairness to you, what I'm about to say might sound a bit strange to a skeptical outsider such as yourself. Just know that I've seen each and every one of these remedies work, or else I wouldn't bother suggesting them to you. Anyways, I'm guessing we are beyond the realm of bandages and doctors by now, are we not? Why else would you be here? Why else would you have come to me, of all people? It seems all we can do now is do all we can do. Agreed?"

He nodded. "Agreed."

And with that, she jotted down her list of potential remedies on the back of an envelope and explained each and every one, point by point. First, she suggested he take the one item his daughter treasured most in this life, wrap it up in a certain kind of leaf, found only in a certain kind of place, and pass it over his wife's body while she slept. "Then tie a knot of five-finger grass to the bedpost above her head, and see if she doesn't rest peacefully after that. If all goes to plan—and I think it will—you'll haven't the need for numbers three through six on this list. Then again, banishing a spirit is never an exact science. So let's review your other options, just in case." Number three on her list, were it to come to that, was to try hanging a colander from the doorknob to their bedroom before bed every night. "You do own a colander, don't you? If not, just say the word, and I'll lend you mine. Haints are said to develop a great fondness for mathematics in the afterlife, though rumor has it, they are not especially good at it. So your third option is to hang a colander on your doorknob, and any spirit that comes that way will stop in the threshold without entering and begin to count all the holes it sees. And if the spirits are as bad at math as folks say they are, they will lose track of their count over and over and over again, right up until the sun comes up."

He himself was no stranger to the quiet labors of fatherhood, and so he had assumed that he could handle anything life might throw his way. Yet this, this thing that he felt, this, this was new to him, this sudden awareness of his own shortcomings in the face of all that he feared, all that it meant to come upon his daughter as a ghost in his own house, a translucent presence felt somewhere and nowhere, like a wind in the walls stalking all the corridors and shelving of his room and hushing up all the laughter in the esophagus of their home. And so it occurred to him then that fatherhood itself might be the quietest of all labors and not a sound louder.

Seeing something on his face giving rise to the terror, Mama Hawa mentioned the last item she had written on her list, like it was some final offering of hope, were all else to fail. "Wishes made under a new moon are said to come true," she told him. "Same as dreams under a new quilt. My mama taught me that, so you and I both know it's true. If all else fails," she said, "Just know that it's true."

Still, he was troubled.

"Tell me honest," she said. "Is there a plot?"

"A plot?"

"A place where she would be buried, were—God forbid—it come to that."

"Well, yes, I guess," he said. "Out in the woods, next to where her mother and I have plans to be buried. Where, someday I hope, all of us will be buried."

"Is there a tree there?"

"Yes, of course there's a tree. It's the woods. There are lots of trees."

"Does she have a tree?"

"Her mother saw to it that we all have a tree."

"Burn that tree," she said.

"What?"

"I said, burn that tree."

"Burn the tree?"

"That's what I said. Burn the tree. You got cotton in your ears or somethin', Berry Man? I am speakin' clearly, am I not? May sound strange to you, but the thing is, we got us a way of doing things 'round here, and it works. Has for a good many years too. My mama told me, like her mama told her, the trees 'round here are alive with souls, and on grave sites most especially. Something about how our lives are connected, I'm guessin'. Trees breathe out what we breathe in, and vice-a-versa. It's how the good Lord made it, so who am I to question? Around here, we don't remove the trees that need removin'. We burn them. Yessir, when souls come up a-hauntin' and a-spookin' from the grave, we burn the trees. Have since long before you. Have since long before me. It's humane, and it works. It's said to release them. It sets them free."

It had occurred to him many times before that most of the Gullah people he knew were spiritual people and had a sort of special relationship with spirits of most every kind. It was like the spirits, they lived among them, especially when you consider how many of the Gullah people's age-old customs centered around the many measures they took to keep from being haunted, from all the many bottle trees that decorated their yards to the ritualistic ways in which they attended their dead.

What he did not know was the reason for this, that it all started when those who had enslaved their ancestors forbid them the practice of reburying their loved ones, like they had back home, a measure they were long accustomed to while living along the West African coast, where necessity had them burying the deceased quickly and without pomp or circumstance, only to dig the bodies back up a year or so later to grant them a right and proper funeral. What he did not know was that centuries and centuries of communal wisdom on the African continent was what was really to blame, for that is what dictated their still widely held belief that the dead would remain restless until their souls were granted the mercy of a second burial, which of course, their captors—being Christians mostly—had quickly put a stop to just as soon as they had set foot in America. What he did not know was that this was how the Gullah people he knew came to believe that their dead could now be doomed to haunt the living. And so to him, there was still a certain abiding strangeness to what they believed, to even what Mama Hawa now offered up as a solution to what ailed his wife. He certainly had his doubts still. But what choice did he have, now that trying anything was all he had left?

"So burn the tree," he repeated back to her.

"Yes, honey. Burn the tree." Then she glanced over her shoulder to make sure no one was listening, before she leaned in a little closer and whispered, "Course, if she does turn up dead—and God help me, I pray she don't—but if she do and that sad day comes and nothing you try seems to help your wife's restless heart, there is another way to free her of the spirit. Can't say you'll like it though."

"Try me," he said.

"Shhh," she whispered. "Keep your voice down. There are ears everywhere. You can't be too careful when speaking of such things. Need I remind you of the lengths people 'round here will go to keep our secrets a secret? Need I remind you of what happened to Tommy Moreland when they caught him rompin' around with that white girl from the city? Or Lil Tina Ginger and Old Man Hamilton? No one can say where Kenna's body ended up, after he went and got himself quoted in the newspaper 'bout us. Jamien Linn disappeared, and that's still a mystery. Secrets stay secrets 'round these parts, and that is because there are people 'round here who will see to keeping it that way. No one's safe. Not you. Not even me. I'm putting myself in danger just telling you this. So look here, do me and you both a favor and keep it down, would ya?" She waited to be sure she made herself clear before starting into her story. "Thing is, Berry Man, there was this one time, a while or so back, I had this woman show up at my doorstep, came to see me from some way away place like Wadmalaw Island or some place like that, and she was all in a panic over something she'd seen, squirming about in her seat and glancing all around, this way and that, like a frightened squirrel or something. Something sure had her spooked, I was thinking. Turns out, her sister had just died from the shakes or some other damned disease. I don't recall exactly. And with her sister now dead and buried and her niece's deadbeat father nowhere to be found, the responsibility of taking the girl on and raising her as her own had fallen to her. She had no problem with that, at first, seeing as her sister's child was one of them easy-going children and hardly ever raised a fuss. And things were all fine and good, until her niece started waking up in screams and fits at all hours of the night. The woman could not, for the life of her, figure out why. She tried and she tried to figure out what was wrong. The little girl was just fine and dandy all day long, but at some point in the dead of night, she would wake up screaming and carrying on for what seemed to be no reason at all. Then it happened. The woman had walked into that little girl's room to check on her, and there she saw it, in the dead of the night: her dead sister standing—not sitting, not laying, but standing, mind you—at the foot of the little girl's bed. She could see it was her sister, just not. 'A see-through version of her sister maybe,' as she told it. She could hardly believe it, and yet there her sister was, just standing there, staring off blankly at the wall, as if she was gazing straight through it. And that is how-come she came looking for me the very next day, visibly shaken, still scared half out of her skin. And do ya know what I had her do? Do ya even wanna know?"

"I'm not so sure I do."

"Well, I'll tell ya, Berry Man. I sent that woman home directly and had her take her little niece out to the graveyard that very same night at around the witching hour, and I had her wave that little girl around by her arms over her dead mother's grave to show her her baby was fine and okay so there was no need to worry about her anymore. And you know what? It worked. It sure enough did. Her sister's soul found peace and was never seen or heard from again." Mama Hawa could see, from the confused expression on his face, that he needed her to explain herself further. So she did. "If the same trick worked one way," she told him, "Then it might could work the same another way."

He searched her face for any signs she was kidding. "You aren't suggesting that I—"

"I am," she said, "If it comes to that, just do it at night. The witching hour is best."

Chapter Six

A ROUND THE VILLAGE, MR. WALPOLE WAS OFTEN THE TOPIC OF whispers. They talked about him, though rarely in public. They talked about him at night, at home on their porches or paired off in the quiet of their bedrooms, often husband-to-wife, often half-naked on their way into pajamas. They said, "I tell ya, that there Berry Man sure can drink and sure drives a hard bargain. How do you suppose he got that way?" some wondered. "Hard living," some said. "Suppose a man like that's got a lotta secrets," others surmised. "I ain't no gamblin' man," some replied, "but I'd wager hard money that he has a skeleton or two in his closet." And perhaps he would've remained only popular amongst the whispers, had his little visit with Mama Hawa that morning not awakened so many of their louder suspicions. They thought it strange enough that he was there in the first place, to say nothing of how long they talked. *About what?* the villagers wondered. And to their credit, it was indeed strange. Everything about it was strange, and every last person in the village knew it. So it stands to reason that, the instant he bid Mama Hawa farewell and set off for home, the entire village was sent instantly into a tizzy of busy-bodies scurrying about from house to house, intent on uncovering the curious nature of his business there.

They all knew that he had his fair share of secrets. What else, besides a good many secrets, would drive a man to abandon everything he knows and escape to an island? There was no shortage of guesses—that's for sure—the majority of which many came to be certain of. Rumor had it that he was, in a past life, everything from a spy doing research for the government to a cold-blooded killer on the run from the law. And all those whispers were awakened that morning once again and did not subside until well after midday when all their frantic inquiries were relinquished for the quiet of their porches where most of the villagers could only imagine themselves in other people's bodies, possessed and stretched from the inside out by other people's secrets. And in that at least, they might've found they understood him better than they imagined they could. They might've discovered that they were not so different from him, especially when the one unbearable constant for all of us is the struggle to outlive the aloneness of our secrets.

THE SUDDEN EMERGENCE OF A KINDER MORE CHILD-LIKE SIDE to his wife was a strange if not downright arresting presence in their house. Every other day or so, the mother the boys had come to recognize as their mother reappeared, as she would on occasion, and revert to the same snide remarks, the same cruelty still harbored down deep in her person. "Boy, ya gone and got all sissified on me?" she would say to one of her sons. "What do you mean you're tired? Man up. Stop whining like a little girl. Need your pacifier and bankey, little girl?" And then that person would disappear again, only to reappear in a day or two with a "Boy, you dumb as a moon rock. What's that you say? Huh? Get your head out the clouds. I can't hear you when you talkin' all kinds a stupid like that." But it didn't take long for that familiar side of her to vanish altogether and give way completely to the earnestness of a child lost in a dream. In the end, she was like a different person to them. And though the change was a welcome one in many respects, change—even for the better—can be a hard thing to swallow. And so feeling the added dread that his wife might be lost to him forever, the first thing their father did when he got home that day was siphon some gas from the engine on his boat and set off into the woods to burn down the tree that he and his wife had selected to, one day, bury their daughter under. It made no sense. Mama Hawa had just finished telling him to wait to see if she will be buried there, but the way he saw it, he could no longer afford the risk in waiting. He doused the whole trunk of that tree in gasoline, said, "Sorry, Little Dewdrop. It's the only way." Then he struck a match and watched as the whole tree went up in flames.

Back at the house, the boys caught a whiff of something burning, and from clear across the island, they could see the smoke. It didn't take long for that smoke to rise, to climb up and over even the tallest treetops, to stack brick-upon-brick into the masonry of the sky, where it appeared ever-growing, like some kind of sooty chimney piling up and up, black upon black and stack upon stack, from the roof of their world. And the boys wasted little time racing off in the direction of the smoke, fearing as they did that something had gone horribly awry, and it was left to the two of them to stop it.

By the time they reached their father somewhere deep in the woods, he was already in the throes of a terrible frenzy. The fire, by then, was nearly out of control. He had this sort of frantic look on his face, like he was genuinely frightened, as he heaved handfuls of dirt at the base of a tree in a fit of desperation, trying in vain to extinguish the fire. "Get some water!" he cried.

And they did.

"Now climb up that tree and douse those branches!" he ordered when they returned with their buckets of sea water. "Good, good! Now those over there!"

When it was all said and done, the tree was reduced to a charred black trunk, a black hand with only an index finger left pointing up to accuse the sky. And there at its base was their father, surveying the scene, still veiled in smoke. He appeared somehow pleased with himself, though neither of the boys could say why. "There," he said, nodding to himself. "A job well done."

"But why?" Ley asked.

"It was the only way, son." And though they were clearly perplexed by his actions, their father did not explain himself any further, leaving them instead to marvel at the mysterious why in this seemingly dastardly deed. And he did not explain himself further because, as their father, he did not have to. He instead kept quiet on the whole matter and watched the wisps of gray smoke escape up through the trees. It was like he was seeing a television in color or hearing his favorite song on the radio for the very first time, and he was leaving it to them to understand for themselves the enigmatic quiet of things even a father cannot explain— things like the morning sun and things like death, things like the feeling of undressing yourself in front of someone new. And their father would never really get around to explaining himself to them, not then, not ever, though he would live to regret it.

He had hoped that, by skipping to the end and burning that tree, the process of fixing whatever ailed his wife would be hastened. For several days, he waited patiently for it to work. But it did not. And so later that week, he went to bed, same as he always did, so as not to alert anyone of his intentions, and he watched the clock tick off into the dead of night, before rolling over to make sure his wife was still fast asleep.

It was two or three in the morning when he snuck out to their shed and gathered what he needed, and it was nearly four o'clock by the time he finally tiptoed back into their room. He had had quite a time of it, trying to decide which of his daughter's things she treasured the most—her long beautiful hair, which she seemed to forever be brushing, or the telescope he'd made for her out of PVC piping and sea glass so that she could keep a lookout for pelicans and sharks and the occasional passing ship. And unable to make up his mind in the end, he decided on both. He stole her telescope from out of her room and went around gathering up every strand of her hair that he could find: from the teeth of her favorite comb and from the knitting in her sweater, a few loose strands from off her pillow and a few more from between her sheets. He wrapped her hair around the telescope and then wrapped the telescope in the leaf that Mama Hawa had told him where to find, then he tied it all off neatly with her favorite blue hair ribbon. He then snuck back into their bedroom and proceeded to wave it back and forth over his wife's sleeping body, exactly as Mama Hawa had instructed him to do.

"See there, Little Dewdrop," he whispered to his daughter, just in case she was somewhere listening. "Ya see? Your mother is doing just fine. Ya see? So you can go now and rest easy. Rest, my dear. Go on. It's time for you to rest."

Every time the floorboards creaked, he paused to be certain that no one was stirring. He assumed he had taken all the necessary precautions to keep from being discovered, but as he reached over to tie a knot of five-finger grass to the bedpost above her head, just like Mama Hawa had told him to do, he caught a glimpse of Ley standing in the doorway. He could not say for certain how long his son had been there or how much he had seen, but it was the look on his son's face that told him already he had seen far too much.

Turns out, while Ley had, to that point, heeded his father's warnings and abandoned his plan to seek the villagers' help to find his sister, he could never quite bring himself to let go of the hope that she was still out there, alive somewhere. Turns out that he too had been sneaking out every night about that time to set off in his johnboat and go searching up and down the coastline for her, wherever she may be. And that is how he happened upon his father carrying on so strangely in the darkness of that room, while his mother slept so soundly. At first, it was hard for Ley to say anything, hard enough for him to breathe. He could hardly believe what he was seeing, hardly believe his eyes. But when he finally did speak up, what he heard himself saying was "That's not right."

"That's not right," he kept saying.

What his father felt right then, upon seeing him in the doorway, was something in the way of regret, regret for all that he had not explained and now could not explain, for all the ways he had failed him as his father. If only for a world of second chances, a world where a father and a son could try again, a world where it was possible to explain himself and the strangeness of his actions. If only for that world. Even then, Ley's heart had yet to be broken, and for so long, all their father ever wanted was to keep it that way, whole and unbroken, same as it should always be. And yet, in a flash, it seemed all that had changed. It seemed his son was all heart now, and his heart too was broken. He knew everywhere there were other fathers who were also rooting for the safekeeping of their sons. He knew that the adult world was a wild and scary place, full of cruelty, abandoned row houses and the staccato of gunfire in the nearby distance. He knew the adult world was a rough and unforgiving place, a bruised city where only a few survive.

The one consistency in a father's life with his sons is that they always find time to wrestle, as if preparing them, in a way, for the baffling violence all men must learn to face in this world. It's difficult to say why the wrestling stops, after years and years of tussling around on the living room floors, and it's far more difficult to say when it stops. Though not in this case. In this case, the wrestling would stop that very night, the moment his son had, at long last, seen enough to give rise to a man. Had their mother been awake to see Ley standing in their doorway, she might have noticed it too: that sudden decipherable change in him, the man breaking free of the sixteen-year-old boy in him, like a dandelion breaking free of the sidewalk. And she would have simply shrugged her shoulders then and likely repeated what her own mother used to say whenever a boy they knew hit puberty: "Whelp, I guess the sap has finally risen in that one. 'Bout time too. And just when I was thinking he would be about as useful as mittens on a snake."

Their father knew nothing he could say would stop him, so when Ley turned and ran out the door and into the night, their father did not chase after him. Lord knows he wanted to. He wanted nothing more than to run his son down, take him up in his arms and convince him to stop running. But if his own life had taught him anything, it's that all men must run from something.

And so their father did not run after him. Instead, he headed off to the one place he knew he could breathe, to a place deep in the woods where he would go to escape his wife when he needed escaping, a place where he had built a moonshine still out of debris he'd found and a piecemeal of borrowed or discarded parts. He would, on occasion, convince an acquaintance in the village to make a special trek into the mainland to buy him a case or two of matured bourbon or, as he fondly called it, his "liquid damnation." But otherwise, this was his place of solace where he could go to find himself and the courage he needed. And there again, in the heart of that island, in the heart of those trees, tapping his still, his sadness took hold. First of his lungs, and then of his eyes. And it was the sadness he felt, right then and there, that reawakened his concern for his son, where he went and where he was going. So eventually he did go after him. He looked and he looked for him everywhere, only to discover Ley and his boat were nowhere to be found.

It was dawn before his now frantic search for his son led him across the water to the village, and that is where his father found him, being led down the street by a handful of men toward Mama Hawa's house.

When they reached her porch, they shoved Ley down at her feet and accused him of planning to reveal their secrets. "An egregious crime," as one man put it. "I'd say," agreed another. "He's been asking around about, um . . . them," a woman said. "He asked me too," said another. "Yeah, and I heard him," a few more chimed in.

Mama Hawa saw the anger welling up in their faces and, fearing the worst, raised a hand to calm the crowd. "Now, now. Let the boy speak," she commanded. "He's just a boy. Let him speak. Come, boy," she said with an assuring smile and helped him up. "To your feet now. Up you go. You hear what they are accusing you of. Now come, it's your turn to speak."

And Ley rose to his feet, a little hesitant at first, but then puffed out his chest and, finding his courage, turned and faced his accusers. "They are right. I am guilty," he said. "I was asking around. I asked her . . . and him . . . I asked him and him . . . and I even asked her. And I'll ask them all the same question a thousand more times, if I have to. I'm not sorry. They took my sister. I saw them do it. I saw them carry her away, with my own two eyes. I demand to know what happened to her, where they took her and where she is."

Were you to ask him, their father would admit, in no uncertain terms, to feeling a deep abiding pride for the fight he witnessed in his son that day on the porch, as well as the willful defiance he clothed himself in, like he was really a man. But what their father mistook for a man's outright defiance was, in actuality, the look of a boy coming upon a kind of urgent realization that perhaps his father's advice had been right after all, that there was something true in what his father told him: "Do your darnedest to avoid confrontation, but if it comes a-knockin', punch first and punch hard." And so Ley did precisely as his father had suggested and came out swinging.

And his father knew that in some ways he was responsible for that, seeing as he had always had some advice for his sons on the ready. You might even say he was full of it, full of advice that is. Advice like, "Don't knock it till you try it, unless it happens to be a door. A good rule of thumb is to assume that all guns are loaded, as is any man who's out past four in the morning." He taught them to shake hands like a man, nice and firm, withholding nothing. "A man is only as good as his handshake," he would tell them. "And always remember: red-right-return will get you home." And he taught them to be gentlemen, above all else, because "here in the South, that's what is required of men." And their father would've done well to heed his own advice that day on the porch, and "only take the blame for what you yourself have done," for if he had, he might still be alive today.

Instead, he stepped forward and accepted all the blame for what his son had done. "If I may, Mama Hawa," he began, approaching the top step. "Don't blame him. He's only a boy. If you want someone to blame, here I am. Blame me. I am his father. I am to blame."

The crowd amassing around her porch was a crowd of people raring for justice.

"Somebody must pay!" a man shouted from the back.

"Yeah! They know the rules! Someone must pay!"

"Quiet. Quiet," Mama Hawa said.

But the crowd would not be silenced.

And so in the end, her hand was forced despite what she considered fair or just. "It appears I haven't a choice in the matter," she said, turning to their father. "Rules are rules, and rules are only rules so long as they're enforced. And Berry Man, you know the rules better than most." The expression on her face said it gave her no pleasure to do what she now had to do. "Berry Man," she said, and a hush fell over the entire village, "I hereby put a hex on you for the transgressions of your son. You are his father. And as his father, I hold you responsible. So hear me now: from this day forward, you, Berry Man, are a marked man. I call down the heavens upon your head as an answer for your crimes. We find you guilty, Berry Man."

Their father would later dismiss the validity of her curse, but only to alleviate the concerns of his family. Secretly though, he knew the danger he was in and spent the next few weeks peering over his shoulder, as if the world itself was out to get him and, at any moment, the sky might fall and crush his head. He had seen enough to know it was entirely possible and even likely. He had heard what became of all the others she had cursed, like Billy Beau Swainee who was crushed by a tree, and Gaston Ricketts who got swept away in the tide, and Sadie Joe Mayfield who choked on her salad.

Nothing their father said, though, could assuage Ley's guilt for what he had done. And as such, that guilt only grew into a kind of mad persistence that weighed on him more and more, until the weight was unbearable, and late one Thursday evening, Ley told his brother he just couldn't take passively standing by anymore. Bohicket and Ley had just returned from an afternoon pirating the waterways with a case of lukewarm beer, a Falcons jersey and a picnic basket full of food and eating utensils. They had camouflaged their little johnboat in branches and dried leaves and were hiding along a riverbank in hopes of spotting one of the Flying Men in the sky and following him back to where their sister was kept. "I'm leaving," Ley said so abruptly it sounded to Bohicket like he actually meant it.

"Leaving? Where will you go?"

Ley cracked a beer. "I dunno," he said with a shrug. "But the villagers were upset, and that means they had something to be upset about. They know what we know. So I suppose I'll search the islands I come across first. Then maybe it's on to Charleston where there are people who can help."

"Charleston's a long walk from here."

"I got legs. Two of them, in fact. Both in good working order, best I can tell."

"Yeah but you're a faster swimmer."

"I can steal what I need, if I have to. Pops taught us good enough how to get by that way. So, ya know, if push comes to shove," Ley said, referring to how, early on, it was their father who first taught them how to run up alongside a bigger boat, how to attach the anchor, along with what to look for and how to get away with it. "I mean, it could get rough I know," he admitted. "Out there on my own. But Bo, I just can't take it anymore."

"Can't take what?"

"I have to believe there is justice for her somewhere, ya know? A way somehow to right this terrible wrong. I have to believe that, Bo. I have to."

"Sure."

"And rest assured, if there is, I will find it."

Bohicket loathed the idea of his little brother wandering the world all on his own, but he could see that Ley had made up his mind already because he chewed at his bottom lip like he always did when a decision was decided. Had he known the kind of serious danger Ley would put himself in by merely continuing to go about asking questions, Bohicket might have tried to stop him. But as it were, Bohicket was not yet privy to the truest reality of living in those parts: that autonomy was still the one essential element to preserving the practices unique to the village and its people and their culture, and as such, the secret of the Flying Men's presence there was equally essential. Though he did not know it yet, it was, after all, the Flying Men's solemn duty, even then, to keep a lookout for unwanted visitors when they came. And on the rare occasion that fish became scarce, it was still the Flying Men's job to come to their aid and point out large schools to the village fishermen and identify animals they could hunt and eat. And it fell to them as well to continue that centuries-old practice of carrying souls to rest in the sky. And yet Bohicket did not try to dissuade his little brother of his plans, largely because, as he saw it, it wouldn't have done any good. Because, if Ley was anything, Ley was stubborn, if not downright bull-headed, once he'd made up his mind.

"I have to think there is someone out there who cares that a girl was kidnapped or—"

"Don't," Bohicket cut him off. "Just . . . don't . . . okay? She's alive, okay? She is. Okay? We just have to find her is all, okay?"

"I guess, if all else fails, I can always go to the local papers or straight to the police. Surely someone, anyone, someone will help."

"Someone," Bohicket said, as if wishing it were so. "And what if, along the way, you happen to find them? The Flying Men, I mean? What then?"

Ley considered the question for a moment, like it was the first time he had thought to consider it. "I'll rescue her," he said. "That, and then avenge her."

"Avenge her? How so?"

"I don't know. Play it by ear, I suppose. Ya know, see what happens."

"You should clip their wings while they're sleeping," Bohicket suggested. "That'll show them. That'll teach them to go messing with our sister again."

"Or tie them to the ground," Ley said.

They laughed like they were really enjoying the whole idea.

"Maybe castrate them," Bohicket suggested. "See how they like peeing from a hole."

"Now that would be justice."

And Bohicket, for safe-keeping, snapped a picture of his brother's sly little smile.

They returned home later that night, and Bohicket helped his little brother pack all his belongings in a small paper bag. And come morning the next day, they set off together for the mainland by boat. Thinking it would be wisest to keep out of sight, they skirted the village, and there on the far side of the houses, Bohicket saw his brother off.

"Write, won't you?" Bohicket said.

"Of course."

"You are still literate, aren't you?"

"Shut up."

"What? It's just you look a helluva lot dumber than you used to. And who's to say how many times you fell asleep on that roof, rolled off and landed on your head? I had to ask."

"Well I'm so dumb now, after all those falls, I can hardly count past ten anyway."

"At least write to let me know what you find out, won't you?" Bohicket said. And for the briefest of moments, he himself considered packing up and going with him. He found he really wanted to. He just couldn't bring himself to leave his parents all on their own, especially now that their mother needed him around to look after her and their father. Well, who knows what was happening to him? "Maybe we can meet up, after you get wind of a good lead . . . and you know, maybe we can hunt them together maybe."

Ley nodded. "Yeah. That'd be nice."

It was early morning, when there was no light but the coming of light.

"Take care of yourself, little brother. Okay?"

"You too."

And Bohicket looked on, as his brother vanished into the woods.

Chapter Seven

IT SEEMS, ALWAYS, LOVE ENTERS THROUGH THE SAME DOOR IT exits. One person leaves and makes way for another, as if our life is a room furnished with space enough for the love we need. And so it was for Bohicket that morning.

As fate would have it, Bohicket saw his brother off and then wandered back through the village on his way home, seizing upon the rare opportunity to appease his curiosity about that place. And as fate would have it, it just so happened that he stumbled upon a girl about his age, sitting cross-legged along the shoreline, mending casting nets for her father.

Her name was Aylin. "Aylin," is how she introduced herself. And were you to ask him, Bohicket would tell you he was struck first by her eyes. Not the color of them, more their size and how they peered out luminously from the evening dusk of her face like two light bulbs two sizes too big or halogen high beams seeing their way down a dark country road. Most other boys in her life had considered her plain, by even the kindest, most generous measures of beauty, from her wholly unremarkable features and almost adolescent figure to her ocean-fed skill with each loop of the net she mended. But Bohicket would've taken issue with that. He didn't know what it was about her exactly, but seeing her there on the beach that day, tucked so slightly into the morning sun, sparked something inside of him. Something he'd never felt before. And while he did not know it yet, the photographer, first commissioned in him as a boy, would later develop an eye for her landscape. "Aylin," he mouthed to himself, knowing, even then, that he would not soon forget her name. "Aylin," he mouthed to himself.

He liked her name. He liked the sound it made on his tongue, so quiet in how it announced itself. Aylin. In his mind, the name itself had a certain persistence to it. Aylin. The synesthesia perhaps, the sound of a taste, the juicy bitterness that comes in being alive out there in so remote a place.

"Still, everyone 'round here calls me Bea, short for Beabuh," she continued. "Beabuh," she repeated. "Means Beaver. They took to calling me that because I'm always making stuff out of wood. But please, if you don't mind, call me Aylin. I prefer Aylin."

"Then Aylin it is."

"Made this here, just yesterday," she said, pulling a small wooden fish from her pocket.

"Out of driftwood?" he asked.

"Yup." She nodded.

"Really? I mean . . . it looks real."

"Stop."

"No really. I've got half a mind to scale it, gut it and grill it for lunch."

"Mama warned me about boys like you. 'Beware of boys and their flattery,' she said."

"Well I, for one, think your mama is right. You'd do well to beware of boys like me," he said. "Especially," he said, "boys like me." And then he gave her a kind of mischievous grin. "All I'm sayin' is this here fish looks real tasty, and I... well, I'm getting pretty hungry."

"Hungry, huh?" She appeared to consider the idea for a moment. And liked it. "Then, a mouthful of splinters might not do. I do know a good fishing spot, not far from here though."

Bohicket always thought he was, at best, an average-looking guy, what with his fog-gray eyes and dusty brown hair that shocked from his scalp like it was surprised to be there. At worst, he considered himself plain, not at all like his neighbors whose skin appeared brilliant with shades and color, rather than bland and white like his own. And so it had never even dawned on him that a girl as striking as Aylin might consider him attractive, much less flirt with him so coyly.

Something about her—perhaps her large cedar-colored eyes—made her seem all the more beautiful to him when she mentioned a spot to fish. Hers was a quiet sort of beauty, the sort of unspoken beauty that speaks to boys like him, like it is itself a kind of secret, a secret she shared only with him. And it was the look she gave him that awakened the stillness inside of him and reminded him, for one reason or another, of the Afghan girl on the cover of the National Geographic he'd read a thousand times as a boy, and the feeling he felt seemed both foreign and criminal as well, in how it drew him in.

Falling in love is like playing with lightning. In the same breath, his mother had warned him about both. "Stay inside. Read a book," she had said at the window, one day. "Bad skies are bad for all God's children." His mother could always summon that hard-and-fast, mothers-know-best kind of charm, if ever she wanted to, and so it hadn't taken long for the eugenics of the world to grow into his one true fear—that he was doomed to be always and forever alone, just another heartless bag of meat that was, as his own mother had put it, "only as good as what the butcher would ask for it." And really, who could blame him for feeling this way, living out his days all alone on that island, in the persistent throes of hormonal adolescence with so few prospects around to see his love through? He wanted to jump at the chance Aylin presented him with, and would have, were it not for the rain clouds that came rolling in from the east, were it not for how readily they reminded him of all his mother's warnings. So he did not, thinking he could see the lightning. And afraid of what it could mean, he replied instead, "Maybe another time," then bade her farewell and headed off across the channel.

BOHICKET TRIED TO FORGET ALL ABOUT HER. HE TRIED HIS darnedest. He knew he had nothing to give her—nothing she'd want—seeing as he was the son of a simple fisherman and that was all, while she . . . she was a dream and, as such, deserving of the life of a dream. He wanted nothing more than to give her that and so much more, but he knew he could not. So instead, he set about doing the only right and decent thing there was to do in his situation, to simply set about his chores day after day and forget about her. But he couldn't. For some reason, he felt himself being drawn to her with each new day, almost organically like steel shavings are drawn in at the magnetic center, and it didn't take long before he was consumed by the mere thought of her face, which had fossilized itself like an insect in the amber of his mind. Every morning, he would wake up and tell himself in the mirror, "Whelp, this is the morning, ol' boy." And yet he could never bring himself to go and speak to her, feeling as if the waters between them were—and would forever remain—an impregnable ocean.

Only after days and days of trying to convince himself, days and days of busying himself with the work of the island, did he begin to truly understand how loneliness makes us idolaters of love. And only then, after days and days of mending things, seeing to this and that, of wading through the marsh and muddy inland creeks to gather up blue crab and oysters for dinnertime, only then would Bohicket become dead-set on outliving the very notion of it all: this celibacy with its unsettling disposition, the colossal quiet of his life alone on that island.

A savage streak of courage is all it would take, and finding it one day, he ventured out across the water on his boat, circled back from the woods through the village and acted surprised when he stumbled upon her, out along the shoreline.

"Hey there, beaver girl. Stomach's been grumblin'. Got any wooden fish I can try?"

She smiled when she saw him there. "No," she said, "but I know where to find them." And after swearing him to secrecy, she led him out to her favorite fishing spot. "This is our little secret, okay?" she told him. "Now I'm trusting you. No one else knows about this place, except you, me and my dead papa."

The spot she spoke of was a mile or so hike upriver, and they had to wade waist-deep through a half-a-dozen tidal creeks to get there. What they found, tucked under an outgrowth of leaves, was a shady spot where they could cool their feet. She explained that she kept her fishing pole and some bait hidden where nobody else could find it. "So close your eyes, while I run and get it," she told him. "And I mean it. No peeking."

"You're acting kinda fishy," he said with a chuckle.

She waited for him to cover his eyes and then went to go dig up her pole from the place she had buried it. "Here," she said, upon her return. "Here's a bit of line for you. Now make yourself useful and find you a stick to use as your pole, while I tie on the bait."

As promised, the fishing was so good they seemed to just leap from the water.

"And here I was, thinking I was the one who was hungry," Bohicket remarked.

"Bet I catch more than you do," Aylin said.

"You're on," he said. "Here, fishy fishy. Got us a bet to win. And there's no way I'm gonna be shown up by some girl."

"Care to make it interesting . . . with, you know, a friendly wager?" she asked.

"Sure," he said. "I'm rich. Heck, I've got all the money in the world."

"Not money," she said.

"Then what? A kiss?"

"You wish," she said.

"No? Have you ever been kissed?"

"Yes," she lied. "Dozens of times."

"No lie?"

"No lie."

"That makes sense," he said with a shrug. "I mean, a pretty girl like you? I bet anyone, born with at least one good eye, has tried to kiss you."

"There you go flattering me again."

"Yes ma'am. There I go again."

Bohicket could see her reflection on the water and knew, had she seen it herself, the way he saw her, she would've known he wasn't simply trying to flatter her. He was telling her the truth. "Still, I'd wager a kiss that I beat you," he said.

"How about this? The loser cooks instead," she said.

"Still like my idea better."

"And I prefer my fish filleted and charred with just a hint of butter."

"Duly noted," he said.

It was her playfulness that he fell for first, her willingness to take a good-hearted ribbing and dish it out in stride. That is why, in a way, Aylin began to remind him of his sister, for how soft she was with her toughness, for the ease of her courage in coping with boys.

"There's five . . . . Now six . . . . Just remember: a hint of butter," she said. And all afternoon, they made a game of it, taunting one another with every catch. "What is that? Three?" she would say. "Better catch up, Berry Boy. I bet you look good in an apron." And it was evening before Bohicket finally waved the white flag and called it quits. "I surrender! I surrender!" he said, whipping his shirt around above his head. "I yield! Uncle! It appears you have bested me."

"Then put your hand over your heart and repeat after me," she said. "I, Bohicket, son of the right and noble Berry

Man . . ."

"I, Bohicket, son of the right and noble Berry Man . . . "

" . . . do hereby admit . . . "

" . . . do hereby admit . . . "

" . . . that, on this very day . . . "

" . . . on this very day . . . "

" . . . that I, Bohicket Whatzurface, got beat by a girl . . . "

" . . . that I, Bohicket Walpole, got beat by a girl . . . "

" . . . so help me God."

" . . . so help me God."

Then Bohicket did as he had promised. He built a small fire, de-boned the fish and cooked their meal. Their conversation softened over dinner, as it often does, once stomachs are satisfied, and their talk turned naturally to more delicate matters, like the verdict of his father's trial. She asked him, "How's he doing? He doing okay?"

And though Bohicket wasn't entirely sure how to answer the question, he felt like he could trust her. His father was coping with this the same way he coped with everything, the isolation, the loneliness, the always disaffected presence of his wife. His father coped by drinking. "Honestly?" Bohicket said. "It's been all downhill since Lil Dew went missing."

"Missing? How so? Oh God. When? How? She's gone missing?"

It wasn't so much what she said, but how concerned she sounded when she said it that made her reaction seem so genuine. "Wait, why do you care? You didn't know her, did you?" he asked, which judging by the sheer volume of her reaction, seemed like a logical question. "My sister, I mean. Did you know my sister?"

"Yes," she said. "Your sister and I, we used to be friends."

He was shocked by her answer.

Turns out that, since Bohicket and Ley had started spending so much time on their boat scouring the waterways and thus leaving Dew all on her own, their mother saw to finding their sister a playmate so she wouldn't have to always feel so alone.

"She really didn't get along with the other girls her age. So when your mother started dropping her off in the village, she began to follow me around instead. At first, she was a nuisance, a pesky kid who refused, despite all my protests, to leave me alone. Then she grew on me. How could she not? Your sister was so sweet. She even offered to help me with my chores. We became friends after that. We had fun together. She turned everything into a game."

Bohicket could hardly believe his ears. How come this was the first he was hearing of this? He and his brother were never allowed to go into the village alone. Never. Not ever. Their father had always told them it was far too dangerous. Not because of who lived there, but because, as he told them, the continuity of them living out separate lives was of the utmost importance. "Games?" Bohicket asked her. "What kind of games?"

And she told him all about their time together. "Oh, even when Dew was little, she could make a game out of anything," she said. "She was creative like that. Games were her gift."

It was the idea of them playing all those wonderful games that had him curious. And it was that very same curiosity that saw him coming back day after day in the weeks that followed. Always, he brought Aylin small tokens of his appreciation for their friendship, like a colorful seashell, a piece of translucent sea glass or a shell with no crab, and sometimes he would just leave them at her door for her to come upon without her knowing who left it because he liked to imagine the pleasure it gave her when she found it. In time, however, the gifts got bigger, as did his feelings for her.

Each time he visited her, he visited her in secret, understanding the rules they were breaking and knowing full-well the danger they would face, if the villagers saw them together. So they rendezvoused every day, well out of sight. And every day, she showed him another game she used to play with his sister. "Here, we made a fairy fort once from old bed sheets and carved them a door and furniture out of wood," she told him. "Then we made them little fairy friends for company. We held hermit crab races and crowned the winners. We made paper boats and hosted regattas. We played dress-up with the clothes we made out of seaweed and hats we made out of dried wood."

And although it sounds strange for a boy his age, Bohicket was happy to take part in all these games. Ask Aylin, and she might even go as far as to say he was really quite good at it, perhaps suggesting he might even have a future in fashion design. "You look good playing the princess," she told him once. He was comfortable enough around her by then to take this as a compliment.

"Princess?" he scoffed. "Try queen."

Bohicket had fun, to be sure. Still, that is not why he continued to play those games with her. It was more that those games made him feel a little closer to his sister, wherever she was, and in time, he could sense a portion of his pain being lifted from his chest. The unfortunate irony of which was not lost on him and how strange it was that, only now in her absence, was he finally beginning to understand her.

THE SITUATION BACK HOME HAD ONLY WORSENED WITH TIME. Ley was gone, and his family was worried. Nothing their father tried could fix their mother, and so their father's paranoia over the outcome only grew with each passing day. In time, his bathrobe had become his vestments, and he stopped going outside altogether, except when he had duties to attend to. Not long after that, he developed a drinking problem, the problem being that he stopped and thereby became susceptible to the unfiltered realities he faced. "If I'm going out, I'm going out sober," he reasoned with himself.

"And if the sky's gonna fall, let it fall. I just wanna hear the thud when it lands on my head."

And a couple days later, the sky did just that. It fell, exactly as he had feared, when their father went out fishing in his boat one day and never returned.

It was Bohicket who found his body when it washed ashore, and it was Bohicket who had to bury him alone, seeing as his mother was now so stricken with grief she wanted nothing to do with the whole affair. So later that night, Bohicket did just that. He buried his father's body out in the woods in the plot that had been delineated for the eventuality of his grave, and there, having covered the site over with dirt and finding himself suddenly stranded without the words to say, Bohicket chose instead to let the bird-cries of the wind give his father's eulogy.

His mother, distraught now beyond measure, holed herself up in her room and closed the door. And despite all his best efforts, she refused to come out. Not for food or fresh air. Not for him. Not for anyone. It was difficult getting past having to bury his father and the grief that came with his daily absence, and Bohicket dealt with it the only way he knew how: by doing as his father would have wanted him to do and look after the woman he left behind. And so Bohicket started sliding her meals through the crack in the door. Whether or not she ate the food was anyone's guess. But he would climb down on his hands and knees each night and call out to her from under the door. "Mama?" he would say. "Eat something, won't you?"

For days, she responded only with silence, until the night she answered, "Yes?"

"Mama?" he said.

"Yes?" she said.

"Try and eat something, won't you, Mama?"

"Sure, son. Sure. I'll just take a few bites of my pillow."

"You think you're funny, Mama. But you're not. You need

to eat something."

"I can make jokes too, ya know? I did, after all, make you."

"I'm serious, Mama. You hear me? Mama, I'm serious."

"Don't call me that."

"Don't call you what?"

"Don't call me Mama."

"Then what should I call you, Mama?"

"I'd prefer it if you called me by my Christian name. Call me April Mae June," was her reply. "Heck, you can call me every month in a calendar year, for all I care. Just don't call me that. Don't call me Mama."

It would be hard to describe what he felt right then, hard even to describe it to himself. Still, were you to ask him, he might describe a gentle jostling at the shoulders that made its way down through the entirety of his person. Perhaps he'd liken the feeling to a seamstress' calloused hands, toiling away at the hemline of all his assumptions. "But Mama," he said, assuming this was but another byproduct of her grief, "That's not your name."

"But it is, son. It's the name my mama gave me. April Mae. Your father gave me June. And completed my chronology. That's how I knew he was the one." She went on to explain herself by way of a story about how they came to settle that island, and all the while, the sound of her voice grew steadily closer, like she too had nestled down on the floor and was speaking to him from the other side of the door. "You see, it was not providence that brought us here, son. No," she said. "Fact is, your father got himself into a good bit of trouble, so to steer clear of the law, we changed our names and just sorta landed out here."

Now, it's quite a thing to find out you aren't who you think you are.

"You were lied to," she told him. "I'm sorry to say it, but you were. We hadn't a choice in the matter. We lied to protect you. Some lies are good that way, son. Some lies simply have to be told. There were so many people after us," she said. "But it's time now you know the truth. It's time you know it was not a curse that killed your father. He died trying to outrun his past."

And Bohicket wanted to understand what she meant by that. But he didn't. He knew he couldn't believe her, not wholly, and yet he felt as if he had opened his front door only to find his home was peopled by strangers, strange furnishings and a strange air. He felt he didn't know a thing at all, that he had been feeling his way through the dark all along.

"That father of yours could be dumb enough to get himself lost on a horse track. But even still, he did not deserve this," she said. "No matter what they say. He was a good man, your father, and a good man should die good, of something noble, like a ripe old age." Bohicket had so many questions, but before he could ask them, she was telling him already of how he swam with her beneath their sheets on their last night together. "Already, he was four-fifths asleep when I asked him if he remembered the plastic flamingo he stole out of the neighbor's yard the day we met. He said, 'Yes, dear, I remember.' 'Honey?' I said. 'It was the way you presented it to me, legs first, that made me think you were confessing your love.'"

Always, his wife had been an estuary to him, something watery and libidinal like a tidal pool, and that is where he got the idea to hold his breath and go under. "Look-a-here, my dear," he had said to her, motioning to their bed. "Jump on in. The water's fine." He knew she loved the water so completely there was no way she could resist. And turns out, he was right, seeing as she just pinched her nose and dove right in, and the two of them went swimming around in their sheets together.

"So many fish," she had said to him. "See 'em all? Well, do ya?"

"What?" he'd mouthed to her. "I can't hear you, my dear. Sort of sounds like you're talking underwater. What? What was that? What did you say?" Then he motioned her up to the surface, and they came up gasping for air.

"Fish," she repeated. "Fish! Can't you see them?"

Then he suggested they go even deeper this time. "Way, way down deeper. Come on, my flower. What do ya say you and I go trolling the ocean floor and see what we find?" And with that, they both took big deep breaths and dove down again. She was doing backstrokes before long, while he plugged an ear with one finger and spoke into his thumb. "Submersible M-47 reporting to dry land. M-47 here," he had said, mimicking the static of a radio. "Reporting from 10,000 feet below sea level. Roger that," he said. "Yessir, Captain April here is doing just fine. Roger . . . Roger . . . Roger that. This is her first-mate, over and out." He had turned to her with a kind of boyish grin on his face that night, the kind schoolboys grow accustomed to when they're looking for trouble. "They said I should check your vitals, Captain." And he took her breasts in his hands. "Just following orders, Captain. Can't fault a guy for following orders. Yep. Yep. All your vitals check out," he'd told her. "Though I really should be thorough and listen for your heart." And so he did. He placed an ear to her chest, and he listened to her heart.

"We did come up for air on occasion," she told her son. "I mean, of course we did. We had to." Then, just like that, they would plug their noses and dive back down, each time hand-in-hand. "The moon that night was sort of lopsided in the sky," she recalled. "And so were the tides. But that did not stop your father and I from paddling our way across the seas of our bed."

Bohicket had plans to meet up with his brother someday soon. Plans to one day set off all on his own in search of his dreams, perhaps enroll in a college and earn a degree, maybe make a career for himself in photography, fall in love and start a family. He had plans to, one day, leave this place and never look back, until at last, he became the man he was meant to be. For so long, he had wanted to be a photographer. But seeing half his mother's face peering out from beneath the door, as she told him that story, Bohicket realized he might be all she had left. So he decided, right then and there, to trade in all his dreams to stay and look after her, realizing that all his plans would be for naught, if he were the kind of man who chose his own wants over the needs of his mother.

Chapter Eight

GIVEN ENOUGH TIME, ALL SOUTHERN SUMMERS START TO FEEL the same, the way the days and the nights sort of meld slowly into one another, the way everything sort of falls in together under the blankets of a hot and heavy sleep. The whole of the world just sweats and sweats, as if to sweat it all out—the trees, the air, the very machination of the earth beneath a person's feet. It's the natural evolution of all summery things in the South to be baptized in water.

Blame it on the caustic heat. Or blame it on something else. But something or another got Bohicket wondering what reasons God had for muting his father. Only a few days after burying his father, and already, the silence was liquid especially in their house. It was near-stifling really in the now audible absence of his father's voice, his breathing. In response, his mother eventually came out of her room and spent hours upon hours at the piano in the den, as if she could die there, just trying to remember how to play. She did not die trying, nor did she attempt to play. Not so much as a single key. She instead just sat there, perched quietly on that bench with her hands hovering about its ghostly sounds. "It was remarkable," she tried to tell him once. "Your father's skill with his fingers."

Feeling completely overwhelmed by the dread he felt for what was now gone and what had yet to come, Bohicket spent the day walking the island and snapping mental photographs of everything he saw for much the same reasons as anyone does: out of a feel for that fruitless struggle to remember what is passing. The film of sweat that collected on his skin felt like the sun's debris, and he was reminded of the ocean when he wiped it away. It was sweat, but in a way, it was ocean water too, in how similarly they both dry on sunburned skin, harden, flake and then peel away like dried paint. Bohicket wanted nothing more than to peel away at his skin, to witness the bone.

He was no longer sure of who he was. At night, even his sleeping body formed a question. He and Ley shared the same mother; that much he knew. That much he could see in how present she was in both of them. It was more his father who was in question here, what parts of him they had inherited. He knew there was no logic to what he felt. Still, he couldn't quite shake the feeling he got when he looked inside. It was like he and his brother were born of the same mother but of different fathers. Nothing about it made any sense, he knew. Their father had at least raised them, and in response to the heat, they had even learned through his example to neglect the top two buttons of their shirts. And they had learned this from the very same man who had taught them to fish and to erect things with their hands and to behave like men were meant to behave. Even still, even despite all the logic that argued the contrary, it just seemed to Bohicket that Ley was more his father's son than Bohicket ever was.

Bohicket once dreamed of convincing his father to share a dinner with him, a meal and a space in time that was exclusively theirs. The conversation he wanted them to have over dinner was one of baseball diamonds and the perfect pitch, of clean getaways and airplanes in flight, of ruminations on the sky and sliding safely into home plate. But always Bohicket felt the conversation he wanted had been Ley's conversation to have. Because, as Bohicket saw it, he and his father had never had much in common, and so he feared their dinner conversation would be mostly dry, even during those hot, wet summer months.

Even now, he practiced for the occasion. Despite understanding the futility of even hoping for the chance, he climbed up on the roof day after day and conversed with the sky. There was no one else to talk to, you see. His mother, it seemed, had taken a vow of silence, and so everywhere, the silence was monastic. So he climbed up on that roof each and every day and carried on with the clouds. He wanted to believe the sounds he heard were replies, the unrooting of a conversation at its inception, but even he was not gullible enough to believe they were. A jet engine, he reminded himself. Two gulls fighting over a fish. A fish. The waves. Wind. The roof's just creaking. "Space junk," he told himself. "That's space junk."

He had made the decision to stay behind and look after his mother because it was the only right and decent thing to do. Despite it all, he did not regret his decision. But just because something is right doesn't mean it's easy. Actually, it was hard, and it only got harder and harder as time went by. It was the silence that got to him first, followed inevitably by the loneliness of finding himself alone in the company of himself. Mostly, his mother was nowhere to be found, now off again to God-knows-where.

His father's drowning should've been his first indication of the real-life danger he would be in, were he to continue meeting up with Aylin, and that would've been enough of a deterrent for him, were he not so unsettled by the greater danger of finding himself now so helplessly alone. It had been only a week or so after his father died, and the island was completely still, out of an almost solemn reverence for its caretaker's passing. It got so bad that eventually the only sound Bohicket could ever really hear was the sound of his own chest as he breathed, which was a wholly terrifying sound, to be sure, and one that Bohicket came to fear, sensing the sudden fragility of it all. And so, frightened of spending a single moment more alone, Bohicket snuck away early one morning to rendezvous with Aylin outside the village.

He found her sitting in the shade of a tree, whistling to herself and carving another animal from a block of wood. "What is it, this time?" he asked, as he reached her. "A seagull? A shark? Or—Oooo!—even better . . . a hungry shark making a snack out of a seagull!"

He could tell by the surprise on her face that she was happy to see him, and he was glad for that. She smiled like she couldn't help but smile, and he was glad for that as well. Glad that someone, anyone on God's green earth, could be happy to see the likes of him.

"I knew you'd come back eventually," she said without so much as a glance in his direction. "That's how-come I've been making you this gift. Just about done now. It's an alligator," she said, holding it up proudly so that he could see it. "It's an alligator. See?"

"An alligator? Really? For me?"

She nodded. "What, you don't like it? You don't. You don't like it, do you?"

"No, no. I like it fine," he assured her. "It's just . . . Why an alligator?"

"I dunno," she said, shrugging. "It's just, you remind me of an alligator somehow."

"Me? An alligator? Huh." He sort of pondered the idea for a moment. "Am I really that scary? I guess I've always kinda fancied myself as more of a mole-rat or something harmless like a squirrel or a pelican with an injured wing. You know, something like that."

She giggled. "A mole-rat, you say?" She looked him over inquisitively. "I guess I can see that . . . from the side at least. Ya sure got a big enough nose on ya. And with those beady little eyes of yours . . . yeah, I suppose I can see it now. I suppose you're right. You could be a mole-rat." Then she giggled again.

"And here I thought we were friends," he said.

"Friends? What kinda girl do you take me for, to just go

around making friends with mole-rats and the like."

"Be careful there, girlie," he said, climbing down on all-fours. "We rodents are a sneaky bunch, ya know?" And to illustrate his point, he went scurrying around and around her a half a dozen times, stopping only to sniff curiously at her head, like a mole-rat might do. "In fact, we rodents are so sneaky we can creep up on you without you even noticing us and just start nibbling at your ears."

"Squeak, squeak," she said.

"Squeak, squeak."

"You know, come to think of it, you make an awful mole-rat," she said.

"So it's settled then, just like that?"

"Yes," she said. "You are an alligator, and that is that."

Bohicket hunkered down beside her to watch her work. "Yes, but why am I an alligator? That is the question," he said. "I mean, of all God's creatures, why an alligator? It's not my rotten skin, is it? Mama says it's hereditary. That and far too much sun. Mama says it can't be helped, that I'm ugly and that is that. She says I should soak my face in sea grass no less than twice a week to keep from looking old before I am young."

"No, no, it's not that. I like your skin. It makes you look tough and sort of dangerous, like . . . like a person you shouldn't go messing with, if you know what's good for ya."

"Dangerous, huh? Tough? I like the sound of that. But if it's not my skin, then what?"

Aylin thought for a moment and weighed her answer carefully before responding. "It's more the idea of you, I think. Ya know? Like you're a phantom or something, disappearing for a good long while and then reappearing, like a plati or a wraith or a banshee, from the water."

"Oooo, don't I sound mysterious?"

"Plus, you've got a big mouth," she added, sort of grinning to herself. "Just like a gator."

They talked for a while with the same ease as they always talked. He cracked little jokes, here and there, that made her laugh a soft and airy laugh that would've reminded him of helium—had he known what helium was—for the weightless way it fainted into the daylight.

The reason Bohicket took to the practice of snapping as many photographs as he did was not so much to remember his life the way it was, but more to imagine his life the way he wanted it to be: as perfectly happy as the people in the pictures that come with the frame. It was his way of hoping, you might say, and it was why he snapped a few pictures of her, before he left that day.

"Come back tomorrow, and I should be done with your gift," she told him.

And he did. He came back the next day and then the next. He came back every day for the rest of that week, in fact. And before long, a few of the fishermen began to take notice of his frequent visits to their shores. Recognizing the danger this might present, Bohicket wised up and devised a guise to hide his intentions. He took to gathering up crate after crate of the island berries and with each new day set out across the waterway to sell his wares in the village, though only as an excuse to sneak away later and visit her. "Just call me Berry Man," he practiced as he crossed the channel. "For I am. I am Berry Man."

Aylin had heard the rumors of his father's untimely end, but not once did she bring it up for fear that he'd stop coming to visit her. One week trailed into the next and then on into the next, and still, he came to see her. Thinking it best to leave the subject of his father alone, Aylin was content to act as a necessary distraction from the sorrows of his life, inquiring about his mother from time to time and lending him an ear, as he shared his mounting concern for her well-being.

"And that is why I've decided to stay with her," he told

her. "Because she needs me. She needs me here. Anyways, what kind of a man would I be otherwise?" he said, almost arguing the point with himself. "I mean, you tell me. What kind of a man abandons his own mother?"

Aylin was glad he was staying, though she knew better than to admit it because tucked away in the firm resolve of his decision was the sound of some undeclared loss, a young man no longer capable of dreaming his own dreams. And that is how Aylin came to understand her duty to him, the responsibility she felt to act on his behalf, to be his friend and to remind him always of all the things he had to live for. She understood too that Southerners as a whole seemed only to have survived this long by laughing it off. And laughing it off, in his case, meant he must first learn to play like there was work to be done, to play as the farmers and the fishermen play, half at work and half enjoying it, which meant he must first make his peace with nature. Why? Because, as Aylin understood it (being a Southerner herself), the only wherewithal a Southerner actually needs to survive such a hard situation begins and ends with his or her approximation to the earth, the sky and the water. Especially the water. And so Aylin took to pointing out the beauty in the waterfowl migrations, the way their wings sort of smoothed out across the surface of the waves in a way that reminded her always of the allure of home, the unmistakable riddles of the sky in the sea.

In his father's absence, it was left to Bohicket to manage the island as best he could, which meant he would need to fish and crab for their dinners, harvest the berries and sell them in the village for whatever supplies they needed. The latter duty gave him a perfect cover for visiting her more and more frequently. Every day for him would begin with tending to the island, traversing the narrow strait to barter his wares and then escaping down the beach to find Aylin. Likewise, every day they spent together culminated inevitably in a walk. Sometimes, their walks would lead them down the shoreline, where Aylin took to humming along with the percussive waves. Other times, their walks would lead them off into the woods, where Bohicket would take the opportunity to teach her the bird calls he knew by imitating them in all their many variations. Every evening, when their walks were done, they would find a quiet spot out along the coast and stand vigil over the sun, while it drowned itself in the sea. And there, every evening, the two of them would nestle in close and take turns searching the privations of each other's bodies, thumbing for ticks and picking at chiggers.

It should go without saying that he found something strangely intimate—if not seductive—about ending their days with the shocking familiarity in the other one's touch, as time and time again they found themselves feeling their way across each other's skin with the subtle suggestions of their fingertips.

"Damn these little buggers," they would say and squeeze so hard at the tiny parasites they sometimes drew blood. There was pain involved—of course there was—but there was pleasure too. And so it was that their relationship gradually took on a strange—albeit, natural—evolution. Strange in that the newness was not lost on either of them. Days passed into weeks, and in little less than a month's time, the shape of their friendship had morphed and reshaped itself into a kind of longing for one another, which was a wholly new feeling to the both of them, seeing as neither one of them had experienced love, much less the means by which it appears.

Still, something about simply being in her presence stirred awake Bohicket's great and slovenly heart, and so he returned to her day after day, as if he was drawn to her by magnet, as if he hadn't a choice in the matter but was driven instead by some primal and brutish need for her. He wanted to come right out and confess the feelings he felt for her, taken at times by the desire to speak his love into being. But he liked what they had; he did. And what they had was just far too important to him to go and risk it on a chance.

Aylin, on the other hand, had been confessing her love to him for quite a long time. Though when she told him, she told him in her own quiet way: by sharing in his concerns for his mother, by asking him how she was doing, by longing for a solution to whatever was troubling her, by kneeling every night in the stillness of her own bedroom and praying to God that something would fix her. It was a Saturday when Aylin told him as much. Told him as much and told him again. She said she had something to show him. "My thinking place," she said. "We need a plan." And she walked him out past the last few houses of the village to where the one church in those parts was located.

They snuck in through a window around back. Bohicket was wary of being found out, so she did her best to reassure him. "Don't worry," she said. "It's safe. No one around here would even think of attending church on a Saturday, especially since, for most, the one service on Sunday is entirely enough."

She climbed through first and then offered him a hand.

"I got it," he said and shimmied on through.

"Saturdays are the best time to come," she told him. "Especially when there's a new shipment of wine and wafers. Care for communion?" she said. She then scurried up to the altar and returned with crackers in one hand and a wine bottle in the other. "Body? Or the blood?" she said, extending both hands. "I like the wafers myself, but I prefer the blood."

Something about her dismissal of all the sacred taboos and ritualistic dangers excited his whole person, made certain parts of him, as yet unknown, come alive with the prospect of joining her in this little criminal enterprise.

"Blood," he said.

"You must first kneel to receive."

So he did.

And it was almost effortless the way she uncorked the wine with her teeth.

"Now, my child, this is the blood that was shed for you," she said. She made the sign of the cross above his head, before pouring the wine straight into his mouth. "And the best part is, we got bread to break when we get hungry."

That evening was one of those instances where she asked him point-blank about his mother, and in response, Bohicket went on and on about how much worse things had gotten. "Something has to be done," he concluded. "Something," he said. "I just don't know what."

"Ya know? I find I do my best thinking lying down," she told him. With that, she slid her whole body underneath the back pew and began dragging herself, arm over arm, under the pews in the direction of the altar. "Come on," she called back to him. "All the best ideas can be found down here, I swear it!"

And so he followed behind her.

She was two rows from the front when she stopped abruptly.

"Right. Here's a good spot."

They laid there together, flat on their bellies, and waited with their eyes closed for inspiration to strike. They laid there together for quite some time. But while Aylin was busy considering a cure for his mother, Bohicket thought only of her. Her eyes were closed, but he was peeking, examining the womanly curve along the small of her back. He knew the carnality alone made what he was thinking wrong. He was in church, for Christ's sake. He knew better. It's just that he couldn't help himself, couldn't help how illicit the sight of her made him feel. How is it that one thing can be so wrong, he wondered. And yet feel so right?

Eventually Aylin opened her eyes and rolled over on her back.

They were so close now he could feel her breath.

"Ever think of bringing her here? I've heard church, in small doses, can work wonders."

But it wasn't so much what she said as how close she was when she said it that had Bohicket agreeing so quickly with the solution she proposed. In all honesty, he probably would've agreed to do just about anything right about then, even cut off his own two arms if only to lend her a hand.

"Can't hurt," she said with a shrug. "Might as well try."

Aylin credited her idea to divine intervention, and he imagined that he too got a sense of the divine, that he too had caught a mortal glimpse of what gives a man wings and a reason to fly, that he himself had finally seen what the sight of a woman can drive up in a man: his need to evolve and civilize the land, to survey cities, plot roads and erect tall buildings. And he believed that he too came to see what drives some men to build coffins and others to build ships, each a means of travel and of seeking out the divine. And seeing what he saw and feeling what he felt that day in that church, Bohicket would've agreed to just about anything Aylin suggested, which was made all-too-apparent by the mischief she got them into later on that night.

It was well past midnight, and they were down at the water still when Aylin rolled a mud ball up in her hands and suggested they arm themselves that way. Bohicket was not stupid. He knew the risks, especially since he needed a working relationship with those he bartered with to ensure he and his mother survived. And yet Bohicket still hungered for vengeance for the curse on his father, so he couldn't deny he loved the idea. And so, without so much as a moment's hesitation, the two of them gathered up an armful of muddy artillery shells and marched back into the village with Aylin, of course, leading the charge. Together they skirted around back of the houses and started pitching those mud balls at all the windows.

It was a mistake, to be sure. But for some reason, Bohicket simply did not care.

"Steady now," Aylin whispered. "Steady. On my mark. And . . . fire!" she shouted.

Thump.

Thump.

Then they'd retreat back into the shadows before racing off into the next yard.

Thump.

Thump.

Even in the darkness, Bohicket could tell whose house was whose. Miss Kaye's house he recognized instantly. She was the village's one and only midwife, and as boys, when curiosity got the better of him and his brother, they had gone peeking in through her windows when word got out that she was to deliver a baby. Typical of boys their age who were still curious about everything and as eager as ever to catch even a glimpse of a naked woman. Still, nothing—not even the memory of where he first caught sight of a woman's naked breasts—would deter him that night. And if that wouldn't, nothing would.

Thump.

Thump.

One can only imagine how their attack echoed through the rooms of those houses, and the start it gave to each and every one of their sleeping occupants. One can only imagine how their startled hearts raced at the prospect of an intruder in their house, mothers springing from their beds, children hiding under their covers and fathers going for their guns. One can only imagine the horrors each of those households faced, as their dreams were startled to waking nightmares.

Aylin and Bohicket endangered themselves that night. They did not know it yet, but they did; they endangered themselves. Had they stopped, for even a moment, and considered the wisdom in this, Bohicket at least would have second-guessed himself, weighed the risk they were taking and adamantly discouraged it, having seen for himself the wrath of the village. Still, if they were anything, they were still young, and everyone knows that with youth comes a staggering blindness to the outcome of our actions.

Aylin got this look on her face by the third or fourth house they attacked, like she was possessed by her own miscreant self, delighted even by the criminal elements within her. A certain wildness overtook her entire person then, and she began to wave her arms about wildly and shouting, "Bring these houses down! Bring them all . . . Bring all these houses . . . Bring them all down!"

To Bohicket, there was nothing truer than the way she yelled this, and nothing more honest than exacting his revenge. "Yeah!" he shouted after her. "Bring 'em all down!" Then he proceeded to pummel all the remaining houses on that block with a newfound ferocity, spurred on by the courage he'd heard in her voice. "Death from above!" he yelled, as he sent one mud ball after another raining down from the sky. "Bring down the heavens!" he shouted. "Bring it down on their heads!"

The shelling continued for one whole block, then it was on to the next. People were up and out of their houses by now, peering out their windows and from their porches, hoping to spot the culprits lurking about in the shadows. Women shrieked and cried bloody murder, as they went ducking for cover. Children began to sob into the arms of their mothers, while their fathers took up guns in retaliation. Even from the shadows, Bohicket could smell the fear on them. The air was thick with it. And no one was safe. There was a breach along their borders, the casualties of the mind. It was almost as if the whole wide night had itself become a battlefield plagued by fear and a dreadful uncertainty. And it appeared, for now at least, that they were winning.

Only later would it occur to him the danger they were in. What were they thinking? But Bohicket was in the fog of it now. He was rash and overtaken by a part of him he had not known before. All he could think to do now was act. Perhaps another way Aylin found to help him heal. Had he the words to verbalize what came over him right then, each bomb he let loose into the walls of those houses would have detonated with a special message from him.

You would have heard, "This one's for Mama!" followed by the explosion.

"And this one's for Pops!"

Boom!

"And here's one for Little Dew!"

Boom!

"And my brother too!"

Boom, boom, kaboom!

"What's that you say? You want to surrender? Well I say tough! I say goodnight, goodnight and kaboom! Cause this is love, and this here's war! So all is fair. I say tough!"

Boom!

Boom!

"And here ya go! Another! Just for good measure!"

Chapter Nine

THAT THEY GOT AWAY WITH IT ALTOGETHER LEFT BOHICKET WITH the kind of deep satisfaction only revenge can bring. And satisfied, he didn't stop smiling all the next day. Even his mother noticed and asked him about it.

"You look so happy. No," she amended. "Not happy . . . glad. You look glad. Pleased even. And you know what would make your mother really happy? If you'd gladly wipe that stupid grin off your stupid face. What's gotten into you anyway? What on earth you got to go on smilin' about?"

He did not answer her.

"So much," would've been his reply.

But he did not answer her because he knew that, despite how relieved he felt to have gotten away with it and despite how pleased he was to have done it in the first place, what he and Aylin had done was a mistake, an impulse acted upon stupidly, rashly and without a single thought to the terrible consequences, had they been caught. And he did not answer her because, chances were, he may have to answer for his actions yet.

Something inside him said it'd be wisest to steer clear of the village for a while. So he did. He wanted nothing more than to go and see Aylin again, but since everyone knows criminals return to the scene of their crimes, he thought better of it and decided instead to stay far far away, at least until the fire was out and the smoke had cleared.

Problem was, his mother had been sharing her bed with that scarecrow of hers for some time now, and seeing as tomorrow would come and she would again go around talking to it like it was a real live person, bathing it in the tub, brushing its teeth and inviting it to join them for dinner,

Bohicket understood the terrible possibility that this was all her way of fulfilling some surrogate need to somehow go on living in her daughter's skin. And so Bohicket decided it was time to put Aylin's plan into action and, just as she had suggested he do, start mentioning church whenever the opportunity presented itself. "Visited the church the other day," he would tell her. "Say? Didn't you and grandpa go to church, once upon a time? Yeah? Tell me, what was it like?" And thinking it was best to let the notion of church sort of dawn on her, he asked her to tell him all about it, about how nice it was to dress up each week in her Sunday best, about how the praise-and-worship used to move her, about God and how close He could feel.

And by Thursday that week, she was trying on old dresses and modeling them for him.

"What do ya think about this one?" she would ask him.

"Mama, you've never looked so beautiful."

"Oh stop it," she would say. "Now you've always been full of shit, my dear, but ya keep piling on like you are, and I might better go and get myself a shovel."

"No, really, Mama. It's just a shame that dress has to stay tucked away in a closet."

And come Friday, he had his mother clearly smitten by all his flattery, seeing as she spent all that day twisting and twirling and singing to herself in front of her mirror. Saturday, she was doing up her hair and putting on makeup and then checking the mirror to remind herself how she looked when she knelt to pray, which in turn, made a believer out of her by Sunday morning when she came into his room and suggested it might be nice if they went to church together as a family.

"Come on, come on," she said excitedly. "Get up, get up. I promise it'll be fun. It'll be like playing dress-up. You can borrow something of your father's, and we'll dress to the tees."

Bohicket, of course, jumped at the opportunity. He ironed his father's suit and put on a tie and then accompanied his mother to church that morning because, yes, he hoped it would do her some good and, yes, because he knew Aylin would be there and he so longed to see her.

Aylin was there, but so was the rest of the village, and he was careful not to stare in her direction for too long, so as to avoid any suspicion. They did lock eyes once or twice, and that was all it took to tell her he missed her, and to realize, in that, he was not alone.

His mother noticed, of course. She did not mention it. But she noticed.

Going to church appeared to work wonders on her tired disposition. From the start, Bohicket could tell something about her had changed, from how briskly she walked home that day after service to how cheerfully she went about her business in the days that followed. He couldn't say what had changed, but something had. That was for sure. It was as if she had discovered a part of her that had gone missing until then. God perhaps? Reason enough to go on and grudgingly relinquish an occasional smile? To just make do with her life and move on?

These were all the plausible outcomes Bohicket had been hoping for. But as he would soon discover, it was not God who changed her, nor was it church. She was glad, yes, of the chance to doll herself up every Sunday morning and parade those pretty dresses of hers down the center aisle. And yes, it was her idea to go back every Sunday over the next three weeks. But in the end, she did not find God there, nor did God find her. No, it wasn't the church or God or some enlivening of the soul in singing those hymns either. No, what had her so excited, in the end, was the sight of that tall, tall steeple rising up and out from the roof of that church.

"Would ya look at that?" she commented once. "Man oh

man, what a sight."

And that should've been Bohicket's first clue as to where her mind was headed and where she herself would be headed the night she snuck out and made her way across the channel. He followed after her, keeping his distance and stalking her step-by-step from the shadows. She took the boat, which meant, unfortunately, he had to swim. Unfortunate because, by the time he finally caught up to her, she was already halfway to the top of the steeple.

"Mama!" he cried. "Dear God, Mama, what on earth are you doing?!"

"Earth's got nothin' to do with it, son!" she yelled down to him. "This is about the sky!"

Only then could he clearly see that she was wearing the very first costume she had made, the beak, the feathers, the wings and all. It seemed her entire person was now glossy in the moonlight, streaks of bluish colors forming ribbons down her back.

"Caw!" she cried.

"Mama, don't do this. Please."

But it was too late. Only upon reaching the top did her whole frail person seem to become a great indiscernible shadow against the backdrop of the night.

"Mama?!" he said. "Mama, please?!"

To this day, he could not tell you what he said that gave her pause. To hear him tell it, it couldn't have been what he said because there was really nothing more he could've said. What she was thinking about up there was anyone's guess, but something had her kneeling into the posture of something resembling a prayer. And maybe, just maybe, that's what it was that gave her pause. The same prayer he had said for her a thousand times, which ended in the same final *amen* and her deciding, almost inexplicably, to abandon her intentions and climb back down.

He never inquired into her reasons for coming down,

choosing instead to avoid the subject entirely. And that night, after they returned home, he sat quietly with her at the kitchen table and, right on through till sunrise, listened as she shared the tales of those they called "The Makers," who she claimed some folks on those islands believed were responsible for looking after them all. Bohicket, however, could never say if these weren't simply flights of her imagination. He only ever heard these tales from his mother.

"There's the Valley Maker," she recalled, "whose job it is to look after the land. And the Water Maker who looks after the oceans and the creeks and the river. Then there's the Cloud Maker who's said to look after the heavens and the sky and all the birds in it." She said, "Some say the Makers appear to us in many forms. A bird. A fish. A stone or the weather. The Water Maker was a wave when I met her last. A big and beautiful wave rocking back from the shoreline and out to sea." And the way his mother recalled what she saw, she sounded so sure.

She had been swearing by these same tales since Bohicket was a boy. "It was lovely the way she waved at me, before she went passing me by. Lovely," she said, as she gazed out the window at the coming dawn. "Still, I dream of meeting the Cloud Maker some day. She might be a fiddler crab with her one giant claw. She might be a tree branch sailing high in a storm. Seems she could be anything nowadays, and someday soon, she'll come to visit me."

"And what of God?" Bohicket asked.

"What of Him?"

"Where does He fit in all of this? You've always been a church-going girl. What of God? What is His part in all of this?"

"Oh God?" she said dismissively. "God got tired of us long, long ago. Moved on to bigger and better things, I'd imagine." It was not until she noticed how her statement perplexed her son that she offered, "But that's where the

Makers come in. God's hired hands. Sent here to look after things in His absence."

And that's when Bohicket got the idea to start calling his mother Birdy. "Birdy the Cloud Maker," he said, chuckling to himself. "If she can appear as anything, then why not appear as you? Sorta makes sense, am I right? It does, doesn't it? It makes a lotta sense. I mean, you got the costume already. See? Ever ask yourself why you made it? Well I'll tell you why you made it. So she can appear in the form of you, that's why. Don't ya see? You. Are. Birdy. Birdy the Cloud Maker, goddess of the sky."

The lost expression on his mother's face spoke to her confusion.

"Don't believe me, I see. Still need convincing? Well here, let me prove it to you," Bohicket said. And he did not ask for her permission or even warn her, before he just scooped his mother's fragile body up in his arms and carried her out into the morning, down the steps, across the beach and into the water. And she did not struggle.

The ocean was so calm that morning it could've been asleep, and Bohicket had no problem walking his mother's body out to where the water was chest-deep. "Now, it stands to reason that, if you truly are the Cloud Maker like I believe you are, you won't need your wings, but still you can fly." And then he set her body loose atop the water.

And she floated there a while.

"See there?" he said to her. "That's right. Arms out. Relax. That's right. Relax."

And she did relax. She did, and she was floating.

"There now, good," he told her. "Now look up. See those birds? Those clouds? The sky up there? Now look again. Now, that very same morning sky is all around you."

And just as he said it would be, there reflecting on the water all around her was a flock of birds, a sky with a sun and a patchwork of clouds. What she discovered was a whole other sky, a second sky, and there, allowing herself to float across that secondary heaven, she imagined she was indeed the Cloud Maker and felt what it was to fly. "Birdy," she almost whispered to herself. "I am, I think. I am Birdy."

THERE IS A PARTICULAR BRAND OF PAIN THAT NO MAN, NO matter how strong he is, can endure for long, and Bohicket's pain was that sort of pain, an ache of the heart that manifested itself in the whole of his person. And after having avoided Aylin for now far too long, Bohicket was sick with it. He ached for Aylin, not in the pit of his stomach, as some might have you believe, but higher up, somewhere between the stomach and the lungs. He could no longer take it, and thinking it was now safe to return to the village, he went there, one morning, to barter off a basket of berries and then go to see her.

Aylin was just as happy to see him, though feeling he might have abandoned her for good this time, she refused to show it. "Oh, hi there," she said coldly.

"Hi," he said.

They sort of circled each other for a while, like that, feeling each other out, until eventually their conversation softened and Bohicket finally felt comfortable enough with her to tell her about his mother. "She was at it again the other night. Found her atop the church steeple in full feathers and ready to jump," he said. "She didn't though. Don't know why."

"I'm sorry to hear that," she said.

"That's why I haven't come. I'm sorry. I wanted to. But I got held up."

"Hmm," she said.

"We got to talkin' one day, and she told me the strangest story. About the Makers," he said. "Ever heard of them? The Makers?"

"Nope. Can't say I have."

Then he proceeded to tell her all about them, about how the job of looking after things was left to them while God was away, about how they are said to appear in many forms. "Mama said she met one, and she said, when they met, it was a wave. But Mama said they can take other forms as well. Seagulls. Rocks. Even alligators."

"What? Really? Alligators? Surely not."

"Yep, even alligators."

Aylin couldn't help but giggle.

Her laughter loosened the stalemate in the air between them.

"I've heard of shape-shifters before," she said. "Though I'm not so sure the two are one and the same. Still, they might be. I've come across one or two of them who live in these parts."

"Yeah?"

"Yeah. I even know where they live."

"Yeah?"

"Yeah. Maybe they've heard of the Makers. I mean, if anybody has heard of them, it would surely be them," she reasoned. "Wanna go see?"

"Sure . . . I mean . . . I guess, yeah, sure."

The thing is, even Bohicket couldn't say why he felt such an urgency to go and seek out the truth about the Makers. He couldn't say for certain whether they were real or completely made-up, or whether they really had anything to do with anything. But an answer to this riddle could present his mother with a cure, so it was worth trying. And even if their little inquest turned up nothing, he would still return home with a story, and hearing him recount his adventures with Aylin would surely awaken the life in his mother's face, if only for a time. And he saw that as progress. Short-lived progress, granted. But progress. A small victory in a losing battle.

And so Bohicket followed her lead.

Wherever Aylin was taking him was about an hour's walk away through the woods, and Aylin took the opportunity to fill him in on who they were visiting and why they'd come to live all alone out there. She said when people learned of their powers long ago, they were forced into hiding, and where better to hide than some uninhabited part of the Sea Islands? "People are afraid of what they can't explain," she told him. "I guess it's just in our nature to turn out this way," to fear the threat we perceive in our differences. And this is why they settled a colony all their own so far from civilization. She said that her people have known about their whereabouts for generations now, but have protected their secret.

They walked for what felt to Bohicket like an eternity. So long, in fact, that Bohicket was just about to suggest they give up and turn back when they came across a riverbank speckled with a single row of houses. "That one there's Annie Goode's house," Aylin pointed out. "Now she and my mother go way back, and my mother is always sayin' how good that Annie Goode is, or as my mother put it, 'good enough to marry that good-for-nothing man of hers,' even despite every last one of her friends having warned her about him."

As the story goes, Annie Goode was also good enough to bear her man four good children, and raise them up good and right all on her own. The sad misfortune is that, back in her day, Annie Goode was full of life, full of that exacting kind of aliveness that made everyone around her feel alive as well. Aylin's mother recalled that, before Annie Goode met and subsequently married her good-for-nothing husband, she had dated her share of suitable boys, boys who went by Boyd and Dickie and Dewey and the like, all names deserving of a character, all characters deserving of their name. She chose instead to marry her husband, which was unfortunate because that is when it all went wrong.

Only now, some fifty years later, could Annie Goode see just how wrong. Only now, late into her sixties, had their marriage reached the point that sometimes she felt as if she was simply living him out, simply living out the rest of her days like she was painting by numbers. She did consider leaving him, more times than she should, and never shied from sharing as much with Aylin's mother. She never would though. She would never leave him. According to Aylin's mother, Annie Goode was far too good to do something like that.

Still, Annie Goode did consider it. And who could blame her, seeing as, when he wasn't off working whatever odd job he could find, Annie Goode's husband spent all of his time sitting in a rocking chair on their front porch, either cleaning his shotgun or shooting at the squirrels in their yard? What's more, he did this most every day and sometimes late into the night. Pest control is what he called it, like his solution for everything was to shoot at it. As chance would have it, that was exactly what he was doing, when Bohicket and Aylin reached Annie Goode's house.

Bohicket and Aylin rather wisely waited till he was re-loading to approach the front door and knock.

"Say, you ain't one of them pesky salesmen, are ya?" Annie's husband asked. "Cause what you got, we ain't buyin'. So skedaddle 'fore I empty this here barrel into both your asses." He was pointing his shotgun at them and sizing them up through the gaze of his barrel. And that alone would have frightened off just about anyone, even the bravest of souls, but especially those who, like Aylin, had heard all the terrible rumors that rightly suggested that a man like this was capable of anything.

Chapter Ten

BOHICKET DIDN'T NEED TO HEAR THE RUMORS ABOUT ANNIE Goode's husband, like Aylin had her whole life, to recognize the danger they were in. The barrel of the gun pointed at their faces told him that much. It was the cold expressionless look on the man's face that told him the rest. One look into his calm dead eyes, and Bohicket could tell that this was a man you cannot reason with, a man who was not only comfortable with firing his gun but who might actually enjoy firing it into someone. The way he sort of fingered eagerly at the trigger, as he squared them up through his sights, said he was just itching for a reason to shoot them dead where they stood.

"See the sign?" the man said, pointing over the door. "Says *Trespassers Will Be Shot on Sight*. There's a slim chance my old eyes deceive me, but I'm pretty damn sure what we got here is a couple of trespassers. Whatcha think?"

"No sir, no sir," Aylin stuttered. "Beggin' your pardon, sir, but we're here to see Mrs. Goode on important business."

"Business huh? Sounds to me like you're sellin' somethin'," the man said.

"No sir, we're not," replied Aylin.

"No sir, we're not," echoed Bohicket.

Right then, the door flew open, and Annie Goode came charging out of the house and onto the porch, and in no time at all, she was stabbing a finger in her husband's chest. "Now look a here, you! Where are your manners, you miserable old geezer?! Have you forgotten everything your mama taught you? Well? Have you? And to think you have the gall to go and call yourself a Southerner anymore. The nerve. Don't you go threatening our guests, and most especially not my guests. And, why, look at them? They're only children. What kind of a man threatens children? What. Kind. Of. A. Man. Come now, children," she said, turning back to them. "Come now. Come on inside. Don't you go payin' that mean old man no attention, no way, no how."

They weren't through the doorway before Annie Goode was asking Aylin how her mother was doing. "How is Esther? Haven't seen that ol' girl in ages. Another lifetime, it seems. She doing alright, your mother?"

"Yes ma'am."

"Good. That's good." Annie Goode then offered them a glass of tea.

"Thank you, but no," Aylin replied. "Me and my friend just came to ask you a question."

"Really? Well do. Go on, do. Do ask me a question. I do love questions. There's lots of them, you know? Sometimes I think all we got in this life is questions."

They sat together in the den, and after taking a moment to gather himself, Bohicket asked her what he came there to ask her. "Ever heard of the Makers?" he said.

"Well no, honey. Can't say I have."

"Maybe you've seen one and didn't know it."

Annie Goode was clearly intrigued. "How so, honey?"

And Bohicket explained how, according to his mother, the Makers were said to take on many shapes and forms.

"Well," she replied, leaning back in her seat, "I might know a thing or two about that." Annie Goode smiled to herself right then, as if let in on her own little secret. "Heck, maybe I am one of them and didn't even know it? Could be. It seems you're never too old to learn something new about yourself."

"Maybe," Bohicket said.

"Because, my friends, it seems I am what they call a skin-walker, better known to others as a shape-shifter." A curious existence which all began, as she saw it, when she turned forty-three and found she could no longer sleep through the night. Instead she would go stalking about the darkness of her house, and coming to hover over her husband's sleeping body one night, she permitted herself a moment of murderous intentions. "Now, mind you, I'd never ever do something like that, you understand? It's not in my nature. And yet it all began with the thought of it, the thought that I claimed that very night. Or better yet, the thought that claimed me. It all began with something ancient on these islands laying claim to me. Reclaiming me." She told them that, in certain circles, she'd heard it said that skin-walkers only claim their powers after killing a member of their own family. "But not in my case. In my case, all I had to do was think about it. Really, I just wanted to be someone else. Anything else. A coyote perhaps. Maybe a fox. A bird would've been nice, especially an owl. And so I became an owl." She could tell, by the worried look on their faces, that the idea itself frightened them, so she went on to explain it as nothing more than mischief. "Mischief" is what she called it. "I've always enjoyed myself a little mischief. Don't you? That is all it was: a little mischief."

Aylin had to force a smile. She knew it would be rude not to.

Annie Goode then leaned in close, as if to confide in them. "And, my dears, here's the secret that no one will tell you. Nobody—and I mean nobody—no matter how old you get, ever really feels like an adult. My advice? Go with that. That's the mischief. That's the power."

This should've occurred to Bohicket as a solution. Turn his mother into a bird. That would have solved everything. But Bohicket wasn't sure if he fully believed Annie Goode and just assumed she knew more than she was letting on.

"Yes," he interjected, "But what of the Makers? What of their powers?" He still believed finding the truth in this was his cause.

Annie Goode, of course, was in no rush to answer him. And rather happy to just have visitors for a time, she again offered them some tea. Again, they declined. "I wish I had a better answer for ya," she said. "God help me, I wish I did, but I don't. Fact is, I know nothing of these Makers you speak of. Nothing, that is, save this: the power to change yourself, as you say they do, comes only in the mischief it takes to actually believe you can change."

Her eyes seemed to become windowpanes then, as if she had just offered them the truest thing that she knew. Her eyes grew deep, a paragon of deep. Her eyes seemed to say that, were it not for the fortune that had allowed her to change herself, to go about seeing without the trouble of having to be seen, the monotony of her own life would have become too much for her long ago, when all the domesticity had turned domestic and her life had become a polyptoton—repeating and repeating until she could no longer bear it repeating. And in that unbearableness, she might have chosen long ago to surrender the plow of her own body to the good earth that it tilled.

She had said as much to her friends, one night some time in early September. It was a Sunday night a good many years ago, as she recalled it. And like most every Sunday night back in those days, her three best friends in all the world—Aylin's mother included—had stopped by for a visit earlier that afternoon once church let out, and somewhere between all the reminiscing and the gossip, they had clucked away the entire day before any of them knew it. It was dark by the time Annie finally came out with it. "I've decided to be an owl," she confessed, without so much as a thought to how her friends might take it.

Her friends, of course, just laughed at the news. They, like most Southern women, could be funny that way, funny in that there was no telling how they'd react to certain news, funny in that they could believe even the most outlandish of things. Take Claudette, for example. She had come to believe almost conclusively that vampires were real and that blood drives were a part of their vast conspiracy. Billie Jean was no better. For the longest time, she thought that Sister Mary Galloway, who taught Sunday school at her church, had gone and gotten herself pregnant simply by eating a communion wafer before it was blessed. Even Esther, Aylin's mother, had a nasty habit of repeating the most ridiculous rumors like they were the gosh-honest truth.

And so, just as she always did when divining the future, Claudette massaged her temples and closed her eyes upon hearing the news. "Yep," she said, nodding. "An owl. I can see you having a future in that." You see, Claudette had been moonlighting as a tarot card reader for some years now and spoke about the future with a certain authority on the subject, and Annie Goode was glad for that.

Billie Jean, on the other hand, was never one to see anything good on the horizon. She was a consummate pessimist and always had been. The result was that most people, back in high school, just assumed she had an addiction to hapless shrugs and dead-end romances. And so it made sense that she would respond to Annie's confession in such a way. "Whelp, my dear. Ya better start munchin' on rats and squirrels first," she said. "Ya know, to see how you like it, before you go off making a hasty decision like that."

Aylin's mother, named after the Esther from the Bible, was the last to respond. Esther had, long ago, taken to the role as mother of the group with relative ease. "Annie dear?" she asked, giving the whole idea another moment of careful consideration. "How exactly do you plan on becoming an owl?"

Annie Goode didn't have a good answer to that, so she listened to the evening around them. Sometimes, when she listened hard enough, Annie could hear the laughter of her children out there in the woods, out where the field songs hung on the air like the moss that possum-ed from the trees there year round. She strained for a moment to hear them. She heard nothing but the buzz of the old porch light and the faintest sound of ancestral crickets taking up homily out along the river.

"Annie?" Esther asked. "Are you okay?"

It was hearing the name *Annie* that struck her. Anne to most everyone else, it was her husband who first called her "Annie," after discovering in her a playful side too. "Annie Bananie," he used to call her. "And our grandchildren will call you Grannie Bananie, if all goes to plan." He was sweet to her back in the early days, so sweet and so godly that Annie came to believe that, if one righteous man could save a city, God would have saved her, were she a city. Back in those days, the early days, it almost seemed as if their love made up all the elements: his eyes of alder wood and hers of oceans. He still had a fire in his belly back then, so she would have gladly tilled the earth. "Annie," he'd said to her, "remember the other day when I said we should look for a house? Well," he said, "we should look for a house." Anne Harden Wyatt was her Christian name. The name she was born with. The name she was given. And yet, from that day on, she preferred Annie.

That night, surrounded by her friends, Annie Goode finally confessed that she was a skin-walker. What she could not bring herself to tell them, however, is how she'd grown to loathe the very sound of the name Annie. What she could not bring herself to tell them is the one murderous thought that led to her change. What she did not tell them was that she had been out driving for most of that morning, that she had skipped church altogether and did not feel bad about it. She did not tell them that country roads were more than country roads on Sundays. She did not tell them the tall-tales those roads will tell you. The lies those roads tell are their way of telling you the truth: that all country roads lead you forever back home. What Annie Goode did not tell her friends that night was that she came by a woman offering discounts in front of a yard-sale sign, as if some treasures come valued in dimes. What Annie Goode did not tell them was that, as she stole away down some back-country road, she got this almost sneaking suspicion that the islands themselves were calling to her. No, Annie Goode did not tell them any of this because, if she had, they would've seen only to laughing about it uncomfortably, and Annie couldn't bear to hear that.

Instead, Annie Goode recounted the scene in her house, earlier that morning. She and her husband were sitting opposite each other in the living room—he in his armchair, she on the sofa—same as they always did right before church. He was reading, and she watched him read. They did not speak a word to each other—not a word—then, just like that, it was all too much for her, having borne that unbearable silence for far too long. Annie Goode could not say what made that morning different from all the other mornings, except that she found she was suddenly tired of everything. Tired of being ignored, tired of him and tired of herself. She was so tired that something finally snapped inside of her.

Taken by a sudden and almost inexplicable need to fix things, Annie Goode snatched a pair of scissors from the kitchen drawer, marched back into the den, knelt down in front of him and cut a head-sized hole in his newspaper. She explained that she really just wanted to see his face.

Annie's friends knew she had always possessed a disquieting, even slightly sociopathic, sense of humor. Back in grade school, she was known for having cut the crotches out of all the boys' gym shorts during PE and later scaring the living bejesus out of a homeless woman when she held her up at banana-point. But this . . . this was something else entirely. Something in her was off, they could tell, something that screamed of desperation. Even her three closest friends in the entire world appeared unnerved by this story, as they sat there, frozen and aghast, startled even into silence.

As Annie Goode remembered it, a wind came down from the whiskers of the trees right about then, down through the screens of foliage, down through a tousle of leaves. And down too came the silence. Out along the river was an ocean of history, kept by women like her, all diligently dead but still flirting in their casual ways, understanding only what lovers need to misunderstand. Annie remembered listening to the rafters of her own house creaking in the darkness, the echoes of some important something lost in orbit in a distant field. Perhaps their love story told soft in her tongue, soft like a snow from a new-moon sky. She still loved her husband, you see. She loved him as only a good woman can. But she wanted, more than anything, to have a vague recollection of her own skin, to discover herself, at last, in the body of someone else. Something, really, anything else. And that is how she came to be an owl. That is how she came to leave him that morning, and later found herself on that old country road.

Annie Goode recounted all of this for her two young guests that day in her living room. And when she finished her story, closing on the silence that befell her and her friends on that night long, long ago, Annie Goode turned her attention to Aylin and said, "Now, you and I both know your mother wouldn't have judged me for wanting another's skin. Not your mother. She's far too kind for things like that. Rather, it's far more likely that she would've laughed at the notion of me flying around in the body of some stupid owl, which as it turns out, is exactly what she did. She laughed so hard that her shoulders shook. You know that laugh, don't you? You do. It's contagious, am I right? It is. Because, soon enough, we were all laughing along with her, and your mother was saying something like, 'Well heck, Annie, you might as well. We all know there are far stranger things 'round here.' And to illustrate her point, your mother brought up one of them flyin' folks that she met, one day. You know the ones, don't you?" Annie Goode interjected. "Surely, you've heard of them. Yeah, you have; you've heard of them. You know? The ones with wings? The ones all the newspapers are going on about? Well, your mother brought up those flyin' folks, laughed a while longer and then added, 'I say, do what you gotta do, Annie. That's what I say. Heck, become a sea slug, for all I care. Or if you'd rather, become an owl. What's another owl in the sky when you've got the men-folk flyin' all about like they do?'"

Something instantaneously alighted in Bohicket's person. "Have you actually met one? The flyin' folk, I mean?"

"Why, sure. Sure I have," Annie Goode replied, as if the question itself seemed silly. "You know, here and there, in some of my travels. Owls gotta share the sky too, ya know. I have to say though, they can be downright rude for my taste. It's just they're so damn busy scouring the coastline all the damn time that they forget to watch where they are going, dashing all over the sky in search of where somebody or another is rumored to have drowned."

Bohicket didn't think to ask her about the Makers again, didn't feel he needed to. He was so preoccupied with the story she told them that the thought of asking her again never even crossed his mind. He was wholly smitten instead with how matter-of-factly Annie Goode spoke about the Flying Men, of how clumsy and unwieldy they were with their giant wings and of how persistently they combed the lengths of the shoreline, day after day and night after night, in search of any poor soul who had battled the ocean and, in losing, drowned.

"Some say theirs is a lost cause," Annie Goode told them, "that no one—not even them—can fly that high. But still, they try. They are always trying, as if their sole mission in life is to act as angels while here on earth, to help the souls of our bodies up and up and forever up into the farthest reaches of the heavens." And she went on to explain that this practice of theirs was almost as old as their time on this continent. In fact, it started soon after their captors forbade the burial traditions they had brought with them from Africa, therein seeing to it that the souls of their loved ones might never truly find rest. "It came as inspiration from the first," she said. "From when they were first introduced to the Scriptures' idea of a heaven above." And believing that the body without ceremony still housed the soul, these Flying Men had taken to the tradition, soon after that, of carrying bodies high into the air, where they believed the soul was permitted its rest. They gone and got taken up was a common refrain around those parts. And the practice they continued still to the day.

Chapter Eleven

BOHICKET LEFT ANNIE GOODE'S HOUSE THAT DAY WITH A NEW-found liveliness in his step, inspired by the tales he had heard. All the way home through the woods, he and Aylin whispered about what they had learned—whispered like people whisper when they have and intend to keep a secret that feels so dangerous to them they might've done better not to whisper about it at all. And reaching the shoreline where his boat was moored late that evening, they swore a solemn pact to never speak a word of what they'd learned that day.

"Not a word," Aylin repeated.

"Not a word," Bohicket agreed. Then he turned to untie his boat.

"Nope," she said, snatching at his shirt and twirling him around. "Not good enough." Her face was twisted all up in a way that suggested what worried her had not been undone just yet. "Blood oath," she said.

"What?"

"Blood oath," she said. "Only way I'll get any sleep to-night is if we take the blood oath."

"Oh . . . okay."

And with that, Aylin bit hard into her hand.

"Ouch," he said.

"There," she said. "Now you go. You bite down till you draw blood."

"Not a chance," he said. "No way, no how. Absolutely not. No."

"Yes," she said.

And so he did.

Her palm was already pooling in a bright metallic red

when she extended it to him. "Shake on it," she said. "Ya gotta shake on it."

And they did. They shook on it. Blood for blood.

Even still, Bohicket was never any good at keeping secrets. With no TV, a broken radio and very little news from the outside world, secrets were like sustenance, and anything worth sharing: a means to survive. But that is not why Bohicket broke his promise to Aylin that day. His mother's illness only grew frightfully worse, and he believed, in his heart of hearts, that the medicine she needed was hope. He would inevitably feel terrible about lying to her, but he broke his oath to Aylin that day because he loved his mother and, in his mind, nothing took precedence over seeing her heal. So Bohicket came crashing into the house later that evening, and even before the door had time to shut behind him, already he was out with it. "Guess what, Mama?! Guess what?"

His mother was up from the kitchen table with a start. "What, in God's name, is it?! Oh no! Don't tell me. Are you okay? Was it an alligator, a shark that got your leg? Heaven have mercy, I cannot bear to look after a cripple! Is it your leg? Is it a storm? Not a storm. Please, Lord Jesus, Risen Savior, tell me it's not a storm." She was now scurrying around the kitchen in absolute hysterics, listing off frantically all the preparations they would need to make, if it was—heaven help us!—a storm. "Don't just stand there looking all dumb and stuff. Though with a face like that, God knows you can't help it. Batten down the hatches! We haven't a moment to spare. No telling if this poor excuse for a house can survive another one."

"Mama."

"What is it?!" she exclaimed. "You sure as hell are a stupid kind of dumb, ain't ya, son? But your mama didn't raise no mute. Ya dumb, but ya ain't no mute. Now out with it!"

"Mama. Come sit down. There's no storm," he said. "Now come, sit."

"No storm?" she asked, peering out at him from underneath the counter, where she stored all of her spare rain buckets. "Well Holy Christ, son! Why, on earth, would you go scaring me half-to-hell like that? You know I got a bad heart," she said, clutching at her chest.

"Just sit yourself down a moment, won't you, Mama? No need to worry. I just came in from outside, and it's all quiet out there. Sky's clear, the ocean is calm. Near-perfect sailing weather, by the looks of it. So whatcha say we sit a while, Mama? Come on, sit."

It only took a bit more coaxing to have her sit down beside him at the kitchen table, and there she listened intently, as Bohicket recounted all he had learned about the Flying Men that day. "See? I told ya, Mama," he finished, never more proud of himself. "See, Mama? Ley and I told ya, didn't we? We told ya they were real. And it seems we were right."

To this point, his mother had appeared to be inspirited by the news he had brought. "Real, you say? Huh. Huh... huh." Then, in an instant, her entire demeanor changed. Her eyebrows furrowed into question marks, and her lips pursed like they did whenever she got dead-set against some idea or another. Even the look on her face said she was suddenly skeptical of whatever it was he would have her convinced of. "We got a letter in the mail today," she told him. "You were out," she told him, "when Mami Granger brought it by."

Now it should be noted that sending or receiving anything by mail was no small matter in those parts. The whole process could be quite an ordeal, faced with all the many deterrents to such a convenience caused by living in the middle of nowhere. First, it took the courier from the nearest post office (which was not near at all) to come out there by boat, which he or she only bothered to do once or twice a month, and even then, it took Mami Granger another few days to get off her fat ass, in their mother's words, and do her job of delivering the mail to their doorstep. It was a whole process, to say the least, with so many moving parts along the way that the system itself typically failed more times than it worked, and actually getting a letter at all was a cause for celebration. The whole family would gather around the table and stare at the envelope like they had spotted something strange and extinct, like some rare, exotic bird had just landed somehow on their kitchen table.

Of course, Bohicket had fully expected his little brother to write to them at some point or another, just like he had promised to do. Not a day went by that he did not think to himself, *Any day now. Should be any day.* So Bohicket was understandably excited to hear about the letter along with the possibility of any news that had his brother closing in on the whereabouts of their sister. "And?" he pressed his mother. "And? How is he? How's he doing? The letter is from Ley, isn't it? It is; I know it is. It is, right? Tell me it is."

It felt like months since they last got word from him, and for all they knew, Ley had gone and gotten himself married to a woman named Jazzy, short for Jazabel, who lived in a rundown rowhouse without a roof, a door or windows and, for fun, painted murals of dead flowers on her bedroom walls. Or perhaps had gone and gotten himself eaten whole by a tiger or a shark. Or worse, Bohicket thought, a tiger shark.

Of course, his mother would've preferred her son been eaten alive to hearing he'd eloped with some deadbeat floozy, as she would've called her. "Better my son go to heaven now with his soul intact than having to explain to the good saint Peter his pickled liver, unopened Bible and thirteen bastard children."

Bohicket, on the other hand, couldn't have cared less what his little brother was up to or who he may or may not choose to marry, so long as he was safe and doing alright. "He is alright, isn't he?" he asked.

"Oh, he's doing just fine," she said, sounding every bit as relieved as he was.

"So? What did he have to say for himself?"

"Here," she said. "Read it for yourself."

The letter Ley wrote was not very long. He sent his love and hugs and asked how they were holding up in his absence. Good, he hoped. He gave no indication as to where he was living now or what he was doing to make ends meet, whether he'd found a job or friends or a means to the justice he was after. Really, the letter would've been of no consequence at all—save for a few pleasantries—were it not for what he penned in post-script, like an afterthought mentioned merely in passing. It was becoming clear to him, he said, that they'd do well to steer clear of the Flying Men altogether. *They are bad news, he wrote. Trust me when I say this, trust me, they are nothing but bad, bad news.*

"Ya see?" his mother said when Bohicket finished reading and put down the letter. "It seems your brother, dumb as he is, knows something that we do not, and it seems your friend Annie Goode's word isn't so good, after all. See what I mean? He said it himself. It sounds like he might be onto something. He was always a wise one, your brother. Intuitive too. Even early on. And well, I got this sneaking suspicion that you and I both should take him at his word."

Bohicket turned the letter over to examine the back then glanced inside the envelope the letter was mailed in, hoping to find something he had missed, some further explanation of what he meant by his warning. But what he already read was all there was. Just a warning. No rhyme or reason to it. No hint as to what his brother's search had uncovered that had him cautioning them so. A simple warning, and that was all. They are bad news, his brother had warned, as if to suggest their very lives could be in danger.

Bohicket couldn't sleep that night, and when he found his mother in the kitchen pacing around from window to window and staring off warily into the deep black sky as if expecting to see the cause of her dread, it appeared that neither could she. It was half-past-three when he gave up on sleep altogether and found her sitting with both legs in the sink and gazing out the window. And though he tried many times to coax her away from that window, his mother refused. At first, he tried to assure her with comforts she knew. "Jesus and His angels are here to protect us," he said. "See them out there? They'll keep guard." And when that didn't work, he tried to sing to her.

"Bo, dear, you sure got a terrible voice," she remarked without looking away from that window. "Now your brother, that boy could sing. Bo, dear, sing like him, won't you, dear? It'd be a shame to keep torturing those beautiful hymns you're singin' with that voice of yours. Won't you try and sing like your brother? Won't you try?"

It was clear that singing to her wasn't what she needed at the time, so Bohicket decided instead to tell her a few stories he'd overheard in the village, followed by a few more he'd heard her tell him. Then and only then, after he turned her own stories on her, could he begin to see her gradually relenting. "You belong up there, don't you, Mama?" he said. "Up there, I mean, with the birds. You do, ya know? You do. Birdy is what they'll call you. Mama Birdy."

"Yes," she echoed with a wistful yawn. "Mama Birdy."

And having tucked her in, later that night, he took care to spread her arms out across her bed. He said, "There now, see, Mama? Dream like you can be anything you want in your dreams. Dream like you are yourself the Makers. That's right, you, Mama Birdy. You, not them."

But even he was not foolish enough to believe his own lies. He hated having to resort to promising her such unattainable dreams. She was no bird, nor would she ever be. There was danger in even suggesting it was so. He knew that. He knew better. But there were far greater dangers out there—if his brother was indeed right—so he lied to her that night and for many nights to follow. And almost sensing those winged men hovering in predatory circles above their house now, he would stand guard over her the rest of the night.

And it was somewhere deep in the well of those very nights that a strange and unexplainable sensation started growing anew in him. He could not help but feel that all his newfound worries, coupled with an encyclopedia of responsibilities, were changing him into a person he did not recognize. Where before he liked to take the world in stride, come things as they may, his sense of obligation to his mother and being left alone now to look after their island meant he had little to no time for himself and the things he had previously enjoyed, like practicing his photography, getting lost in his thoughts, fishing for the fun of it and enjoying the commonplace leisure in moments of passivity. Though he did not know it yet, the change in him was a thing he had come by naturally: the subtle maturation of a boy becoming a man.

Only when dawn came and the coast was clear did Bohicket dare to venture out again in search of Aylin. And in time, the strangest thing began to happen to him when he did, though it happened so gradually he hardly even noticed. And so it was that merely existing in Aylin's presence began to change Bohicket in a number of slight and indistinguishable ways, and he came, in the end, by way of a quiet healing.

In time, certain aspects of Aylin began to remind him of what he had loved most about his sister. Her penchant for laughing at her own stupid jokes. Her irrational fear of being crushed by a falling tree branch or jet engine. Her habit of issuing daily salutations to the sun. It could've been any one of those vague similarities they shared, or it could've been how excited Aylin got at the notion of the mystery of the

Makers and the Flying Men, whenever another whispered tale or unsubstantiated rumor surfaced so that they could go and investigate together. It could've been how big her eyes got at the prospect of magic nearby, and her unrelenting belief—nay, insistence—that it was, it always was. It could've been that he grew to love Aylin as deeply as he had loved his sister, though it's impossible to say for sure. And yet one thing's for certain: in seeking out the mysteries of those islands together, what he found was not his sister or his sister-in-Aylin, but rather Aylin herself, filling that void that his sister's absence had left in his chest.

And so he did not confess to her his growing fears nor so much as breathe a word of the warnings in his brother's letter, afraid it would frighten her, make her leery of everything—even the magic she saw inhabiting the four corners of her world—and that, he could not bear. So rather than mention it at all, he asked Aylin to take him someplace new each and every day in order to retrace the steps that she took with his sister, long, long ago.

Aylin, of course, was happy to oblige. And together they visited many new and magical places in the weeks that followed—from a little-known spot where her ancestors, as fugitives, were said to have hidden a cache of stolen gold, to a singular spot atop the river where a curious moon was said to have come down to earth one night on a whim, only to be buried there forever beneath the river's waters, where she sleeps to this day under the watchful eye of her twin sister in the sky.

And he took tales of all their adventures back home with him to his mother, and he found that, in time, those tales did her some good, lifted her spirits, if only for a while. And bright and early one cheerful morning, he decided to share the good news with Aylin, as a means of encouraging her about the good she was doing.

"So she's doing better?" Aylin asked.

"Yep," he replied, while the worry on his face betrayed his words. "I suppose, yes, yes she's doing better." But even he knew good-and-damn-well that this was a lie, haunted still by whatever he saw behind his mother's eyes: the look of someone entering the vault of a big empty room. He could not bring himself to tell Aylin the unadulterated truth. He could not tell her how often he still found his mother reading the formations of birds in the sky, convinced their shapes were telling her something. "V-shapes point to the things we need to survive, things like love and friends and a good long nap," she would tell him. "Ws are a reminder to look inside, to eat your vegetables, drink more water and remember to pray," she would say, so sure that she could master the signs, read the birds like a prediction in tea leaves. "No shape at all," his mother would tell him, "now that's the worst. All you can do then is brace for high winds and bad, bad weather." And he could not tell Aylin how uneasy his mother got when she foresaw this, the way she clenched her fists so tight, like she was holding a one-way ticket to a far-off place.

"I'm glad she's doing better," Aylin said. "But an idea dawned on me, just last night. Can't believe it didn't occur to me sooner, but the Healing Tree," she said. "The way my mama tells it, a tree like that is sure to work."

She took him to see the tree, that very morning, and standing at its base and staring up into its tall, tall branches, she explained that the tree was rumored to possess certain healing powers. "The joke is that love is just a means of validating ourselves," she said. "But the mere fact that this tree exists seems to say otherwise. For centuries, people around these parts have been coming here on behalf of their loved ones. The story goes that, if someone you love is sick or dying, you need only hang an article of their clothing from these here branches, and they will be healed." And to illustrate her point, she shared a few stories of mothers who saved their children from smallpox or some other disease with nothing more than a pair of pants, along with all the many shirts that had saved men from the sea.

"Outsiders may call it a fairy tree. Others, the Lazarus Tree. But most people these days have forgotten all about it. Not me though. I still believe." While Bohicket was taken by the sheer height of the tree, Aylin went on to explain that, while she might be naive about a lot of things in this world, she understood the many vagaries in this life. "It just so happens that love ain't one of them is all. It ain't. Love ain't one of them."

They sat down side-by-side against the tree's trunk, and Aylin told him it was her father who made her a believer in such things. "Tell me the story of the fairy tree, Daddy," she would say, back when she was just a girl. "Tell me the story of the fairy tree. And don't forget the voices." And her father would tell her that story, night after night, until her eyelids grew heavy with emerald dreams. "But it was how he told it that had me believe," she recalled. "He said someone's cousin or something from *off* had plans once to build a house in its place, and my father, he tried to warn them. Course, they didn't listen. 'Can't go cutting down a tree like this,' he told them. But when the first tractor sputtered to a halt mere inches from its trunk and then would not restart, they just assumed it was a malfunction with the motor. When the second tractor did the exact same thing, it was strange, but not unsolvable. They got the second tractor up and working again, and were on their fifth attempt to raze it from its roots when a branch broke free of an otherwise healthy tree and split the driver in two. And it was hard for anyone to argue with that."

Hang an article of clothing from a fairy branch, and they will be healed is how it goes. So Bohicket stole a pair of his mother's socks, and the following night, he did just that. In the coming weeks, he began to slip bras and panties from her dresser drawers and shoes from her closet, and night after night, he and Aylin ventured out to that tree and dressed up its branches, until the articles of clothing outnumbered the leaves. And he would sit back and marvel at all the colorful fabrics that hung there—the reds, the blues, the yellows and the greens—still all too aware that there was more than laundry on the line.

Chapter Twelve

ONLY DECADES LATER WOULD BOHICKET SEE WHY HE WAS so easily convinced to trust in the healing powers of that tree, to take Aylin at her word and go on stealing his mother's clothes for days and days, draping them from its branches. Only in time would Bohicket realize how convincing your first love can be, given as he was at the time to the persuasions of young love. It would take him a good many years to see this clearly, to see that Aylin was not his first love, like he was so sure she was, but rather his second. It would take him that time to see that he was not smitten so much with Aylin at first, as he was with how strikingly similar she was to the first girl he loved, the Afghan girl on the cover of his *National Geographic* magazine, the girl he'd stared at for so long as a boy that he'd memorized both her face and the person, he felt, behind it. There was a certain practicality to what both their faces said to him, a certain matter-of-fact presence to their eyes. And so, without knowing it, he had learned to love them for the same exact reasons, for what they each appeared to be hiding—some facts about surviving, some context of pain and something that spoke still to the endurance of joy. And that, he would later see, is what made his loving them as essential as uncovering their truths, believing that acceptance itself was love alone.

He had stolen nearly half his mother's wardrobe before she caught on. She was holding up a handful of mismatched socks the morning she came marching from her room to confront him with a mix of confusion and despair all over her face. "Bo!" she shouted, as she came stomping down the hallway. "Bo? I know you're behind this! What sort of shenanigans have you gotten yourself into? Look at all these socks, and not a single matching pair! Not a one!"

Bohicket was in the kitchen when she found him stooped over a bowl of fruit, and he had to answer her mid-chew. "What? No. Me? I'm as clueless as you are, Mama. Strange though," he said. "Really strange."

"Bo."

"Yes?"

"Even you are smart enough to know that socks don't up and run away on their own."

And Bohicket knew it was time to come clean. "It was me," he said. "I stole your socks."

"What in God's name, Bo?"

"And like one or two of your shirts."

"You are kidding me, right?" she said.

"And maybe a few of your bras as well."

"What? Why?"

"You might be missing some shoes too. Just sayin'. And that green dress of yours."

"Damn it all, Bo."

"What? You don't ever wear it anymore. And well," he said. "I needed it."

"You needed it? Good Lord, help me! Good Lord. Good Lord. Tell me you haven't been w-w-wearing my clothes?!" she stuttered, as if merely the thought of her son doing such a thing was hard enough to say.

"No, Mama, I haven't been wearing your clothes."

"It's alright to be curious, ya know? Not a thing wrong with being curious from time to time. No sir, not a thing wrong with that. We are all guilty of that at some point in our lives."

"Mama. It's nothing like that, I assure you."

"Come to think of it, you always were an odd one," she continued, rubbing at her chin. "Seems, by now, a boy your age would've, at least, begun thinking about girls."

"Mama," he said.

"I mean, I suppose it'd be nice to have someone around here to play dress-up with, while your sister is away. It's just . . . It's just a lot to take in, is all."

"Mama!"

"Look, ya got your mother all flustered now. Oh dear Lord, I think I'm gettin' dizzy. Shame on you for breaking the news to me like this. For shame." And with that, she dropped herself down in the seat across from him, as if her legs were going to fail her.

"It's not what you think, Mama. I swear to God," he said. He then proceeded to tell her all about the Healing Tree, where it was located and the curious powers it was believed to possess. And the look on his mother's face, as he told her about it, suggested she was more than relieved that her suspicions were wrong.

"Well praise the Lord Jesus for sparing me my fears!" she exclaimed. "Praise the Good Lord above! Praise Him! Praise the Lord! Otherwise, I'm not entirely sure what I would've done with you," she said. "Okay. Well. Go on. Tell me more."

And so he did, and when he was through sharing everything he had heard about the tree with her, her whole demeanor was one of ecstasy. Bohicket mistook this look for wonder, a child's curiosity. While in reality, it was the look of a person newly pregnant with an idea, an idea that would've had him frightened for her well-being if he had sensed it.

It had seemed, for a while, that she had seen the error of her ways and abandoned the very notion that she could fly. She stopped gathering feathers, stopped making plans and stopped jumping off rooftops, which all in all, made Bohicket extremely pleased. And yet, his mother was so taken by the idea of that tree that, the very next day, she could be heard screaming her elation from the top of its branches. In fact, her screams were so loud that Bohicket and Aylin could hear her screaming a mile or so away, and they came running. By the time they reached her, all of her yelling and carrying on had drawn quite a crowd of curious onlookers, some intrigued, others concerned. But not Bohicket. Bohicket was terrified, not only because of the spectacle she was making of herself, but also because she was making that spectacle here in broad daylight.

He tried to talk her down.

Aylin tried too.

And concerned for her safety, a few of the villagers tried to as well.

In no time at all, it seemed the entire village had ventured from their homes and encircled the base of that tree, which made the whole situation that much worse when his mother spread out her arms and claimed that she too was one of the Flying Men.

In an instant, Bohicket's voice caught up in his throat and then went hoarse, as he came face-to-face with the loathsome prospect of what this proclamation of hers might come to mean, what with the whole village there to hear her say this and the terrible atrocities that had befallen so many others who dared speak their name.

"Look at me now!" she yelled at the top of her lungs. "Look at my wings! Watch me fly! For I am Mama Birdy, the Cloud Maker, the mother of all Flying Men! I am one of them and all of them! I am all of them at once! And now, I am off to rescue the drowning!" No sooner had she leapt from that branch did she come crashing back down to earth, where she crumpled with a thud.

And all while the whole entire village looked on.

Her body hit the ground with such violence that the onlookers let out a collective gasp. It was hard to make out the shape of a person in the awkward way that she landed. One leg was tucked completely underneath her, another bent sharply above the knee. As for her arms, her arms were both misshapen and broken in several different places. And yet she did not cry or let out so much as a whimper. In fact, she hardly made a sound at all as Bohicket rushed to her side.

"Is she dead?" someone asked. "She's not moving. Ya think she's dead?" And yet it wasn't so much what the people around him were saying as the way they glanced around at each other, most out of concern, but some almost suspicious of her.

Aylin and one of the older women from the village raced over with Bohicket to the place where she had fallen. Aylin checked for a pulse, said she was breathing. "Good. That's good," the old woman said. "But that leg is broken, by the looks of it. Her wrists are too. Let's get her to Mama Hawa's house, see if she can't look after her." And the old woman helped heave his mother's limp body up onto his shoulders and then led the way back into the village.

Mama Hawa wasted no time hurrying them inside. "Lay her down here," she said. "Put her on the sofa while I get my things." And a moment later, she returned from the kitchen with a makeshift brace for his mother's leg. Mama Hawa felt around her fractured bones and commented to herself, "Uhuh. Uhuh. There now, I see." She put a stick lengthwise across his mother's mouth and said, "Now bite down on this, my dear. You've gone and done a fool-ass thing. You're lucky to survive such a fall. But this is gonna hurt. I'm warning you." And the cracking sound of her leg bone when Mama Hawa set it in place was enough to turn anyone's stomach. "Now for your wrists. Deep breath now. One . . . two . . . three . . . "

The pain his mother was in must've been excruciating, and yet she did not squirm or utter a sound. She did bite down so hard on the stick though that it broke in half, and Aylin was tasked with clearing her mouth of the splinters.

"There now, my dear. There, there," Mama Hawa said, brushing the hair back from his mother's face. "That's a brave girl. Seems you're a lot tougher than you look. The worst is over. Now you heal. Let me mix you up something for the pain." And then she disappeared into her kitchen for five good minutes before returning with a makeshift splint and an herbal brew she had just bottled. "Your mother's gonna need some tending to for a good long while," Mama Hawa explained. "Give her two teaspoons of this twice a day. Once in the morning, and once mid-afternoon. Should help with the pain, okay? And whatever happens, keep her off that leg, ya hear me?"

Bohicket nodded.

"I mean it now," she said. "She's your mother, and it's your job to look after her, same as she looked after you when you were a baby. Good, as long as we're clear. I'll get a few of the boys to help you carry her back to the boat. Then you will take her straight home and make sure she's good and rested." Mama Hawa headed out to the porch and whistled a few men over. Each man took an arm or a leg, lifted his mother from the sofa and helped Bohicket carry her out the door.

That, however, was as far as they got before having to put her back down, for an angry crowd had already begun gathering around the porch, making it impossible for them to pass. A woman in the back said something about what she'd heard his mother say before she jumped. Another said something about the Flying Men.

And Bohicket knew then that they were in trouble.

The angry voices in the crowd grew louder and louder, and before long, a few more angry voices joined in, announcing their agreement that something should be done, that "something had to be done." And in no time flat, the situation became dire, just as Bohicket had feared it would. But then Mama Hawa emerged from the house, approached the steps and lifted her arms to calm the crowd. "Not today, my friends," she said. "Not today. This woman is hurt, so make way!"

And that was all it took for the crowd to disperse.

Several men helped Bohicket carry his mother out to the boat, and he made sure to thank Mama Hawa as he left her porch. "Thank you," Bohicket said. And she smiled a smile that he could not misconstrue, a smile that said, *You are welcome, my dear. Of course you are welcome. You are right to thank me, and you are welcome, just this once.*

After getting his mother home safe and sound, Bohicket gave up on the Healing Tree entirely. He stopped stealing her clothes and hanging them from its branches, and he almost stopped hoping altogether. The final straw came by way of a letter that his brother sent a few days later. In it, Ley openly questioned what they saw that evening on the river. *Dead end after dead end, he wrote, and now I've begun to question it myself. Big birds maybe. Pelicans or some other species of bird leftover from dinosaur times. Now wouldn't that have the scientists baffled? Tricks of the eye maybe, he wrote. I just don't know. Maybe she's still alive somewhere and will somehow, someday, wander back home. Maybe so. Or maybe we watched our sister die that night, and what we saw was just our way of seeing her off to heaven. Maybe that is all. Maybe we see only what we want to see.*

And that got Bohicket thinking that maybe his little brother was right.

It took him a while to go and face Aylin with the news of his hopelessness, and even then, he only told her at a loss for anything else to tell her. He wore his resignation on his face the day he did it, as if hopelessness was all that remained of his life, and despite all her attempts to dissuade him of it, even Aylin proved to be of little help to him.

It wasn't until Bohicket visited her again, a few days later, that Aylin told him she had had an idea. "I've got just the thing to fix what's ailing you," she said, nearly jumping out of her own skin with excitement. "Now cheer up, won't you? Stop all this moping around you're doing, or I'll be forced to punch you right in the mouth. And don't you think I won't. Just you try me."

And Bohicket forced a smile, just to appease her. "There, happy?"

Aylin understood there were great dangers involved in the idea she would propose, but there were dangers involved in not proposing the idea as well, dangers namely to him and his mother, dangers Aylin was only willing to risk for him. And so she did. "What would you say if I told you there are real-life angels among us?" she asked him.

"I'd say you're better off punching me."

"There are, you know? I know because I've met one."

"Here. I'm tough. I can take a punch standing," he said. "Which one? Jaw or square in the mouth?"

"I'm serious," she said.

"Jaw it is then. You'd never forgive yourself if you knocked out my teeth."

"I can take you to meet him, if you like."

"Be sure to close your fist real tight, like this, so you don't go breaking those precious little fingers of yours, alright?" And with that, he closed his eyes and braced for the impact. "Okay," he said. "Okay, I'm ready. On the count of three, alright? Ready? One . . . two . . . three!" He paused a moment before peeking open one of his eyes. "Well?"

"Well, what?"

"Well don't go wussing out on me now. A promise is a promise."

"I'm not wussing out."

"I'm waaai-ting," he sang.

"Do ya wanna meet him or not?" she asked, crossing her arms.

"Fine," he said.

"Fine," she said. "But I still wanna punch you in the mouth."

Chapter Thirteen

For days, Aylin's mind was plagued with the gloom that had overtaken Bohicket's whole countenance whenever he came around. Whatever sadness had befallen him manifested itself on his face, somewhere between his eyes and nose, like a tree weighted down impossibly by a long and heavy snow. It was as if his shoulders and head were merely being dragged along with him wherever he went, and the sight of him like this was in itself cause enough to worry. And so Aylin had spent many a sleepless night pining away for a solution, until a solution finally dawned on her and she made a plan. She was up with the sun early the next morning and set about, all that day, seeing it through.

Her plan would require some deception and a little white lie, neither of which were in her nature, but since what Bohicket feared the most scared her even more, Aylin put aside any apprehensions she had.

And that's how Aylin managed to convince Bohicket to follow her across the island that day, on the promise that she would take him to meet a real, live angel.

Bohicket had his suspicions, of course. How could he not? He had grown to be suspicious of everything in those days, even things that could be explained by the senses, things like the wind and the tides, even things that could be proven by science, like migrating birds and a change in the seasons.

Aylin suspected this and spent much of their journey to an adjacent island trying to convince him that there really are angels among us. "And I'll prove it," she said.

"Yeah, yeah. We'll see," Bohicket replied. "We'll see."

Still, Aylin was insistent. "We've seen far stranger things

together, have we not? I mean, if Annie Goode can change into an owl, then surely there are angels among us."

Bohicket did not argue, did not see the point in it.

"And you yourself saw the Flying Men, am I wrong?"

"I don't know anymore," he said with a shrug. "Maybe."

"You said you believe in the Bible."

"The holy and inspired word of God," was his reply.

"Doesn't the Bible speak of angels? Surely, you aren't calling God a liar, are you? Cause if so . . . man . . . I fear for your soul."

Like so many other boys who grew up in the South with a healthy fear of hellfire and damnation, Bohicket was quick to refute the dangerous accusation. "I'd never call God a liar."

"Then admit it is possible. Admit it's possible that there are angels among us."

"Fine," he said. "It's possible you're right."

"Good," she said. "Because as long as there are still angels around, there is hope."

After reaching the far side of the island and wading through the shallows to the other side, Aylin confessed that Eustace Clearle, a boy from her village, had first introduced her to the angel. "He claimed they were friends, and in time, he paid for their friendship," Aylin told him. "You see, rumor around those parts had it that Eustace Clearle had business with the Devil. The curmudgeonly spinster Miss Tenishaw even swore to it. She had claimed to have seen Eustace Clearle with her own two eyes, keeping company with a shadowy man with large black wings. 'I know cause I seen it,' she told the other villagers. 'With my own two eyes . . . whatever it was.' She said the shadowy man he kept company with was taller than any man she'd ever seen. 'Must've been twenty or thirty feet tall,' she had said, 'Taller even than the trees themselves. And God knows, only angels and demons are that tall. I say demon,' she told everyone. 'That's what I say. I say demon.' When Miss Tenishaw described the shadowy man's wings, she did so with both her arms. She would reach her arms out as far as she could, and exclaim, 'Like this! Black as midnight too.' But Miss Tenishaw was wrong about that. The shadowy man's wings were not black; they were white, so white, in fact, they were nearly translucent with tips that glowed in the presence of the light. No one in the village knew Eustace Clearle like I did, and I know Eustace Clearle would never ever make friends with the Devil."

Now, tales such as these were not uncommon out on these islands. In fact, tales such as these fully inhabited them, particularly out there along the Carolina coast. Everyone in those parts had heard them: the tales their grandmothers and grandfathers had whispered into their fireplaces at night, tales that dated back well before any recorded history on those islands. Eustace Clearle had heard the stories, same as everyone else had. He had heard them so many times growing up that he came to believe they were true. He came to believe in the supernatural, spirits in particular, angels and demons, not only because he took his Bible at its word, but because he was convinced that he too would have wings one day, that all God's children would, the day they die.

"I suppose, Eustace Clearle was what you might call a believer," Aylin explained. "And he really only had his mother to blame for that. She was a Southern woman to her core, you see, and as is the case with some Southern women, she had herself convinced of outlandish things. Sadly for him though, Eustace Clearle had more of his mother in him than he cared to admit, which is why," as Aylin told it, "he wasn't surprised in the least when he happened upon an angel."

They were somewhere along the back side of the island, where the land gave way to a field of marsh, when Aylin finally stopped and said, "Here's where I last met him." And then she continued out into the marsh, snapped the head off one of the reeds and returned to sit with Bohicket.

"Eustace showed me once how to call for him," Aylin sai,d then put the marsh reed to her lips and blew. "It's a quiet noise," she said. "But he will hear it. 'Stop by when you want,' the man told me. 'It gets lonely out here sometimes. I do love the company.'"

Aylin blew once and then waited a moment before blowing again.

Only after the third time did the trees begin stirring and the sky fill with retreating birds.

Strange, Bohicket thought.

Then Aylin noticed a black dot along the horizon. "There!" she exclaimed. "There!"

The dot appeared to grow bigger and bigger by the second, as if something was approaching and approaching them fast. In a matter of seconds, Bohicket realized this dot was not a dot at all, but rather the lanky silhouette of a man with wings.

Aylin stood to greet the man, as he descended from the sky and came to land in front of them in a big tornadic gust. "My dear, dear Bea," the man said, calling her by her nickname, "You've come at last to visit me. It's been too long." He seemed sincerely overjoyed to see her.

Bohicket was understandably taken aback, and seeing this, the man extended his hand to him. "No need to be afraid, my boy," he said. "Allow me to introduce myself. I go by the name of Piedmont Black. But my friends call me Pete."

It took quite a lot of courage for Bohicket to shake his hand. "I'm Bohicket," he said. "And no one calls me Bo."

"Then Bo it is," the man said with a hearty laugh.

And with that, the man folded back his wings and took a seat beside them. "Sorry I'm late," he said. "I was fast asleep when you called. Been pretty tired, as of late. Not sure why. Then again, you'd be surprised how much energy it takes to go flapping about everywhere on these fool-ass wings."

"Asleep?" Aylin asked. "You sleep up there?"

"Well, sure I do," he replied.

"But where?"

"Ship masts mostly. Sometimes a cloud. And you won't believe how much trash is just floating around in the ocean. Enough to make a nice comfy bed out of, is how much."

"A cloud?" she asked, genuinely intrigued. "You sleep on a cloud?"

"Where better to grab a little shut-eye? One of the only perks to lugging around these enormous wings."

Bohicket would admit to believing him from the start.

After all, in every tall tale, there is an inch of truth.

"Ya mind taking me some time?" Aylin asked.

"Perhaps. If you promise to be good," he said. "Then again, it's risky business when you don't have wings of your own. I've seen more than a few men fall to their deaths, just trying."

Bohicket imagined himself soaring up into the sky and bursting through the clouds.

"Clouds are really the only place someone like me can sleep," the man said, sounding to Bohicket as if he was referencing some great weight on his conscience. "It all feels somehow lighter up there," the man said in a way that seemed to recall all the angels who were cast out of heaven for want of what they most desired, only to miss home.

And when Bohicket looked up to where the man had pointed, he thought he recognized something vaguely familiar along the rooftop of the heavens, something vaguely good in gazing down to witness it all.

They talked and talked for quite some time, though Aylin and the man did most of the talking, mostly to catch up with each other since last they met. Bohicket had questions, plenty of them, but he had been brought up right, and in the South, that meant minding his manners. So he stuck mainly to small talk and laughing at the man's good-hearted jokes. Of course, it did occur to him to inquire about the wings, but that, he assumed, would be rude. And while his allegiance to the dictates of proper etiquette would have seen to it that a question like this never be aired, eventually Bohicket's curiosity got the better of him, as it so often did. And it was nearing sundown before he got up the nerve to part with the pleasantries and just come out with his question. "I'm sorry," he said, "but I have to ask. Excuse me, if I'm overstepping my boundaries . . . I mean, where are my manners, right? But, Piedmont, I have to ask: what's with those amazing wings?"

They had been sort of skirting the idea of where men go when they die, when Piedmont had shrugged at the mention of heaven. "Pete," the man said. "My friends call me Pete." And almost knowing what Bohicket was really asking, he extended one of his wings to him.

And Bohicket reached out his hand and touched the feathers.

"Pete," said the man.

"Pete," said Bohicket.

Each feather was aghast with evening light, which seemed to vein out in rivers from Piedmont's back to the tips of his feathers. And yet Bohicket saw it all a different way, like the illuminations came instead from within. "Aylin says you're an angel," he said. "Are you an angel?"

And the man just laughed. "Oh she did, did she? Well, let's see. I drink too much bourbon for one thing, and I cuss like a sailor, if that answers your question."

"So you're not an angel then?"

"I never said that, now did I?"

"So you are."

"Yes, I suppose. In a manner of speaking, you might say that."

"Oh don't be coy, Pete," Aylin said. "It's nothing to be ashamed of. Go on and tell him. He wants to know. It's why he's here."

"Fine then," the man said. "I've been outed. I'm embarrassed to admit it, but yes, Bo, I am as she says; I am an angel."

Bohicket looked away out over the marsh to where the sun was readying its goodbyes.

"Not at all like you expected, I see," the man said. "Thing is, the Bible seems to have breezed over this part. You wouldn't be the first person I've disappointed. Nevertheless," the man said, fanning out his wings, "here I am in all my glory, coming to you live and in person."

"If you are an angel," Bohicket said, "shouldn't you know a thing or two about heaven?"

"One would certainly think so."

And Bohicket reached out again and touched the man's wings. Not sure why, but were you to ask him what he felt when he did, he might've had trouble finding the words to describe it. He would have said they felt sort of feathery, in a harder not-at-all-feathery sort of way. He would have said they had substance to them, a heft even, with an odd weightlessness you must feel to understand. "They were warm," he would've told you. "That might surprise you. They were warm like skin." He would've tried to mimic the way the feathers pulsed, same as an artery does at the wrist or neck. Were you to ask him, he might've even drummed out the rhythm he heard with his fingers, a sort of metronomic thump-thump-pause-thump-thumpthump. But Bohicket never told anyone what he had felt for fear of what atrocities men are capable of when keeping a secret.

He did tell his mother a few days later, after swearing her to secrecy. "Cross your heart, and swear to God. Good. Now, here's the thing about angels." And Bohicket told her there are angels among us, and he told her how he knew because he thought, at the time, she needed to believe in such a thing.

He was still touching the man's feathers when he asked

the question. "My sister," he said quietly. "Her name is Dew. Have you seen her? Up there, I mean? Have you happened upon her in all your comings and goings?" He didn't know why, but Bohicket was thinking about his mother when he said this. He didn't mean to, yet he was.

"Your sister? Hmm. Let me think," the man wondered. "Her name is Dew, you say?" And he paused for a moment to think. "Yes, come to think of it, I have. Dew. That's right. She's a sweet one, your sister. If my memory serves me correctly, I believe she's an angel now too."

It would be impossible to describe what hearing this meant to Bohicket. In an instant, he felt like he could breathe again, breathe like it was the first breath he'd ever taken.

"And while they could have my wings for telling you this," the man continued, glancing over his shoulder warily, "the word on the street is the bookies have your sister as the odds-on favorite to win the derby this year. She's a fast one, you know? Hand to God. No girl, I can recall, flies faster."

It seemed then, with this momentary respite from his concern for his mother, that Bohicket found himself startled by how deeply he missed his sister.

"You miss her, don't you?"

"I miss her."

"You aren't a betting man, are you? No? That's probably for the best. I tell you what though. It's a safe bet, this one." Then he leaned in close and whispered, "Slide me whatever you got in that wallet there, and when I get home later tonight, I'll get my buddy Puggy Collins to bet it all on your sister. What do ya say to that? Do we have a deal?" And the man let out a big hearty laugh, and the air felt a bit lighter after that.

Bohicket didn't inquire about his father, and their talk turned to simpler things. And before they parted ways, an hour or so later, Aylin asked for a moment alone with her friend. Bohicket obliged and went off to wait for her at the treeline, which is unfortunate because what Bohicket didn't hear Aylin say to her friend was, "Thanks for your help." What Bohicket didn't hear her say was, "Heck, ya almost had me convinced you were an angel, so thanks. You'll always be an angel in my book for that."

Had Bohicket thought to take a picture with the lens of his mind, he undoubtedly would have. Indeed, the thought never occurred to him. Any one of us would have recognized, at some point, the similarities between Piedmont Black and the Flying Men he saw carry away his sister. Bohicket did not. And he did not because conviction is sometimes born of need. He instead simply looked on from just beyond the treeline, as Piedmont Black spread his wings, waved farewell to his friend and rose swiftly into the sky, where once again he vanished like a vision into a nest of waiting clouds.

Chapter Fourteen

N0 FACT, IT SEEMS, IS TRUER THAN THIS: TRUTH IS A LAN-
guage spoken in tongues. Despite what Bohicket believed or did not believe, whom he actually met that night
was no more an angel than he was, and that is a fact. That
Bohicket was lied to is also a fact. A fact, yes, but not the
truth. Because even a lie can be true, in how it bears out
other truths. It all depends on who is listening and what is
heard. The fact is, Bohicket heard exactly what he needed
to hear that night: the truth in the lie he was told, and the
deception that had become so necessary to how honestly
he'd go on facing this world.

There was no malice in what Aylin did that night, the
show she put on for him, the favor she called in for the sake
of her friend. What she did that night, she did out of love.
She lied, yes. But she lied out of concern and out of a desire
to rescue him from himself. For she had seen what comes
of men who are stripped of hope so completely. She had
walked with skeletons. She had outlived her father, and she
was afraid that Bohicket too might lose himself among the
walking dead, a shade of his former, better self, a stick figure
of a man, erased of all material skin and heart and bone.

She knew the ends rarely justified the means. But she
risked it, and the risk paid off. From that night on, Bohicket's
whole demeanor changed, starting with his eyes. Then his
head tilted upwards and his shoulders broadened slightly.
Gradually, his entire person sort of rose with the hope he had
found, the hope she had given him. In a matter of days, the
resurrection was complete, and Aylin had her friend back.

The realization of her true feelings for him came as a
shock to her. At first, Aylin flat-out rejected the whole notion

completely. But try as she might, she just couldn't shake the sensation she got whenever he was around. The feeling was wholly foreign to her, and as new emotions often go, the experience was horrific, frightening her so completely that she decided against admitting it, even to herself. Especially to herself.

It would take a solid week or two of fighting back the whole notion of her loving him before she wised up to the notion that this was one battle she could not win. And so, night after night, she practiced telling him in front of a mirror. "It seems, ya see, well, I think perhaps . . . well maybe it turns out that, um, yeah, well, I love you, Bohicket," she would repeat again and again. "I do, I guess. I do love you." And she began to dress for the occasion too, to tie up her hair with a ribbon the way he liked, sneak a touch of her mother's makeup, though not too much, so as not to be obvious about it. But the moment she was sure today would be the day she would tell him, she would just as quickly chicken out. *What if he doesn't love me back?* she feared. *What if he thinks I'm just some silly little girl with some silly little crush? What then?*

This went on for days and days, until she was ready to just be out with it already, if only to be free of its burden. She was decisive that morning, even in how she dolled herself up for him. Just let him try and say no to this, she told herself in the mirror. Girl, you're a fox, that's what you are. He'd be a fool to pass you up. Let's see him try. And she went out that morning fully prepared to tell him exactly how she felt about him. But as chance would have it, that was the first day in a long, long time that Bohicket didn't stop by to see her, and what's worse, he wouldn't stop by to see her for nearly a week, which begged the question, why?

You see, without so much as a warning as to his plans to drop in for a visit, Ley just showed up one day completely unannounced. He didn't knock on the door or look to tell anyone he was home. He just let himself in and settled into an armchair in the living room, where Bohicket found him an hour or so later.

"Ley?" he said. "Ley? Holy God, really? Is that really you, Ley?"

"The one and only," Ley replied. "Coming to you live and in the flesh."

Bohicket charged over, snatched his little brother up in his arms and embraced him like he might never let go. "I can hardly believe my eyes," he said, unable or unwilling to hide his excitement. "I mean, it's you. It's really you . . . I mean, of course it's you . . . but holy cow, holy cow, what are you doing here?"

Ley gave him a sort of sideways smirk, the kind of shit-eating grin he was famous for. "Well, um, last I checked, I actually live here. That's what I'm doing here," he said. "Got any more dumb-ass questions for me? I mean, I can see, by the general smell of you, that you're bathing a little more regularly. And that's good, I guess. But you're still as dumb-as-a-rock stupid as you were when I left ya."

Taking little jabs at each other was just a part of how they got along and always had been, so Bohicket doled it out in turn, slugging his brother in the arm and saying, "I can still take your scrawny ass, any day, any time. 'Specially now that you've gone and gotten yourself all city-fied. I mean, what's with the get-up? Look at you. A button-down shirt. Polished shoes. You haven't gone and gotten all soft on me, now have you?"

"I'll show you soft!" Ley shouted and leapt from the chair, and the two of them went rolling around the living room floor, kicking over a table and a lamp and each trying their damnedest to pin the other one to the ground.

Eventually Bohicket got the better of his little brother, as he often did when they wrestled, and he straddled him with both legs, pinned his arms to the floor.

"Say uncle!"

"Never!"

"Say. Uncle."

"Over my cold dead body."

"That can be arranged!" Bohicket shouted. And with that, he landed two good punches into Ley's ribcage, making his brother squeal. "Say. Uncle," Bohicket said. "Or I'm afraid you've breathed your last, good sir!"

"Uncle!" Ley cried. "Uncle!"

"That's more like it," Bohicket said, as he rolled off his little brother and onto the floor beside him, where the two of them remained for a while, side-by-side, catching their breath.

"City-fied," Bohicket said.

"Dumb ass."

Daylight was escaping the sky outside, and it camouflaged the two of them in long thin shadows that yawned and grew and stretched out lengthwise across the floor of that room.

"How's Mama holdin' up?" Ley asked.

"Not good," Bohicket said.

Ley suspected as much, and sensing how deeply it pained his older brother to even hear her name mentioned, Ley left it at that. "It's all their fault, ya know? Just as we had it figured."

"Whose fault? The Flying Men?"

"Yeah. Who else?" Ley said. "God, Bo, what's with the questions?"

Bohicket postured himself over his brother like he just might attack him again. "Once wasn't enough for ya? Wanna go again? Well, do ya? Keep it up, flea bag. See what happens."

But Ley didn't so much as flinch at the threat and instead laid there, as calm as ever, staring up blankly at the ceiling. "I'd almost given up completely, ya know? I even began to question my own two eyes. But then, just like that, fully prepared to admit I was wrong, the old lady I rented a room from, started to tell me about her cousin who happens to live in these parts. One morning over coffee, she said her cousin swore she saw things that no one would believe. She said the newspapers were onto something. 'Flying Men,' she said. 'Men with wings.'" Ley went on to explain, in great detail, what he had learned from the old lady's stories. "And that's why I'm back," he concluded. "Because she gave me clues as to their whereabouts. And look, I know I wrote you and said it's best to steer clear. That those Flying Men are dangerous and not the sort we should go trifling with. And look, I know we made promises, and I'm not saying we shouldn't be cautious, but the way I got it figured, as long as there's even the slightest chance that she's still alive, I, for one, am willing to risk life and limb to find her."

There was something serious in the tone of Ley's voice. Serious, Bohicket thought. If not wholly hell-bent.

LEY WAS ALREADY LOADING UP THE JOHNBOAT WITH SUPPLIES when Bohicket found him early the next morning. "Where are you going?" he asked his little brother, but he already knew the answer. "Never mind," he said. "Dumb question. But I'm coming with."

Ley looked as if he might protest the company, but he thought better of arguing with Bohicket. "Got a day's supply of food, two extra canisters of gas, and Ol' Betsy here," which is what he had named his gun. "Ole Betsy," he said, kissing the long barrel. "How I've missed you, my dear. This ol' girl can do me no wrong."

That morning, small quadrants of light peered through the cathedral windows of sky and ignited the waves like flambeau. This, to the two brothers, was a religious experience. And they started their day on the water with a bit of piracy, as they had done too many times to count. There was a certain expertise, born out of years of experience, to how they hunted down and boarded those boats, to how swiftly they made off with whatever they found. By midday, they were all stocked up on cases of beer, a new fishing rod, two or three tackle boxes, a pile of mostly beach-reads and several trashy harlequin novels, thirty-eight dollars and a handful of loose change.

Satisfied with the morning's bounty and preferring not to push their luck, they spent the rest of the afternoon in search of the Flying Men. Ley insisted on driving since he claimed to know the way, while Bohicket took up his perch on the bow.

"Be on the lookout," Ley told him.

"Aye aye, Captain!" Bohicket replied. "But on the lookout for what?"

"For wings," Ley said. "For men with wings and other terrible things."

And they scoured the waterways along the coast late into the evening, and finding nothing but boats and fishermen, oyster beds and such, they continued their search day after day the rest of that week. Ley hardly said a word the whole time, which was entirely out of character for him, seeing as he typically talked so much one might rightly assume he was in love with the sound of his own voice. But Bohicket knew better. He knew there was something pressing on his mind, some larger plan he might soon put to action.

Only once, and after a good deal of prodding, did Ley admit to what had been occupying his mind for so long. They had anchored on a sandbar and were eating their lunch when Ley said, "God help me, I know it's only right to forgive and forget. And I know we made us a promise to let this go. But they took her, Bo. They took our sister. And I haven't slept right, ever since. It's not the Christian way. I know that. But I have to sleep, Bo. Bo, a man has to sleep."

If only Bohicket understood the extent of his brother's

rage. But he didn't. He couldn't have. The only conceivable ends he could imagine his brother seeking at the time was to find the Flying Men, rescue their sister and call the Flying Men to account for what they had done. He didn't once consider the violence in his brother's voice—not once—despite all his talk of finding them and exacting his revenge, nor did he think his brother capable of any of it, were it to ever come to that.

"This is a hunt," Ley told him. "It's not a search. Let's clear that up from the get-go."

Bohicket tried to caution him as to the dangers they might face. "You've seen it yourself, how well they are protected and how far some people will go to protect them. Pops said to drop it, and I have to say he was right. Anyways, I'm not so sure you aren't wrong about them. Ya see, I've got this . . . friend who's assured me they mean us no harm. She says—"

"Wait a minute. 'She'?"

"Yes. She. She says they think it's their duty to go flying around the islands, searching for people who've drowned so they can carry their bodies up to the heavens. She says they think of themselves as angels this way."

"Angels? And you believe that?"

"In angels? Yes. In their claim to be angels? No. Not in the slightest. Thing is, even if they are angels, as they claim, it seems they aren't very good at it. However many times they've tried to reach the heavens is exactly how many times they've failed to. More often than not, it appears, they simply give up and dump the bodies out in the ocean, which would, in the very least, explain why so many bodies have been washing ashore as of late."

Ley pressed him for an answer to who this "she" was, but to no avail. "At least tell me her name to validate your source," Ley tried. But seeing as Bohicket simply refused to satisfy his brother's curiosity, no amount of reasoning with Ley would dissuade him from seeing his plan through. So

Bohicket was more than relieved when, by their fifth day out, their search turned up nothing and it became more and more apparent that it could all be for naught.

Bohicket had begun to drop hints to those ends, and by the end of day six, even Ley appeared to be weighing the wisdom of giving up the search. Of course, that is when it just so happened that the highly unlikely became likely.

It was nearing dark, and they were halfway home when Ley spotted a disturbance of shadows in the distance. It, at first, looked to be nothing more than a flock of seagulls in a feeding frenzy.

Strange, Ley thought.

"Strange," Ley said.

Only upon closer investigation did they realize what they had stumbled upon. Ley cut the motor upon their approach. And sure enough, there, just a few yards away from them, were the faintest figures of two men with enormous wings, which they had to flap only once to clear the surface of the water. And the two men carried what appeared to be a body, held fast by the ankles.

And though they'd seen this all before, neither Ley nor Bohicket could believe their eyes.

Still, there it was, plain as day.

With each flap of their wings, the two men rose higher and higher, as if setting a course out over the ocean in a diagonal rise into the sky just above the horizon line. Ley waited a moment, and once they were far enough away, he quickly revved the engine and started after them. The two men did try and try with all their might to break through the clouds and on into heaven, as Bohicket suggested they might. But they were about five or six miles out from the shoreline when their wings clearly began to tire and give way. And though they struggled a good bit longer to summit the cloud line, their wings slapping at the air more and more frantically. Eventually, they had no choice but to quit their endeavor and release the body they carried to the ocean depths.

A certain horror overcame Bohicket as he watched the body plummet head over heels several times over before finally landing in the water with a muted splash. It was the horror of witnessing the moments immediately after a person passes. But it was also the horror of witnessing the gracious failure of how hard those Flying Men had worked to see to a proper end.

"Now!" Ley exclaimed. "Now we've got 'em!"

And knowing full well they'd return to land, Ley followed after them.

"Think about what you're doing," Bohicket said. "Pops warned us about this."

But the pitfall of revenge is its consuming greed, and in the end, nothing—not cooler heads nor wisdom or reason—would deter Ley from following them. And so he steered that little boat down the coast in the direction of where the Flying Men were headed, eyes firm, jaw fixed, and appearing as if he were possessed by something beyond his control.

Chapter Fifteen

THE SUPERNATURAL CAME NATURALLY THAT NIGHT, AS LEY HIM-self was taken with an almost supernatural determination to follow those men down the coast, to find them when they landed and finally call them into account for what they had done. The moon rose over the water like one single giant eye. And even Bohicket understood that God was watching.

Supernatural too was how quickly and quietly, despite all Ley's efforts, those Flying Men simply vanished from sight, upon reaching the shoreline and disappearing over the trees.

Ley had run the johnboat aground, cut the motor and wasted no time racing off in their direction, with his older brother following warily after him.

Bohicket finally caught up to him a mile or so inland at a clearing in the midst of the tall, tall trees. Ley stood quietly, gazing up in a frantic search of the treetops, whereabout he'd last seen them.

"Damn it all! Damn. It. All," Ley said. "Do you see them? They were here. They were just here. Dammit! Dammit! Do you see them?" There was a hint of desperation in his voice now, some terrible need that Bohicket had not heard before.

"No," Bohicket replied, "I don't."

"Dammit. Damn it all. They were just here. Right there, right above those trees."

There was a certain stillness in the trees, a stillness that belied a presence there. No birds, No wind. Just a certain stillness in the irrevocable quiet, in the wide canopy of petrified branches and leaves. And for all they knew, the Flying Men were still there, hidden somewhere in or above those trees, listening, watching, waiting them out.

"I know you're here!" Ley shouted up at them. "Show

yourselves, you cowards! Stop your hiding, and show yourselves, if you dare! Come out and face me like a man!"

Silence.

The night itself was silence.

"Marco?!" Bohicket called.

Ley turned and shot him the sternest of looks. "It's not
a joke!" he barked at his brother. "It's not," he said. "This
is not a joke."

Bohicket shrugged. "Figured I'd try something."

"Well don't. Just shut your stupid mouth for half a second,
and let's see if we can't hear them moving around up there."

The brothers just stood there quietly for a time. Thunder
clapped from some far off place, as if rising from the cradle
of the ocean itself, followed then by lightning in the distance.
Lightning then thunder. More lightning, and more thunder.
Then came the scent of rain. Otherwise, the night was so
quiet that even the birds seemed to be in cahoots with the
men in hiding.

"Damn cowards," Ley said, almost to himself. "Ya hear
me?!" he shouted up at the trees. "A bunch of cowards is
all you are! A bunch of lousy, no-good cowards!"

In time, it became clear their search was for naught, a fact
that soon became apparent even to Ley. But before giving
up entirely and starting back to the boat, Ley lifted his arms
up to the heavens and let out a ferocious roar that echoed
out across the island in such a raw and animalistic way that
even Bohicket was startled by the sound of it.

The whole way home that night, Ley swore to God—"if
there is one"—that he wasn't through, that he'd be back and
that this wasn't over. And he was right about that.

You see, unbeknownst to either of them was just how
quickly word travels on those islands. And somehow or
another, news of their near run-in with the Flying Men that
night got back to the people of the village the very next day.

The boys were fast asleep when they were awakened

suddenly by a loud knock at the door. At first, they imagined they were hearing things. Then came the second knock. The boys met as two shadows in the hallway and crept to the window to peer outside. On the porch were five men from the village.

The boys opened the door cautiously.

"Come with us," one of the men said.

The boys hesitated.

"We don't want to, but we will make you."

The boys could tell they were serious. And it wasn't long before they found themselves standing on Mama Hawa's porch, there to be called to account for their crimes.

Ley was always the belligerent one, hot-headed and quick to anger, and already, he was beside himself with rage. "Get your hands off of me!" he shouted, as he reared back and started swinging his fists about wildly. He caught one man in the jaw and sent him reeling. He caught another man in the chest, which accomplished nothing more than further inciting the man's anger, and with one punch to the abdomen, Ley was on his knees, writhing in pain.

Now Bohicket was never one for violence—that is, with one exception. When it came to defending his family, he could be an animal uncaged and thirsting for blood, and seeing his little brother collapse on the ground like that, struggling to catch his breath, was all it took for him to start in after the men surrounding them. But he stopped the moment he heard Mama Hawa shout, "Enough! Enough already! What is the meaning of all this?!" A voice like hers commanded respect.

One of the other men stepped forward to address Mama Hawa, and judging by how he moved among men like a variable threat, he must've been a village elder. A lifetime on the open ocean had charcoaled his skin, until it was now more hide than skin, more alligator than man, and that fact alone told Bohicket that he was the kind of man who possessed the rarest of tempers, exclusive to those who scrape out twelve-hour workdays trolling the waterways in search of their dinner. He was a large boulder of a man, as big as his voice was. He stepped onto the porch and said, "Mama Hawa, these two boys ya see here before you are guilty of an unspeakable crime. Word is, they have been hunting our friends for play."

"Friends? Hmm." Mama Hawa stopped to ponder this for a moment. "I must say, Mister Gruffton, I didn't know you had any friends." This had a few of the others chuckling behind him.

"Crack all the jokes you like, but you know, good and damn well, who I mean," he said.

"I do," she nodded.

"So I sent the boys out to fetch 'em."

"Now? In the dead of night? Certainly not."

"Yes ma'am, I most certainly did. Here they are now, and we want justice," Mister Gruffton said. "And respectfully, Mama Hawa, this is your duty."

Mama Hawa then turned to the boys. "And what do you have to say for yourselves?"

Bohicket could feel his brother's anger welling up inside of him, could see it coming to life on his face. He knew he should do the talking for now. "They are right, Mama Hawa," he told her. "We have indeed been searching for your friends. I offer you no excuses in our defense, save for this: my brother and I have seen what we have seen, and what we have seen is those friends of yours taking away our sister."

There was a commotion in the crowd, a "Nonsense!" and a "They are liars!"

Mama Hawa considered the serious look on Bohicket's face for a moment. "It seems you are pretty well convinced of this. Problem is, dear boy, I've known our friends for a long, long time, and I'm really quite sure they are no more capable of kidnapping someone than you or I."

"I hate to disappoint you, ma'am," Ley interjected with a certain kind of rage welling in his voice, "But we both saw them do just that. Isn't that right, Bo? Swooped down and carried her body off right before our eyes, they did."

By now, all the commotion had awakened the village, and sleepy-eyed and dreary, an ever-growing crowd of people had begun gathering outside Mama Hawa's house.

"So you admit it?" Mama Hawa asked.

"That we do," Bohicket said. "That we do."

"Then I'm afraid my hands are tied."

"Wait!" someone yelled from the crowd. "Wait just a minute. Wait, okay?" Then the crowd parted, and Aylin appeared. She approached the porch and came to stand at Bohicket's side. "Before you go casting judgment, Mama Hawa, I ask only that you hear me out."

"What are you doing?" Bohicket said to her. "Please," he said. "Don't. Please."

Mama Hawa was clearly surprised by Aylin's appearance. "You two know each other?"

"No," replied Bohicket quickly, thinking only of her safety. "I haven't a clue who she is."

"Oh but the concern on your face says otherwise, my dear. Your concern, it betrays you."

"Please," Aylin said. "Let me speak, I beg you."

Mama Hawa nodded. "Go on then, girl. Go on."

"You see, ma'am, this whole thing is all my fault really," Aylin explained. "I'm the one who's to blame here, not them. They were only doing what I suggested they do. Their mother is very sick, you see. Sick in the head. So I suggested that, if their mother's really so dead-set on flying, then maybe perhaps our friends could help."

"That right?" Mama Hawa said, while her thoughts had clearly turned to something else.

"No!" Bohicket protested. "No, that's not right. It's clear

this girl is lying. I've never met her before, never seen her a day in my life, much less asked her for advice."

Out in the yard, thin beams of moonlight parsed the trees, as if the whole wide world was just longing to be touched by some narcoleptic seizure, and this had Bohicket thinking of Aylin, the way he himself had only dreamed of touching her. Yes, he thought of her then, before leaning in close and whispering to her. "Stop. Stop," he whispered. "Please."

But undeterred, Aylin just continued. "So you see, ma'am, if anyone is to blame here, it's me. I gave up our secret. Not them. Me. I did."

Mama Hawa looked the two of them over for a moment then, and surprised by what she inferred from their eyes, said, "Oh I see what's happening here. Oh yes, I see it now. Oh my dear, dear children. Your eyes have given you away. They have."

It's unmistakable really: the look of love in the young.

Only Aylin could say why she had rushed to his side, though Bohicket imagined he knew the answer, or rather felt it in his bones, the way a carpenter feels the angles of the wood before it finds its shape. But what gave them away, in the end, was how readily Aylin had rushed to their defense, finding herself so in love with him she simply could not help it. Though what they were faced with now was a whole different degree of danger, with consequences far more dire than ever before. Aylin's attempt to speak on their behalf and Bohicket's attempts to silence her spoke volumes for how deeply they cared for each other. Which, as it happens, is how their secret came out and how the nature of their feelings for one another was brought to bear, finally, under the examining eye of Mama Hawa's porch light.

The unfortunate reality they were faced with now was that a romance like theirs, between a person from the village and any outsider was strictly forbidden by laws that were established long, long ago, out of a basic need to preserve the integrity of the villagers' way of life and to see to it that their culture and their traditions, which they treasured above all else, would survive for generations. And so it's easy to see why word of the scandal sent the whole of the crowd into tumult, and why the sheer number of angry faces that night only served to prove the danger Aylin, Bohicket and Ley could be in. The initial uproar alone was palpable, to say nothing of the voluminous pitch it reached in only seconds. To the three of them, it sounded like a signal to run for it, to flee the scene while they had the chance. Still, they did not run. Instead, they turned and faced their accusers, braver now than ever, held fast by the convictions of love and youth and the atrocities they had witnessed in living with both.

Every man, woman and child in the yard that night had a need on their faces, a need to right things. A need for justice, for a return to peace, perhaps by way of violence if necessary. Even the crowd, among all their chaotic cheers and demands for vengeance, was merely seeking a sense of order to it all, same as everyone does, and Bohicket could not fault them for that. Not that. Not with all the other fictive hopes we must learn to live with and survive.

Were it not for Mama Hawa calming the crowd that night, there's no telling what might have happened, whether they would've been banished forever or tied down together to drown in the rising tide. But Mama Hawa was there to raise her arms and shush the crowd. She was far more forgiving than anyone else in that village and offered them a chance to repent and be forgiven. "Confess your sins, and we'll grant you mercy," she said. "We've all been guilty of the crimes of our youth."

But neither Bohicket nor Aylin would repent. They were in love, you see, and only now, faced with the danger of admitting they were, could they see what being in love actually means. *Yes, they realized, we are in love.* And for that, they knew they could not be forgiven.

"I love him," Aylin said. "Do what you will to me, but I do. I love him."

"And I love her," said Bohicket. And with that, he took her in his arms, and he kissed her as if for the first and last time. "There," he said. "No one but God can forgive me of that."

Not even Mama Hawa could control the crowd now, and the crowd of people cried out for justice. It was as if they were intent on getting it by her hand or theirs. And Mister Gruffton pressed the issue by citing Mama Hawa's own agreement with the boys' father way back when, and it seemed there was no stemming the tide that was to come. Mister Gruffton argued that, if the boys' father understood the gravity of abiding by their laws (like Mama Hawa had assured them all he was), then the boys' father should've explained the dire consequences the boys would face, were those laws broken.

Mama Hawa understood well that a love like theirs was always a force to be reckoned with in this world and should never be weighed lightly. But in the end, Mama Hawa was left with no real say in the matter. In the end, her hand was forced. And having no other option, and hoping to curb any chance of violence, she had no other choice but to curse not only Bohicket, but his entire family with the devastation of a flood. "Hear me now!" she cried, lifting her hands into the air. "Hear now! Hear this! From this day forward, I call down the heavens upon your heads, and I call up the seas to swallow you whole. This is the punishment for your crimes: justice by way of a storm."

Chapter Sixteen

PERHAPS THE TRUEST COURAGE IS SIMPLY WAKING UP THE NEXT morning. Simply opening your eyes and placing your two feet on the cold floor and, there by your bed, rising again from the gravity of your own life. Perhaps this is the bravest act of all. And perhaps this is all that is required of us sometimes, the spiritual discipline it takes to muster your will and merely press on, like a stone that must skip and keep on skipping across the face of the water.

Certainly this was true in Bohicket's case. It was all he could do to wake up the next morning and face the day. But when he did, when he finally did, he found his little brother eating in the kitchen. And it was clear, by the solemn way his head bowed over the bowl, that Bohicket was not the only one who was troubled by what had befallen them the previous night.

Neither one of them spoke a word over breakfast. Neither one had the words to speak, both afraid to even look the other one in the eyes, for fear of seeing what would surely be a cautionary tale. And so they ate in silence, and once they were through, the two of them set off in different directions, attempting to escape, it seems, the certainty of what would come.

Good men at low tide are just biding time. Bohicket and Ley were no different. Out there, they got a sense of how the tides pulled along the bows of history. Ley fished the shallows for most of the day, while Bohicket went traipsing through the pluff mud, spearing blue crabs and digging out oysters with his hands. And between them along that inland shore, the two tended a precarious distance from each other. Though always mindful of his role as big brother, Bohicket made especially certain he kept his little brother in view, as if to stand vigil over both him and this place. The same went for the next day, followed then by the next. But no amount of distance succeeded in making either one of them feel any better, not when the feeling they both felt was one and the same. A heaviness with its own sort of heft. A heaviness that hung invisibly about their shoulders and neck, weighing itself heavily on both of their minds. As if the two of them had together become a single Atlas, encumbered by the weight of the same world.

And you should see no coincidence in the fact that they both sought out the water respectively, for that is where (for island folk, at least) all catastrophes and all peace give rise. One might say that they went to the water to keep watch over it, expecting more so than fearing the inevitable danger in the currents. To them, the ocean was itself a kind of birthright, where the hazards of small local knowledge forced men and boys to measure their worth by the rubric of the tides. And so they did; they went to the water. And day after day, Bohicket walked barefoot through the sand, as if to gauge even the slightest variations in water levels. Ley did the same, eyeballing the channel for the sudden and instantaneous surge he knew would surely come.

You see, more often than not, living in the Lowcountry means outlasting its water, and Bohicket and his brother knew this to be true. They knew what all the many generations of people, who've managed to go on surviving out there, knew: that everyone returns inevitably to the water. In the end, everyone does; everyone always does. Cities and towns, parents and children, irrespective of age or experience, precautions or dumb luck, people are subject to the fate of those waters, a fate not a one of us is spared.

And so it was, just as Mama Hawa had predicted, a hurricane came ashore late one night just a few days later, and hit their tiny island with the wrath of someone's call for vindication. What made it far worse was that, when it came, it came wholly unannounced, and it brought with it the skies and the sea. By midnight, the winds were categorical, complete with a ten-foot surge that came rushing in from the ocean to flood everything in its path: their family home, their land and, yes, the whole of their island. It was exactly as they had feared.

To that point, their tiny island had seen its fair share of tropical storms and even the occasional hurricane, so much so that enduring them was just another aspect of their life out there. And so, having survived more than a few close calls, their family had gotten really quite good at battening down the hatches, weathering the high winds and the high waters and living to tell the tale. Problem was, despite dreading the inevitable for days and days, the boys never once thought to prepare for it. It was as if they saw it coming but never saw this coming.

And so, as the water levels rose steadily higher and higher, eventually the high seas began leaking into their house, first under the doors then up through the floorboards. And yet even when the floodwaters finally reached the windows and blanketed the world over outside, their mother appeared clueless to the danger they were in and simply pressed her face to the pane, like a child, and gazed out in hopes of seeing a fish swim by. And it took a good bit of coaxing to convince her away from the windows.

"But I wanna see the fish," she said. "It's like an aquarium out there. And I wanna see the fish."

"Yes, Mama, we see, it is like an aquarium. But won't you come and join us on our raft?" the boys pleaded, but to no avail. "We'll play a game. You can be the captain, Mama." Once the boys had realized how high the waters were getting, they had lashed a few chairs to the sofa, using a spool or two of fishing line. And hoping to coax their mother onto the raft, they began to shout, "Land ho! Land ho! Beware them rocks! Look out! Oh no, Mama, help us! Help! It's a giant sea monster!"

And they made the game sound so fun their mother finally did agree to join them.

"Captain on deck!" they shouted with a firm salute, as she climbed on board. "Raise the anchor, and hoist the main sails! Where to, Cap'n?!" they yelled. "Where to?"

Gradually, the waters climbed higher and higher up the walls and filled their house. And together they floated up with it on their makeshift barge, until they had to crane their necks to keep from hitting their heads on the ceiling. It is a terrifying thing to have only a few inches of air to breathe. The wind that night was so strong it nearly lifted the roof clear off the house, and with their ears almost pressed to the ceiling, they had no choice but to listen to the sound the roof made as it creaked and groaned and threatened to give way.

"Breathe," Bohicket told his brother. "Just try and breathe."

One of Ley's few fears was of small, enclosed spaces, and the look on his face said this might be his undoing. "This is what we get," he said, panic-stricken. "See? Now we're all gonna drown."

"No we're not!" Bohicket yelled back. "No we're not! Not on my watch! Not just now! Time to breathe, little brother. Breathe." Though, were you to ask him right then, even Bohicket would admit he wasn't as sure as he tried to sound.

Thankfully though, the floodwaters would subside eventually, and the storm would pass. And as the three of them waited for the water levels to retreat back out into the world from whence they came, Bohicket suggested they play a game of tic-tac-toe on the ceiling to pass the time. "I mean, why not?" he said. "When else will we get such a rare opportunity?"

"You got a marker on you or something?" Ley asked.

"Uh, no," Bohicket replied.

"Then I tell you what. I got an idea. Let's sign our names

to the sky." And perhaps Ley was a bit out of his mind at the time because, almost without thinking, he bit down on his index finger till blood came out, and then he scribbled his name out on the ceiling in big bold letters. "There," he said, apparently satisfied with himself. "Now everyone will know that Ley was here. Your turn," he said to his brother. "Go on. It's your turn."

Bohicket was never keen on the sight of blood. It made his stomach turn. But merely the prospect of his little brother getting a chance to call him a wuss saw to it that he followed in suit, and so he bit down on his finger and signed his name on the ceiling.

"Now we've gone and done it!" Ley exclaimed. "You and I both just signed the sky."

"Mama," Bohicket said, "wanna try?"

But their mother was clearly lost already in the recesses of her mind, bunkered down in the corner of that sofa with her knees tucked squarely into her chest, so frightened it seemed she was paralyzed, balled up so tightly into herself she was barely a shadow, if anything at all.

"Ya really must try it, Mama," Ley added. "I have to say, it's a lot like flying. And you like flying, don't ya, Mama?"

Her face was buried deep in her knees, and it appeared too that her eyes were closed.

Outside, the storm clouds started to roll away, much the same as they rolled in. Lightning blued the cracks in the heavens, and the rain surrendered its vibrato on the rooftop. The ceiling was leaking now. The corners of the sky quieted. Still though, she could not bring herself to speak.

"Mama?" Bohicket pressed. "Are you still in there somewhere?" He understood that she, same as all mothers, carried around inside her the Sisyphean stones of worry. But this, he saw as something different, and he could not bear the sight of her like this. So he did what he could to ease her mind, and rocked her back and forth in his arms, brushed the knots from her hair and told her a story. "It all began long, long ago," he began, "when this world was but a glint in its father's eye." And he told her the whole long story of how angels came to be, how they came to roam the earth among man and beast. "And still to this day," Bohicket concluded, "those very same angels walk among us."

Slowly, her head lifted from her lap. "Really?" she said, appearing for a moment to be delighted by the idea.

"Really."

"And how do you know?"

"Because, Mama, I've seen them," he said. "Aylin took me to meet them, one day."

She was silent for a while, as yet unsure what to believe. "Aylin?" she asked.

"My friend," he said. "Aylin." Then he went on to tell her all about the night he'd gone and seen one. "An angel, that is. As real as you or I." But it wasn't until he told her what the angel said about their sister that their mother's whole countenance changed.

"He said that? Really and truly? He said that?" she asked in a way that sounded more like a plea than an actual question. "He told you he actually met her? That she is up there, even as we speak, floating about on angel wings?" And there was a certain relief in her voice, upon hearing this, along with the glad sort of pain that comes with losing someone you love to the gateways of heaven.

"Sure did," Bohicket said. "And he said she can fly."

"Fly?" she said, as if smitten by the idea.

"Not only that, but she flies real fast. Some say, there's no one faster."

And as he told her a tale of the races she had won, word for word, as it was told to him, the floodwaters slowly receded, almost without them noticing, until at last, the last of the water was all but gone, and they disembarked their vessel and ventured outside to survey the extent of the damage that had been done.

It was dawn, the storm clouds parted, and even in the faint slivers of light, they could see the havoc caused by the storm. The hurricane had ripped off large portions of their roof, destroyed their fishing nets, sunk their fishing boat and left the receptacles and the aqueducts they used to gather and deliver rainwater in total disarray.

Only then, only upon seeing all the destruction that had waylaid their island, did Bohicket stop to consider the hefty price Aylin must have paid for the crime of their love. *If she were forced to pay even a fraction of the cost we have paid, he thought, Then God help them. God help us all.* And that is when it first began to take shape in his mind, the seeds of blame he would reserve exclusively for himself. "And God help me," he said.

That morning, Bohicket, Ley and their mother walked the whole of the island, surveying the damage in what could only be described as a hapless quiet, and when there was nothing more to say, nothing more to see, they set about divvying up the tasks and fixing what they could.

The boys started with the rain catchers, knowing they could not live without drinking water, and over the next few days, they scurried around the treetops with hammer and nails, mending all the receptacles and patching up the aqueducts. When that was done, they turned their attention to re-stitching the frays in their fishing nets to keep from going hungry. They knew enough to know that a storm that size would have inevitably claimed the boat their father had sunk with cinderblocks in the channel. Rescuing their own boat seemed, at first, to be a lost cause as well. But Ley dreamed up a plan, and together they waded out into the channel, dove down to the bottom, found the boat and, fastening ropes to the bow, dragged it onto dry land.

It took a good deal of patience on his part, but Bohicket knew enough about motors to save the engine, after taking it apart piece-by-piece, drying it out and oiling it down. The entire endeavor was a test of his will, but in the end, it proved a success by any and all measures of that word. And thinking it a cause for celebration, Bohicket and Ley took the boat out for a spin that very night in search of their dinner.

A return to the sea is a return to the womb. Nothing is more essential. Nothing more true. Especially in their case. Especially now. Even their father had deified the fisherman at sea. "Gods are men with time," he used to tell them. "Time enough to be out of work and still working." And their mother used to say, "Eat. Eat," like it was the way of the world. "Either eat, my loves, or be eaten." And so they ate.

Two weeks in, and things were going better than they'd ever expected. They had fresh water to drink and food on the table. And in a week's time, they'd have the roof as good as new. Not only had they survived the whole dangerous ordeal, they were well on their way to being all the better for it. Where once their hopes of making it at all were slim-to-none, things were starting to look up. And yet, unbeknownst to them, a far more troubling problem was yet in store. For the storm, you see, had disinterred their father's body from its grave. Their mother had good reason to insist, as she did, on keeping the whereabouts of his body secret, though the boys could not, for the life of them, see why. Little did they know, but even as they worked away day after day to piece their lives back together, the receding tidal surge had carried their father's body out to sea, only to then return it again to their shores one bright and sunny day.

A fisherman from the village was the one who discovered it, or rather what little was left of it, and he was the one who brought what he found to Bohicket's attention. That it was a human body at all was, at first, difficult to believe. But upon closer investigation, Bohicket realized what the fisherman had stumbled upon was indeed the body of his father. He would have kept the discovery to himself, had he not needed some assistance to carry his father's remains back into the woods and bury them. So he told his brother about it, and together they returned their father's body to the ground.

The whole dastardly circumstance would've ended right there, were it not for a bit of bad luck that had their mother, purely out of chance, happen upon them en route through the woods. It was all they could do to console her, now that she was forced to relive the pain of burying her husband once again. But bury him they did. And for the sake of their mother, they took care to say a few words while they lowered him in the ground. And that, they hoped, would be the last of it. But they of all people should have known better.

The boys awoke the very next day to discover their mother was not in her room, and fearing the worst, they headed straight into the woods and, there, found her lying on top of their father's grave. Simply by the look of her, covered so completely in dirt and filth, they knew what all had transpired the night before. At some point the previous night, she had grown restless with the idea of being so inescapably alone and had fled the house under the cover of dark, wandered out to his gravesite and, there on her hands and knees, started to dig. She was halfway to him before she stopped digging and fell asleep with no more than a foot or two of dirt left between her and her husband. By the time the boys discovered her that morning, she was rubbing her eyes and yawning awake from a long and restful sleep. She shrugged away the horror she saw on their faces, telling them instead how much better she slept with their father close.

"It's a mystery to me how I ever took him for granted," she said. "Because last night was like one big and beautiful dream, and your father was an angel when he came to me in my dreams and wrapped me up so tight in his big, wide, gigantic wings that I had no choice but to dream." She then sort of chuckled to herself, as if laughing at a joke only her husband and her were privy to. "And look what else," she said, rolling over on her back, "it appears God Himself, in all His infinite mercy, has seen to lending us these bunk beds for the night. As for your father, well, your father never ceases to amaze me. He always was so good to me, you know? Just you look at how lucky I am to have him in my life. Even now—Bless his heart, even now!—your father was good enough to give me first choice and took the bottom bunk."

To this day, Bohicket couldn't say why he just left her there. Perhaps it was the calm on her face that had him so resigned to just leave her be. Perhaps because she was so bright with sleep, he simply could not bring himself to wake her from that waking dream. Perhaps, in a world far less cruel than his own, he could've seen to waking her first before he left, but as he saw it, that would be far more cruel. So he did leave, and he did not wake her. And for one reason or another, Ley did not argue with his older brother and just followed him home, perhaps seeing it all the same himself.

Still, Bohicket would be haunted by this for days to come. Haunted by the sight of his mother cradled so wholly in that shallow grave, alone but still dreaming, having reverted finally to the fetal position, as lost as ever in the throes of her own helplessness. Yes, Bohicket would be haunted by this image of his mother, until at last, he himself was possessed by her ghost.

Chapter Seventeen

NEITHER OF THE BOYS SPOKE OF IT FOR DAYS, THEIR MINDS haunted by the sight of their mother on their father's grave. It was as if they had witnessed her laying her own soul to rest that day in the woods, and her reappearance in their house, later on that afternoon, was nothing more than the ghost of a dead woman walking. There. Around. But not really. And it seemed too that the resurrection of ghosts would be the theme of their week because a sudden knock at their door, early one morning, was all it took to disinter a few others.

He was a crafty man who showed up at their door that day, given away by the purposeful expression on his face. It was clear he had a chip on his shoulder, while the hard-and-fast grip he had on the papers he carried spoke volumes as to the serious nature of his business there. "Bohicket, I presume. Let me see here . . . " he said, glancing through his papers. "Yes. Says here you are the man of the house. Am I wrong?"

"Yes sir, I'm afraid you are. That would be my father."

"Is he around?"

"No sir. Can't say he is."

"Your mother then?"

"Seems you just missed her as well."

The man could tell Bohicket was lying. He wrinkled his brow at him suspiciously and then, without skipping a beat, continued into his purpose for being there. "Well then, mind if I steal a moment of your time, Mister . . . ah . . . "

"Bohicket. And as for you stealing anything of mine, well, I do. I must say I do mind. That, you see, would be criminal," Bohicket replied, a little too pleased with himself. "Tell you what though, my good man. I'll let you borrow it for the time being, as long as you promise to make good use of it."

"Mind if we sit?" asked the man.

"Can't say I mind that at all."

They sat across from each other on the porch, Bohicket sensing the harm that could come if he had let him inside. The man spread his papers out on his lap, cleared his throat like someone preparing to share bad news, and said, "Ya see, Mister . . . ah, Bohicket, my boss back in Charleston got word recently of a certain body washing ashore near the village."

"Anyone I know?"

"That's the thing, Mister Bohicket. It seems this certain someone is of particular interest to the police." The man smoothed out the wrinkles in his pants to bide his time. "My boss has reason to believe that this certain someone is a wanted felon, and we've been on the lookout for this person for quite some time."

Bohicket felt a lump rise in his throat. "Do tell," he said, leaning forward in an attempt to appear more interested than he was concerned. "Appears we got us a real whodunit, am I right?"

"Appears so." The man then shuffled through a few more pages, before continuing. "I've been inquiring in the village, these last few days, and so far, no one has seen a thing. I was beginning to think our lead was nothing more than another dead end, until someone suggested your father might be a bit more helpful."

"And so here we are," Bohicket said.

"Yes indeed, Mister Bohicket. So here we are."

"If you don't mind my asking, what did this man do? I mean, what was his crime?"

"I never said he was a man."

"Really? Huh. I could've sworn you did."

"Nope. I never said he was a man." The man was looking at him a little more suspiciously now. "Got something to tell me?" he asked. "Now would be the time. The sooner you do, in these cases, the better. I mean, it'd be a shame if a boy your age went down as an accomplice for someone else's crimes. Yes sir, that would be a real shame, Mister Bohicket. A terrible, terrible shame."

"So he is a man then," said Bohicket.

"What?"

"You just said his crimes. So I was right. He is a man."

The man had moved in so close Bohicket got a sense of the man's breath as he uttered his next words. "You're a bit scrawny around the edges, aren't you? Such a shame," the man said. "A boy as flimsy as you are would be swallowed up whole, if he were to find himself in prison. Yep, I've seen it happen far too often, even to the best of 'em. Soap on a rope. The shower's empty, save for the two of you. The next thing you know, the biggest and blackest man on cell block six is tucking you in at night, singing you lullabies and calling you his girlfriend."

"Well who doesn't love a good lullaby from time to time?"

"Suzy," the man said. "Yep, you'd make a damned fine Suzy to someone or another."

"Suzy?" Bohicket replied, sounding indignant. "Over my dead body would I ever go by a name like Suzy. I've always seen myself as more of a Beatrice than anything else. A name with a little more heft to it, ya know? A little more meat around the bones. So if it's all the same to you, I'd just as well go by Beatrice, so long as he doesn't shorten it and call me Bea. I hate that name. Bea. I'll go down fighting, if he ever calls me Bea."

The man leaned back in his chair once more and sort of chuckled to himself. "Oh you'd go down for sure," he said. "Fighting or otherwise."

"So?" Bohicket asked.

"So, what?"

"I asked you a question, didn't I? What did the man do

to have ya coming way out here?"

"Oh I think you know," the man said.

"Do ya now?"

"Oh I think you know. I've been at this a long, long time, ya see. And I got a pretty good nose for when somebody's lying to me." It was the look on the man's face, more so than the accusation he made, that had Bohicket worried he'd been found out. Government work can, after all, do a number on a man's soul, can leave him without a trace of compassion for other people, given all that he's seen during his years on the job. And the hard way that that man glared at him, as if he could see straight through him, was all it took to convince Bohicket of that.

Even still, Bohicket kept quiet. He was startled to his core by the news he was hearing, but he was wise enough to know he'd fair far better if he admitted to nothing. "I've sure been called a lot of nasty things by a lot of nasty people in my life," Bohicket said. "And while mostly all of what they said about me was true, the one thing I ain't is a liar."

"Then it appears we are done here," the man said. With a good firm slap of his knee, the man gathered up his papers and handed Bohicket his card. "In case ya ever wise up and come to your senses, that's where you can reach me," he said and left.

The man never mentioned his father by name, but Bohicket knew. He knew. Only after the man left did the full weight of what Bohicket had learned about his father sink in. Was the man right? Was his father really the wanted criminal they were after? What had he done? Could it be? How could it be? Alone with his thoughts and outlandish conjectures, Bohicket began to see his father in a whole different light—a harsher more criminal light, a light that only made impossible words, like kidnapping and murder, seem suddenly possible.

No, not his father. No way. Impossible, he reasoned. Still,

maybe. Just maybe.

Bohicket set about finishing his daily chores around the island, checking the crab traps, watering the berries and fixing a tiny leak that had sprung up in his boat. At some point along the way, he lost all track of time. Hours went by. And only when his mother appeared from within the quiet belly of their house did Bohicket finally snap to. "Mama? Where have you been? Where are you going? Where have you been? A man stopped by to speak to you earlier."

"Ooo, really?!" she replied, apparently delighted by the idea of having a visitor. "Do I know him? What was his name? Wait, wait, don't tell me. Was it Seven? Tell me Seven stopped by, please? He sure loved your father, that Seven. And what a delight his visits always were. Your father called him Lucky, as in the lucky number seven. Get it? They were close like that, like nickname-close. Maybe that's how he introduced himself, said his name was Lucky. Was that the man's name? Did he say his name was Lucky? Oh please, tell me it was Lucky."

"No, Mama, it wasn't Lucky."

"Then, who was it? Surely, you got his name. Tell me you weren't rude to our visitor. You're a Southerner; you should know better. If we Southerners love anything, it's a visitor. And I do, most especially." She was nearly hopping up and down, by this point, no longer able to contain her excitement.

"He said he was working with the police on some case or something."

"The police? Oh . . . well . . . that is strange. What do you suppose they wanted with me?" She appeared then to sober up from her excitement, and sort of melted down into the chair beside him. "The police," she repeated to herself. "The police, you say? Really, the police? Well, what did the policeman want? Did he say?"

"That's just it, Mama. They were asking about dad," he said to gauge her reaction.

The air between them thinned, as if the atmosphere itself was slowly deflating into nothingness, evacuating the perimeter of their tiny island so quickly that soon there would be none left for their lungs. And it was how that air seemed to asphyxiate in his throat that had Bohicket feeling more desperate than ever to get at the answers, and so he flat-out refused to hear her excuses. He had heard enough excuses over the years to know there were no more to be had. Something about the policeman's accusations had a tinge of truth, especially when Bohicket considered how casually his father had taught them how to board other people's boats, how to steal from them and how to get away with it. Something about it all just made sense, as if his father had been well acquainted with a sort of criminal knowledge all along. "The man said things about him that, while odd to be sure, seem to be true," Bohicket said to his mother. "Why are they looking for him, Mama? What did he do? I know you know. Tell me."

And to Bohicket's surprise, it didn't take a whole lot of convincing before she came out with it, perhaps done now with all the secrets herself, with a lifetime of lies. She was not shy about telling him the truth either. In fact, she told him everything, every last detail of everything: the crime his father had been accused of, who had accused him of it, and why so many people were after him for what they said he had done.

It was a long story, to be sure. One that began with his father's previous life as a young fighter pilot in the Navy, which later led into a career flying commercial jets up and down the eastern seaboard. "And then one day, the engine just up and quit on him," his mother said. "They were a mile or so from land when his plane gave way and went crashing into the ocean," she said. "The damn sad fact of it all is that only your father survived. Sad," she amended. "But not really, seeing as your father did come out alive, and that's all that mattered." She pointed out over the water, as if to say the accident had happened not far from where they were sitting. "Out there," she said. The introspective look in her eyes said she was reliving the story once again in her mind. "For one reason or another, God saw to it that he—and only he—survived. They blamed him for that. They did. They blamed him for surviving."

His mother paused for a moment, as if expecting the news to incite a response. Then she continued on with her story, explaining that the families of the deceased—perhaps out of some need to hold someone, anyone, responsible for their pain—insisted his father be charged with criminal negligence and worse. "Your father, even back then, was a close friend of the bottle, which made charging him easy. Though his real punishment was enough," she told him. "Having to live out the remainder of his days with only himself to blame. The goddamn truth of it all is that your father never had the guts to off himself. So instead he was drinking himself to death in retribution for his sins. Tides just got to him first. You see, your father never really spoke of what happened that day," she told him. "But on the rare occasion that he did, the story he told was a short one, a vignette really, because your father was knocked unconscious at the moment of impact, and when he finally woke up, he found himself being carried away into the sky by two men, who (as your father said) looked to be really quite ordinary, were it not for their extraordinary wings. He said they were so startled when he began to scream that they simply let him go, and he plummeted down into the ocean and somehow managed to swim back to shore. But your father was always haunted by the carnage he witnessed that day from the beach: the distant screams of all those passengers, the slow descent of the fuselage that would eventually drown them all, and that sky so full of winged men circling high above the wreckage. He swore they saved his life that day.

Why him? Who knows? Perhaps he was the only one they had time to save before the plane went under. Your father believed it shouldn't have been him they saved; if there was a God in the universe, it shouldn't have been him. Someone, anyone else, just not him."

Too much news, good or bad, tends to add up rather quickly. Especially when it comes at you all at once. What it amounts to is a sense that it's all bad news, or so it was in Bohicket's case, as he came upon the most horrific news of all, that day on the porch: the simple discovery that all the truths in his life were all untrue, which made it feel as if the whole of his world was turned upside down. And so it's entirely understandable that, while he was looking out over the water and his mother finished her story, Bohicket found himself wondering if his father had washed ashore the day he died, only to find he was relieved by the incalculable justice that saw to it that he departed the same way all his passengers had, taken by that same wide ocean, by the same sad misfortune, and all under the same blue sky and the same watchful eye of those men with wings. And it's entirely understandable that Bohicket also found himself wondering if hearing her husband's story, told so true so many times over, had been what inspired his mother's insatiable desire to do as her husband had done: to grow wings and fly.

"And that's why we were forced to escape to this island," his mother concluded. "We didn't want to, mind you. We had to."

All the terrible ways that this could play out raced through his mind, in one horrific scenario followed by another. "They heard about the storm and how the floodwaters resurrected his body, Mama. I don't know how they heard, but they heard. I lied and said I didn't know anything, but they know about the body, Mama. Someone must have gone and told them. And oh God, what if the villagers talk?" he said, the terrible prospect only just dawning on him. "What then, Mama? What now?"

And yet nothing in her demeanor suggested this was a cause for concern.

"They won't," she said.

"What do you mean, they won't?"

"They won't talk. They wouldn't dare."

"And what if they do?"

"They won't."

"But they will, Mama; they will. Don't you see that? One of them already did."

"Yes but we have a pact, us and them."

"A pact?"

"Yes, a pact," she said. "Your father and Mama Hawa made a pact with each other a long time ago. We keep their secrets secret, and they keep ours. And the price of betraying the bargain we struck is a mutually assured destruction: with the atomic weaponry of our own secrets and the promise of a nuclear holocaust if ever those secrets are revealed."

Still, despite all her assurances that their secret was safe, Bohicket couldn't shake the feeling that it wasn't. Night after night after night, he lay awake in his bed, mulling sleeplessly every terrible scenario he could imagine, whether it was them being forced off their land or him being forced to become somebody's Beatrice. And yet nothing in his mind could be worse than the possibility that they would find the body, put two and two together and charge his mother with aiding in her husband's crimes. What he feared most was that someone in the village, perhaps someone who had had it out for his father from the start, would think *Agreement be damned* and put in a call to the authorities. So Bohicket felt he had no choice but to venture off into the village once again and there plead for Mama Hawa's help in keeping the whereabouts of his father's body a secret.

Chapter Eighteen

I T'S BEEN SAID THAT MISERY NEEDS COMPANY. BUT SO DOES DREAD, particularly when what you're dreading is a wholesale loss of all that you love. Bohicket did not want to go and seek Mama Hawa's help in the matter. But fearing his mother could be implicated and serve time enough to kill her, he was left with no other choice. And so he spent the better part of the next day shoring up his nerves, and then come late that evening, just after twilight, he set out in his johnboat across the channel to speak with Mama Hawa face-to-face in hopes of securing the village's secrecy as to the whereabouts of his father's body.

Down at the docks, the boats were all moored and abandoned for the day, each pregnant with tackle boxes and empty live wells, rods and reels and casting nets, inanimate objects left only to be animated by their dreams of a favorite fishing spot tucked away somewhere upstream. And Bohicket knew, as he passed them by, that even the homily of the stars above him would've quieted for big-fish tales such as theirs. He made his way into the village, where only a few windows remained lit, evidence of a village readying itself for sleep. Most of the lawns he passed were clean and mowed, while a few others resembled graveyards with their headstones of rusty junk and collected beach chairs, deflated rafts and outboard motors, empty kiddy pools and bikes with flat tires or no tires at all.

Even the sky that night was heavy with the threat that, at any given moment, it all could come down on his head. He just assumed the investigation was ongoing, and it seemed to him that there were detectives and reporters, legions and legions of them, lurking around every corner, and it seemed that every household he passed was filling up, even then, with whispers and clues, answers to the riddles the authorities were after.

It was a priestly quiet he found himself traipsing through, as if houses themselves make the finest confessionals. The village itself was so quiet he could almost hear, in its silence, every last family disclosing whatever they had to disclose, whatever willpower that they possessed breaking under the pressure, until at last they were all confessing the very thing that would end life as he knew it out there.

He stood outside Mama Hawa's doorway for what felt to him like hours and hours, at a loss for the bravery he needed to knock. He had every good reason to just turn back, to leave the whole outcome of his life up to the fates, and he nearly did just that. He nearly turned back, and really, he would have, had he not recalled how closely his mother slept to his father's lifeless body in the well of that ground because that image, in the end, granted him all the courage he needed to see his plan through.

Whatever she had or had not been responsible for doing in the past, whatever part she had played in the plight of his family, Mama Hawa was, despite it all, a good and decent woman. And recognizing the danger he would be in, were he discovered in the village, she quickly ushered him inside to have a seat.

"Care for some water? A coffee? Sit, sit, my child, have a seat. You look parched," she offered. "Can I get you a drink?"

"No thank you," replied Bohicket. "No thank you. I'm fine. But thank you."

"You sure?"

"I'm sure."

And so Mama Hawa sat in a chair across from him and asked him what brought him to her doorstep at such an odd hour of the night. "Whatever it is, it must be important," she said, "Judging by that look you got on your face. Come now, smile, child. It can't be that bad, can it?"

"I'm afraid it is."

"Really?" she said. "Surely not? Is it your mother? How's she doing these days? Holding up, I hope. I have been prayin' for her, ya know? She's been a staple in my nightly prayers for some time now. How is your mother? Is that what this is about?"

"Well no," said Bohicket. "No. And, well, yes. It's more a secret she told me the other day after a policeman came by asking questions."

"I see," she said, leaning back in her chair to consider his meaning. "I see, I see."

"Do you?" Bohicket asked. "Do you see?"

"Yes, my child, I do. Mama Hawa sees far more than she puts on."

"Good, then you'll understand why it's so troubling to me that that investigator is here snooping around and asking questions about my father."

"So you do know?" Mama Hawa said. "Good. Now it's all on the table."

"It's my mother, is all. Nothing would be worse for her," he said. "All I'm asking is that we let the dead alone."

"Seems fair. Let bygones be bygones, am I right?"

"Let my father's secrets be buried with him."

Mama Hawa could see how earnestly Bohicket needed this, if only in how his voice seemed to plead for it. He had lost his father and probably his sister, and chances were, he was still rebuilding his life after the storm had come through and ravaged his home, and so she knew that, whatever crimes he or his brother or his father had committed in the past, surely by now, Bohicket had paid a hefty enough price for the lot of them. At least the sullen and whip-weary expression on his face, the weight of all the concerns he had yoked around his shoulders, said he certainly had. And losing his mother to something like this would simply prove too much. In a way, he looked older now, too old, she imagined, for a boy his age. Hard times will do that to anyone, she supposed. And that, she thought, was a shame. The mother in her, the kind and caring woman that she was, couldn't help but feel sorry for him, right then, couldn't help but sympathize with the terrible plight that had befallen him and his family so recently. "What can I do to help you, my child?" she asked. "You wouldn't be here, if you didn't need me. Chin up, my child. I promise you I will do what I can."

But Mama Hawa knew already what he would ask of her and what he had risked to come there as well. Sensing how difficult it might be for him to make such a request of her, she offered him a solution, and offered it freely. "I will help keep them quiet," she said. "I can see how much this means to you, and I understand why. So I will help, my dear," she said, "if that is indeed what you need of me."

Bohicket could not hide the relief he felt, upon hearing her say this. "Thank you, Mama Hawa. Thank you," he said.

"I only ask one thing of you in return," she continued, sounding as if it pained her having to ask. "It's an unfortunate request, I'm afraid, but as it were, it's a matter of necessity, circumstances being as they are around here."

"Anything," Bohicket said.

"My one fear is that the rest of the villagers might not be so receptive to what I ask of them, without suggesting we've struck a bargain."

"Whatever it takes, Mama Hawa. Just ask."

"Bea," she said. "Aylin."

It was the sound of her name being mentioned at all that struck him so completely. The sound of those two syllables, Ay- and -lin, hit the shell of his ear and tore its way down clean to his heart and there constricted his chest. He had thought of her often in recent weeks. In a way, she never quite left the front of his mind. He loved her, you see, and he would've given anything to see her again, would it not have endangered her and were he not so busy rebuilding whatever semblance of a life he had left after the storm.

"Aylin?" Bohicket asked. "What about Aylin?" He was afraid he already knew the answer.

"Whether you realize it or not, if there ever was a darling in this village, she is it. She is well loved, for sure. So much so that most of us think of her as our own daughter, and so we are all understandably protective of her, perhaps overly protective. That's why they took the news of the two of you together so hard. Why am I telling you this? Because I'm afraid you must promise to never see her again. I'm sorry to ask this of you, but I'm afraid it's the only way."

How hard it was for him to agree to her terms cannot be overstated. He had fallen in love with Aylin, and as it is with anyone who finds themselves so helplessly in love at so young an age, Bohicket felt he would've cut off both his arms at the elbows and his legs at the knees and walked the whole entire face of this earth on all four stubs, if that's what it took to be with her. However, his mother was still his mother, and despite all her many faults, how nasty she could be, how mean and how cruel, he loved her. So really, he was left with no other choice but to agree, especially when he considered his mother and whatever punishment the law had in store for such a willing accomplice to his father's crimes. Being arrested, dragged away in handcuffs, a long and drawn out court case, the families of all the victims sharing their tragic testimony, prison time, the stress of it all, the reporters sniffing around for an interview, the inside scoop, he knew well she would never survive it. So in the end, Bohicket agreed to Mama Hawa's terms with a reluctant nod. And he would have every moment for the remainder of his life to regret it.

The whole matter appeared to pain Mama Hawa so much she began wringing her hands violently, as if to be freed of her own guilt. "And what's more," she added, "for this to work like we want it to, you must declare it to her publicly. You must go there tonight, and you must tell her face-to-face." Mama Hawa was now so riddled with guilt over what she was asking of him she offered to go with him, if that would make it any easier. "It's the least I can do," she said. "I feel like a monster, having to ask such a horrible thing of you. Really I do. It's an atrocity, I know. And one for which I will not easily be forgiven. It might be hard to believe, but the woman you see before you was not always this old. I too have been privy to the treasure that is young love and know as well how rare and wonderful a thing it can be when you've found it. But it's a cruel world, I'm sad to say. So the least I can do is go with you. The rest, I'm afraid, I leave to you."

And so Mama Hawa did just that. She accompanied him all the way to Aylin's doorstep and, there on her porch, knocked at her door for him. And when Aylin's mother came and answered it, Mama Hawa took it upon herself as well to ask to see Aylin.

"Now?" Aylin's mother asked.

"Now," said Mama Hawa.

Mama Hawa then ducked away into the shadows of the porch just out of sight.

Bohicket must've reconsidered his decision at least a dozen or so times before Aylin finally appeared in the doorway, and seeing her face illuminated by the porch light and her silhouette backlit by the fragile lights inside, it was all Bohicket could do not to make a run for it, right then and there, to bolt off in any and all directions, finding he wanted to be anywhere else but there. "Hi," he said, unable to look her in the eyes and letting his gaze fall to his feet instead.

"Oh! Bohicket, what . . . what are you doing here?" Aylin said, the confusion on her face made evident in even the darkness. "What an unexpected surprise. And oh . . . um . . . my, my, where are my manners? Won't . . . won't you come in?"

"I can't," Bohicket said a little more sternly than he intended.

"Of course you can, silly. Ya needn't stay long, but come in." And with that, she reached out to take his hand, so as to lead him through the door.

"No," he said, jerking away his hand, "I can't."

"Oh," she said. "Oh, I see."

"Aylin, I'm here because I have something to tell you."

"Oh, I see. So you're not here to repair the sink then? Pity. Darn thing's been acting up since my baby sister, Marmie, got the bright idea to stuff all her doll hair down the disposal."

And he loved the way she chuckled to herself, always had.

Her family was not discreet about it at all. In fact, her mother, her two little sisters and her aunt wasted very little time in coming to huddle around the interior of the door, like it was their God-given right to eavesdrop on any conversation they liked.

"The thing is, Aylin . . . " Bohicket started with a frankness that surprised even him, "Well, the thing is, Aylin... " And he kicked at the doormat with his shoe. "The thing is, Aylin . . . the thing is, I just can't see you anymore. Not now. Not ever."

The expression on her face told him how wholly and completely his words had crushed her. "Well, why not, Bohicket? Why not? Why? We can, at least, be friends still, can't we?" Her voice was almost pleading with him now, as if so much of what dwelled inside of her depended on his recanting and taking it all back.

"Because," he said flatly.

"But why?"

"Because I said so."

He hated himself for making her cry. And now, she was crying.

"I'm sorry," she said. "I'm sorry for whatever I've done. I'm sorry. I am. I'm sorry."

Bohicket wanted to turn to Mama Hawa in hopes of finding a reason to call it all off, for any excuse at all to keep from going on, but understanding he would find only affirmation on her face for doing what they both knew needed to be done, he instead braced himself for the words he would utter next. How he managed to say them would be a mystery even to him. But he said what he said nevertheless, perhaps to save her the pain of holding on to her hopes. "No need to be sorry. And no need to go on crying about it either," he heard himself saying. "It's just . . . it's just . . . I just don't love you anymore."

Now, it might rightly be said that an island is the perfect place for boyhood mischief, and for so long, their island had been exactly the place for such good, harmless fun, fun like peeing on frogs and leering at bikini-clad sunbathers on the bows of their boats. Still, where boys are involved, there's always a chance it can all go horribly wrong, much like it did for Bohicket and Ley one day while traipsing through the woods. They couldn't have been older than six or eight at the time, when they stumbled upon that bird with a broken wing, flapping around on the ground and squawking loudly as it tried to stand. So fascinated were they by the sight of that bird that it did not occur to them, for a good long while, to try and help it. And even then, whatever they tried only exacerbated the problem further. Then they got the bright idea to tie the bird down to a piece of wood in hopes of inspecting the problem more closely. What started off as scientific curiosity and an attempt at helping the bird turned quickly to a sense of helplessness in both the boys, followed then by pity. It was Bohicket who first offered up the possibility of putting the bird out of its misery. "What good is a bird that cannot fly?" he argued. "Look, she seems to be asking us for mercy. Look, it's asking us for it." And so he carried that plank of wood down to the water's edge and held it afloat in the shallows. It was Ley who dared his older brother to get it over with already. "Go on!" Ley jeered. "Do it! Don't be a wussy, do it!" The bird was still trying to flap its one good wing while chirping a loud chirp of sheer panic, when Bohicket finally lifted that board over his head and sent it flipping face-down into the water. There were very few things he would regret more than what he did that day because, as long as he lived, he never forgot the startling stillness, the moment it drowned.

It had been years since Bohicket had thought of the bird he had drowned, and chances are, it might've been a good many more, had he not said what he said to Aylin that night on her doorstep. It was Aylin's sudden expression of pain that reminded him again of the quiet desperation he saw in that bird's eyes, the look of an injury that could not be undone, the prospect of something so precious being drowned once again by his own two hands. Call it a moment of clarity or call it insight, call it whatever it is you like, but Bohicket knew, the instant he saw that look on Aylin's face, that she too was that bird, and coming right out and lying to her like that was no more an act of mercy than drowning a bird twice.

Aylin was crying so much now that it appeared the skin on her face had melted into rivers. "I don't believe you!" she shouted. "I don't! I just don't believe you!" She looked him dead in the eyes, like she was seeking out the lie she was positive she would find. And finding no more than a trace of one, she buried her face in her hands and vanished back down the hallway into the shadows of her house.

It was quite enough having to break her heart like that, but had he known the kind of malevolence she had been forced to endure by way of the other villagers for the simple crime of loving him and doing so without apology, Bohicket might've never forgiven himself. (A young heart would have proven too fragile a thing to survive such a catastrophe, knowing he had stolen the one thing she had sacrificed so much for.) As it was though, his heart too was broken, same as he himself was broken under the weight of what he had done, of calling the single most honest thing he had ever known false. And this is what made it all such a terrible shame because, as he would soon find out himself, no ghost haunts you like a broken heart, and no crime feels quite as egregious as calling true love a lie.

Chapter Nineteen

ONLY NOW, FACED WITH THE OVERWHELMING LOSS OF IT, DID Bohicket see how a man in love is a man with wings. Only now did he see that love is what grants the appendages of flight because only now, without Aylin in his life, did he know what it was to feel so helplessly grounded. It seemed his feet were leaden weights, heavy with the earth's gravitational pull. He kept his head bowed, and not once did he look up from the work he was doing. Not once did he gaze into the sky. He wouldn't dare, for fear of having to, at last, bear witness to the clouds, the birds and the great insurmountable distance he felt he had fallen.

So this is how the fallen angels felt, having betrayed themselves, he thought.

So this is the curse of being alone, of a man without God.

And just when he assumed things couldn't possibly get worse, his mother took up yet another strange habit, born perhaps out of the hope she had discovered in the word she got of angels or, far more likely, the long-forgotten past that was awakened finally by a nosey investigator who'd come asking after her husband. And so it was that Bohicket's mother could be found, at all hours of the day, curtsying to herself in front of the mirror, nodding agreeably and introducing herself to her own reflection. And what made it all far stranger than that was the name she started to answer to, a name that Bohicket had heard before but which, according to Ley, was most assuredly not her name. According to Ley, her name was Robin Walpole, not April June. He knew that. Everybody knew that. Still, she insisted. Either they call her April June or Mama for short.

When they finally confronted her about this curious

new habit of hers, of practicing her curtsy in front of the mirror and introducing herself by an entirely different name, when they finally set about inquiring as to who exactly this "April June" was, it was late afternoon and their mother just beamed a big wide smile at the both of them, bowed her head in a subtle greeting and said, "Oh, April June? That ol' girl? Why, that's just me."

Ley looked at his brother like she had finally lost it. "Well, I guess, that's it," he said. "It was bound to happen someday. And there they go, the last of her marbles." But while he was chuckling to himself, even Ley knew that this was not funny, not in the least.

"But that's not your name, Mama," argued Bohicket, a little wary of how she would respond. "You do know that, right? You do still know your own name, don't you?"

"Yes, course I do, silly," she grinned. "Like I said, it's April. Miss April June."

It took the better part of an hour before they convinced her finally to explain herself, but terrified beyond words by the way she was behaving, the boys were insistent. So, come around evening, she was left with no choice but to answer for herself.

"Okay, okay, fine then. You've got me by the toes. So let me explain," she yielded. "April is my Christian name, the name my mama gave me. And when I married your father, I took his name, June, as is the custom around these parts. And I know, I know . . . I know what you're thinking. And to answer your question, yes, it is awfully unfair to us women-folk, having to abandon our family names and all, but that's just the way it goes in polite society. A good wife takes her husband's last name, and that is that. You'll understand that someday, when a nice young girl catches your fancy, and y'all settle down, and y'all get married."

"But Mama, we are Walpoles, remember?" Ley protested. "I am Pawley Parker Walpole, your youngest and far better-looking son. And this here is my half-witted older brother, Bohicket Walpole."

"Oh, don't be ridiculous, son," she said. "Of course I remember who you are. I mean, your mother might be old and all, but she's sure as hell not senile. Not just yet."

Bohicket could feel something terrible enter his mind. And he appeared a little sterner than before, as if only just stumbling upon the possibility of this story of hers as real and actual truth. "You and Pops changed your names, didn't you, Mama?" he surmised. "Makes sense that you would, seeing as y'all were on the run from the law and all."

"Wait, what?" Ley interjected. "The law? Who's on the run from the law?"

Their mother looked away for the briefest of moments and smiled, like she was remembering herself in a previous life. "That might've been the funnest part: picking us out some brand new names. Yep, your father and I were a regular Bonnie and Clyde back in the day, and new names meant a whole new identity and, even better, a fresh start. I always felt I was more of a Robin than an April anyway," she said with a shrug. "Robin like the bird. Suiting, am I right? Now your father, his real name—the name his mama gave him that is—was Prescott Anson June. Captain June to some. Scotty to others. Though I have to say, your father he made a damn fine Cal, that's for sure. I guess we settled on Walpole because no one would so much as blink at another family of Walpoles living out here. And no one did. No one was the wiser."

None of this was easy for Bohicket to hear, much less come to terms with. Once again, he felt betrayed as if for the first time. He did, however, feel a lot calmer than he imagined he should, perhaps because the story itself was not news to him. Ley, on the other hand, was near frantic with impatience, and he demanded to know what exactly the two of them were going on about. "I insist you tell me, and you tell me now," he said. "Now who did you say was on the run from the law, and who's changed their names? And for the love of all that is sacred and holy, who the hell is this Bonnie and Clyde?!"

And so they started from the beginning and told Ley the whole story. Their mother worked through the gist of it, while Bohicket filled in the gaps, until at last, when the story was through, Ley looked as dumbstruck as Bohicket had felt when he first heard it told.

"Come now," said Bohicket, gathering his little brother up in his arms, "It isn't quite as bad as all that, now is it?" He was also trying to convince himself. But to his surprise, what his little brother took from the revelation was not so much a sense of betrayal (like Bohicket himself had felt and now couldn't shake) as it was a sense of being wholly taken with curiosity, in particular the part about their father being a pilot.

"So Pops flew planes?" Ley asked. "As in real-life jet planes?"

"He sure did," their mother replied.

Bohicket couldn't believe that that was all his little brother took away from their story. Though really, if you think about it, it did make sense, seeing as Ley and his father had always shared a special bond that centered mostly around their common love of airplanes. They could spend hours and hours sitting on the beach and picking out planes, squinting off at the horizon and trying to identify each and every one of them by their make and model, as the planes made their way across the clear blue sky. And yet Ley's newfound fascination with his father went well beyond his career as a pilot. It seemed also to awaken questions in him about who his father had been.

For the rest of that night and from sun-up to sun-down over the next few days, Ley barraged his older brother with question after question, most of which Bohicket did not have an answer to, though he tried his darnedest at an educated guess. Taking their boat out fishing seemed, as it always had, the best of all places to go and discuss such things, to work their way through some of life's more difficult questions. And so the two of them went out fishing together every day for the rest of that week. And that is how, most every evening, the boys went steering their boat into the horizon, like two misfits howling deep into the embolism of sky. And that is how, as fate would have it, they were drifting along the currents of a channel late one particular evening, and came upon a handful of Flying Men making their way across the sky toward home.

This time, they numbered about five or six. Or maybe less. Maybe just three or four.

It was nearly dark by then, so it was anyone's guess.

Three, by Bohicket's estimation. "Yes," he said, counting. "One . . . two . . . three . . . "

A half a dozen was Ley's best guess. And inspired by the sight of so many of them in the sky, Ley suggested they follow them. "Come on," he said. "What have we got to lose?"

Bohicket himself knew this was a bad idea. He knew he had made Mama Hawa certain promises that were best kept. And he knew what would happen if they weren't kept. And yet Bohicket was still young and impetuous, and was as eager as his little brother was to end this tale conclusively. So he did what any big brother would do when presented with even the smallest chance of saving his sister. He answered, "Alright," and steered the boat off after them.

Ley was alive with excitement, as he pitched his rod into the well of the boat and took up watch on the bow. "That a way, big brother! Now we've got 'em!"

Upon reaching the shoreline, the men paired off in several directions.

"What now?!" Bohicket cried.

"Them!" Ley pointed. "We follow them!"

Bohicket was quick to agree to it since giving chase to the closest of the pairings would give them the best chance—if they had a chance at all—of catching up to them.

"Maybe it's a tactic to try and throw us off!" Ley cried. "Maybe they're all headed for the same place! Maybe they're like bats and live together in the same cave! And maybe," he said, nearly consumed with the possibility, "that's where we'll find her."

Bohicket ran their tiny johnboat ashore, cut the engine and started off after his brother in the direction the men were flying. Being the oldest, he was faster than his little brother was, and so it didn't take him long to overtake him, stride for stride, and bounded out into the lead.

"Can you see them?!" Ley yelled ahead to him.

"Yeah," Bohicket shouted back. "Yeah, I see them!"

They were somewhere deep in the heart of that island when, after sprinting for a mile or two, Bohicket and Ley finally came upon the spot where the men had landed, and there, the boys disguised their presence behind a nearby tree.

"Shhhh," Bohicket warned.

"Where are they? Do you see them? I can't see them. Can you?"

"They landed over there," Bohicket said. "Right there, beyond those trees."

Ley gazed out in the direction where his brother had pointed, and what he saw when he squinted into that dark was the silhouette of two fully grown men enfolding their wings behind their backs and continuing off into the woods on foot. "Where do you suppose—"

"Shhhhh!"

"Right," Ley said, lowering his voice. "Where do you suppose they are going?"

"Just wait, and we'll see."

The boys followed behind the men for a good long while,

making sure to keep hidden in the shadows and the trees. Where they found themselves, five or ten minutes later, was on the outskirts of what appeared to be a whole village of thatched houses tucked high in the trees.

"Makes sense, if ya think about it," Ley said with a shrug.

"Sure does," Bohicket agreed. "Ya know what they say . . . birds of a feather."

"Think it's safe?" Ley asked, as if recognizing, only now, the danger they were facing. He had been so eagerly awaiting this moment for so long, ready to confront the Flying Men as to the whereabouts of his sister, and yet only now did it begin to occur to him what confronting them actually meant, the dangers they could be facing. He would never admit it, but all that pent-up anger only now served to remind him that he was but a boy and frightened through and through.

"No, I don't," replied Bohicket. "Not at all."

Ley swallowed hard. "I think maybe . . . well, maybe it's time we turn back."

"Look here, little brother, this was your idea," Bohicket said, scolding him. "Surely, you wouldn't turn back now when she is so close? She needs us, little brother. She needs a rescue party. Your sister needs saving."

"Are you cold?" Ley asked. "Cause I am. I'm shivering."

"Wuss."

"Am not."

"Prove it."

The mere sight of all those many houses, perched like a murder of crows in the blackness above them, was enough to have Ley again rethinking their whole endeavor. The walls and the roofs of each of those houses—fashioned as they were out of driftwood and branches and covered over in a canopy of leaves—resembled the kinds of nests that birds would make atop power lines and trees, were there birds so big. And this is how Ley found himself imagining birds that large, birds so terrifically huge their size alone made them positively prehistoric and equally terrifying. What made the whole scene all the more horrific, though, was that every corner on every house appeared so sharp and so nasty to the touch that Ley just assumed that a good deal of harm would await any fool soul who dared venture up there, much less knock.

So, understandably, it took a great deal of courage (and quite a long time to find it) for the boys to swallow back their fears and apprehension, before it was all said and done, and quite a bit longer to gather up the nerve they would need to see their plan through. Ley nearly up and quit entirely a few dozen times, and Bohicket too found he needed all of his capacities not to give up and run away alongside his brother. But they did not quit, nor did they run. Rather, they stood their ground, if only for the off-chance that their sister really was up there in need of saving. And eventually they stumbled upon the courage that they needed, the way boys often do: by challenging the other one's manhood, by calling one another "pussy" and "yellow-bellied" and adding yet another "pussy" for good measure, until at last, they were both sufficiently threatened by the prospect of being labeled one permanently that they were left with no choice but to act. (Shame, after all, is an awful catalyst amongst boys.)

"Fine," Bohicket said finally. "Beat you to the top."

And up they climbed, hand over foot, till they were at the doorstep of one of the houses.

Where Ley found the nerve to do it is anyone's guess, but almost without thinking (and perhaps wanting, more than anything, to have it over with already), Ley stepped up to the door, shut his eyes and knocked.

No answer.

"Whelp," Ley said, "it appears no one is home. Out to dinner. Be back later. Suppose we should leave a note?"

"Try knocking again," said Bohicket. "No? Fine then. Let

me, ya coward."

But the door swung open before he had a chance to knock a second time, and there, towering over the two of them, was a man with a bearded face grizzled by both time and the sea. The man's shoulders were so erect and so wide that his sudden appearance in the doorway was near-menacing, along with how shockingly tall the man was. According to their best guess, he stood a good seven or eight feet tall. His whole frame appeared ready to lunge at them at any moment. The topography of wrinkles above his eyes gathered up in a threat. "Why are you here, what do you want?!" the man thundered. "Who are you hoping to find all the way out here?!"

Bohicket was at a loss. Anything he could've or would've said in response to the man got caught up decisively in his throat, as if all at once, all his words had just up and abruptly quit on him, which is what made it all the more surprising to him when his little brother found his own voice somehow and spoke out on their behalf.

"We're here for justice," Ley said. "That's who!"

The man appeared just as shocked as Bohicket was by Ley's bold response. "Justice? Nobody by that name lives here; I can tell you that," the man said. "This is my house, and I live here alone. Come to think of it, I can't say I've ever heard of a Mister Justice living in these parts. And trust me, I'd know; I'm as old as time itself (or at least I feel as old), and this has been my home for as long as anyone 'round here can remember. Sorry to say it, ol' boy, but I'm afraid you two have gone and gotten yourselves lost. Chased a rabbit trail, so to speak. A little advice though: cut your losses now and scurry on back to wherever it is you came from, before things get sticky for you."

"Sticky? Ha!" Ley said, sounding all too indignant now. "Do you know who my father is? Well do ya? Cause that's where ya got me figured all wrong. My brother and I were born and bred on sticky situations. Our father saw to that. So God help me, I'll show you where you can stick those hollow threats of yours!" And then, recognizing the fleeting chance to save his sister and perhaps exact some revenge, Ley, taken up wholly in an instant of righteous indignation, reared back and caught the man square in the jaw with his fist. "That's for my sister!" Ley shouted over the crack of the man's jaw. "There ya go! There now, I found him! There he is! That there is justice!"

Unfortunately for the both of them, it would take a hell of a lot more to render a man of his stature helpless. And while Ley could pack a punch (enough of one, at least, to send the man reeling back on his heels), the man had recovered in no time flat, snatched Ley up by his earlobes and was dragging him into the house. "There!" he shouted. "There, ya see?! You'll find no Justice here. No one by that name. Just me, myself and I. And the three of us live here alone." And with that, the man threw Ley down on the living room floor and unfurled his gigantic wings, as if to issue his last and final warning. And the warning worked, if only for how instantaneously the sight of those wings spreading out from wall to wall, casting a darkness over the whole of the room. If only for how it gave the two of them pause. "Look around, if you like," the man said. "Go on. I don't enjoy beating the snot out of little boys. But I will if I have to. Try me. I will."

Perhaps it was the ease with which the man had lifted Ley's body clear off the ground, the sheer strength it took to do so. Perhaps it was the look on his face that promised he'd do it again if it came to that, that had both Ley and his brother second-guessing the wisdom in attacking him again. But they were second-guessing it, all the same, cowering even in an admission of defeat.

"Now what's all this about your sister?" the man asked, bending over to catch his breath in long, heaving huffs of air. "Is she dead? Gone missing? She's dead, isn't she? There now, use your words, and tell me. I'm far too old for this shit. Out with it already," he said. "Well? Is she, or isn't she?"

Ley glanced back at his older brother, who was still standing in the doorway, as if to ask him for his permission, before getting it, clenching his jaw and answering the man's question directly. "That's just it," Ley told him. "She's dead, if you killed her. Alive, if you didn't. That's why we're here 'cause we don't know nothing, but we intend to find out. What we do know is we saw you—we did—we saw you take her. And so dead or alive, we know you are to blame."

It was the way his voice cracked mid-sentence, as if in the throes of puberty, that saw to a wholesale change in the man's demeanor. His face eased with empathy. And something in the man's eyes seemed to be reflecting perhaps on the person of their sister. "What was her name?" he asked softly, tugging thoughtfully at his beard. "Your sister, I mean. What was her name?"

"Like you care."

"What was her name?"

"Dew," Ley said. "Dew was her name. Her name was Dew, and you best start remembering, before my brother and I help jog that memory of yours."

The man sighed a resigned, sad-sounding sigh and then sat down calmly in his chair, where he thought for a moment then said, "Well, you're welcome to go on blaming me, of course. Just know you'd be wrong to. I'm not in the business of killing people, you see. Nor of kidnapping them. Never have been. Never will be. Not exactly my thing, ya see. Never really had the stomach for it honestly. Helping people out, sure. Rescuing them from drowning, sure, yes. But not killing or kidnapping them. Let me be clear."

Bohicket could see his little brother needed him now, so he started cautiously through the doorway to the center of the room and helped him to his feet. "We saw you," he told the man. "Say what you will, but we were there, and we saw you. She was in the channel. We would've found her, we could've saved her, were it not for the likes of you."

The lamplight caught the look on the man's face midway between being reminded of something and remembering it. He looked up and then away then back at them. "It was evening, as I recall. Dusk almost," he said. "And there were two boats in the water, yes? No? There were two boats, correct? Y'all were swimming about so frantically we could tell something or another had gone horribly wrong. Yes . . . it's starting to come back to me now. The pieces. They are coming together. It's all making sense. Y'all were the two boys swimming in the channel that evening, were you not? You were, weren't you? Yes, I believe you were."

"So you admit it?! You admit you were there!" Ley shouted and stared accusingly in the man's direction. Ley was never one for sadness, you see, nor was he one to admit it, if he was sad. Rather, his go-to reaction was always anger, to lash out at any cause that would otherwise recommend his own sadness.

Bohicket, on the other hand, was never that lucky because, unlike his little brother, everything he felt he felt deeply. He had, to that point, held out hope, until word of their sister's untimely death was finally realized and came crashing down atop his head with all the force of some gigantic tidal wave, which threatened now to drown him. Of course, a tiny part of him had somehow always suspected that she was dead and gone and he himself was nothing more than a lightning rod waving around in anticipation of the storm. Then again, no one is prepared for the thunderbolt when it strikes, and expecting the grief is no consolation when faced with grieving.

"Admit it!" Ley shouted, stabbing a finger in the man's face. "Admit it!" he cried. "If you're sorry at all, for the love of God, for the love of anything and everything, for love of God, have the decency to admit it!"

"I admit it," the man said, yielding with both of his hands. "I do. And for the life of me, I am sorry I have to. I'm sorry she died. I'm sorry you lost your sister. I'm sorry that bad things happen to good people, and I'm sorry that it happens far too often to see any justice in it. I'm sorry we weren't there in time to save her. God knows, we tried; I'm sorry we weren't. Really and truly, I am. I'm sorry we weren't there in time. I am. I'm sorry. Still, I did not kill her. Blame me all you like, if blaming me helps with your loss, but you and I both know that the ocean is a bastard, and that bastard, the ocean, she is to blame."

Still, try as he did, no matter what the man said, no amount of excuses he had to offer them, nothing the man said forgave him their blame, and in the end, it was all Bohicket could do to drag his angry brother, kicking and screaming, from the man's house.

"I'll get you still!" Ley cried. "I will; I'll get you! This is not over; ya hear me?!" he shouted, as Bohicket ushered him away across the island by the collar of his shirt, all while Ley continued screaming and yelling his curses high into the trees.

And that might've been that, his words just words, had Ley left it at that. But rarely are words just words, and as such he would eventually endanger them both, without ever meaning to, with the promises he made by way of those words, by way of the curses he shouted up at the Flying Men, even from the boat, where he issued the one promise both he and his brother would live to regret. "I know where you live!" Ley cried. "And hand to God, I will not rest until the world comes knocking at your doors!"

Chapter Twenty

WHAT LEY'S PROMISE TO REVEAL THEIR WHEREABOUTS DID WAS cause the Flying Men to panic because the one thing that concerned the Flying Men the most was the prospect of any outsider discovering that they existed. Their very lives, after all, relied on them operating in secrecy, and they knew what humans are capable of when faced with anything they cannot explain. And so they did what they had to do to keep their existence quiet; they sought help from their oldest allies: the people of the village. And really, who could blame them, humanity being what it is: a living, breathing mass of terrible apprehension?

Unbeknownst to either Bohicket or his brother, the village had formed ranks to defend the Flying Men's secret. Seeing no other way, they set out decidedly to chase Bohicket and his family from their land. How was the easy part, considering Bohicket and his family were wholly reliant on the villagers to barter and trade for their everyday needs. So when Bohicket learned of the embargo, he approached Mama Hawa to plead for some grace, only to discover there was no grace to be granted.

"Take it back," Bohicket told his brother, upon returning from his visit. "It's the only way. You have to apologize and take it back. Tell them you were angry, tell them you were kidding, say whatever it is they need to hear, but fix it. Take it back."

"I can't," said Ley, like it had become a mere matter of fact.

"You have to."

"I can't."

"Then you have doomed us all."

"If that's how it is, then that's how it goes. They killed my sister, and I'd sooner die than give them the satisfaction."

They were each grieving in each their own way, Bohicket with his tears and Ley with his anger. Though Bohicket tried and tried, no amount of coaxing or bargaining or rationalizing with his brother would change his mind. Only time, and the now real and looming inevitability of having to leave their land for good, would change his mind. And it would be a good many weeks before it came to that. A good many weeks before the effects of the dried-up trade lines were finally felt. Then and only then, with the rain catchers leaking their only source of fresh water, after the ceiling in Ley's bedroom had cracked wide open above his head and drenched both him and his mattress in rainwater, only then did Ley see fit to yield to the pressure.

"Fine," Ley agreed at last. "I'll take it back. But I won't apologize. Not now. Not ever."

"Praise be to God!" Bohicket exclaimed. "Seems you might have a brain in you yet, little brother. Despite all evidence to the contrary."

Problem was, it wasn't the villagers who needed convincing. The Flying Men had initiated the affront, so only they could call it off. And realizing this, the boys set out in search of their island that very day, but wary now of any and all newcomers, there were no Flying Men to be found. They went back there day after day, only to find the island seemingly abandoned again and again.

So Ley at last had the bright idea to head out there, and set traps in the trees. Bohicket tried to dissuade him, understanding that this was no way to offer anyone a sufficient apology, that a man will pretend to forgive just about anything to be freed of his captors. And so rather than take part in his little brother's plan, Bohicket looked on from below, as Ley bounded from tree to tree and branch to branch, webbing the woods around the Flying Men's houses with spring-loaded traps, which he had fashioned out of discarded casting nets. It was a tactic their father had taught them to quench his unquenchable taste for rabbit stew. And every morning for the remainder of that week, the boys returned to that island, hoping and fearing the traps had worked.

They had not.

And just when it appeared all hope was lost, Bohicket had a bright idea.

"Aylin," he told Ley. "Aylin will know where to find them. She will help us." Though in his heart of hearts, he wasn't so sure. Of course, his motives were not purely about undoing the harm Ley had done. Bohicket had been quietly haunted by his memories of her for weeks on end. Memories of the two of them together and the love that had come to mean so much to him, especially now in her absence. Day and night, his thoughts of her had trailed after him, dogged him like something sinister was onto his scent. He couldn't shake the thought of her, couldn't shake the memories he had of the two of them playing tic-tac-toe on the beach, a game which Aylin always started with an X she drew in the sand. "You be the hugs. I'll be kisses," she'd explained. And he loved that about her, how playfully she always flirted with him.

By now, the color of Aylin's eyes had all but escaped him. Were they brown? Yes, brown. Brown sounds right. Brown with specks of green. Simply knowing there was green hidden in them made the knowledge seem so intimate, like he alone was privy to their secrets. And yet the more he tried to remember the rest of her body, to account for the length of her legs or the smallness of her hands, the more the thought of her escaped him completely. (Time can be cruel this way.) Still, day after day, he tried his best to commit her to memory, to recall even the subtlest of creases in her knuckles, the joints that went riding in and out on the torque of her muscles, on the causal fuel of her veins. And so it was that he returned, almost daily, to whatever memories he had left of her: the times she would take his hand in hers and how the act itself would have him thinking, *Oh. Now this is something. This right here, this is something.* Her touch felt like benevolence. And it seemed too that, with every touch, came a smile—he seemed to slowly forget that too; how she was always smiling. With every touch, she was smiling, like she too saw their intimate encounter for the gift it was.

He was all too aware of the promise he made Mama Hawa. He was also aware of what happened to anyone who crossed her. And he knew what he was risking in going back on their bargain. But finding his little sister took precedence. And the feeling of missing Aylin happened upon Bohicket so quickly it was tough to get a sense of it, the same way that it's tough to know when that tickle in your throat marks the beginnings of a cold. And yet the thought of her occurred to him so frequently that he knew full-well what the feeling was. Warm and aching now from head to toe, Bohicket found he was indeed sick with it, stricken even with a feverish need to go and see her once more.

So it was decided. Rashly and perhaps naively. But it was decided.

Early the next day, Bohicket and his brother set out across the waterway to find her.

Outside one of the houses along the waterfront was a man on his porch, playing his guitar and singing loudly as they passed. Was the tune he played a good one? Well sure. As good as any. Then again, what did he know about how a song is supposed to be played or not played? Their father was the only one in their family who had played the guitar and played it well. In fact, he had seemed always to be playing it. So Bohicket was well-accustomed to the sense he got when a song struck a chord, and this song did strike a chord. He didn't want it to, especially not this way, especially since, in his mind, it shouldn't have. He had grown up singing along to the very same song. And though it did affect him, he tried to hide it. The memories that that song conjured up in his mind—of their father with a guitar ever-present on his knee, singing the same songs he always sang—alerted his whole person to the danger his family now faced. Still, Bohicket did not mention it, for fear of admitting that all life here in the South is born and dies on porches such as these.

They were a good ways down the coastline before they caught sight of Aylin. She was down on her knees, collecting an armful of driftwood. Seeing her again startled something inside Bohicket. He just assumed, rather naively, that Aylin would be equally glad to see him, that all would be forgiven and she would just come running over and kiss him so hard and so squarely on the mouth that he would chip a tooth. This, he quickly realized, was a foolish assumption. Instead of being delighted, she just stood there, as still as if she was frozen, looking him over from a safe and calculable distance, as if she did not recognize him at first or, worse, no longer wanted to.

"Hi, Aylin. Hi, it's me," he said, stepping closer.

"I'm sorry," she replied, rubbing her eyes and backing away. "Do I know you?" She pointed a plank of driftwood at the both of them in warning. "Stay back," she said. "I'm warning you. Stay back. I know a girl out here all on her own may seem like an easy target to a couple of perverts like you, but I'm warning you: this girl packs quite a punch."

Bohicket should've expected such a cold reaction from her since a young girl's heart is a precious commodity and is nothing to be toyed with. "Oh come on, really?" he said. "Come now, you know I didn't mean it. You know I love you and you love me. I was lying. That's all. I had to. You have to believe that. I lied to protect you."

"Help!" she cried. "Someone please! Someone help!"

She swung the driftwood around wildly and slowly backed away. And it was all Bohicket could do to keep from being hit upside his head, as he continued to inch closer.

"Stop it. You know me, Aylin. So stop it," he said. "You do. You know me," he said. "You do. Now stop it." And after a few swift dodges and a few more close calls, he was finally on top of her and wrapped her up tightly in both of his arms. "Stop," he said. "Just stop. Now go on, drop it. That a girl; drop it. That's right. Now, now. There, there."

Aylin kept on fighting him, even after she'd been disarmed, but fighting him any longer was of little use. His grasp was as strong as his determination to not let go, to never again let her go. So she did eventually give in to him, and then, and only then, did she allow the weight of her person to crumble wholly into his arms. She was sobbing on his chest now, and Bohicket knew, right then, that he alone was to blame for this.

"I'm sorry," he said. "I'm so, so sorry. I didn't mean it. If I could take it back, I would; you have to believe me. You know I didn't mean it. Please believe me. I swear I didn't mean it."

What finally had her believe him must have been how sadly he pleaded this into the shell of her ear—how he gathered her up so desperately in his arms like he might never let go, how he repeated his apology again and again like there was honesty in the echo. And once she stopped crying, she placed her hand on his chest and whispered something into his open mouth, only to then seal it inside with a kiss.

"Look at me. Jesus. I'm a mess," she said, finally pulling herself away from him and brushing herself off. "Oh, Bo, what choice do I have but to believe you? I mean, look at me. Just look at me. You must love me," she said, looking herself over and laughing. "This must be love. It must be, if only because you can appreciate my snotty kisses."

He wiped her face with the sleeve of his shirt. "There now, good as new."

"Pretty as ever?"

"Even prettier."

Ley had remained completely silent up to this point, observing the whole messy exchange from a safe distance. He wasn't entirely sure what to make of what he'd just witnessed. The whole thing came as a surprise to him, especially since he had taken Bohicket at his word that Aylin was just a friend and nothing more. He didn't know much about love himself, but he knew enough to know that friends don't kiss like that. "Enough," he interjected. "Enough. Can we get on with it already? I'm feeling a bit queasy with all this kissing and tonguing and smooching and such, and I'm starting to second-guess your whole plan."

For the first time, Aylin noticed Ley standing there. "Why, Bo," she said, "who is this handsome hunk of meat you've brought along with you? Well, what's the matter with you? Aren't you going to introduce me? A girl counts herself lucky for the company of one good-looking man, but two? Bless my soul, I think I've gone and won the lottery."

"Oh, don't mind him," Bohicket said. "That's just my dim-witted brother, Ley. He just likes to follow me around wherever I go . . . that is, when he's not busy mindlessly gnawing on barnacles or walking face-first into trees."

"Ley? As in *the* Ley?" she said. "So this is the famous Ley you're always going on about. Well it's nice to finally meet you, Ley. I am Aylin," she said. "And judging by the way your brother here is always talking about you, he sure does think the world of you, Ley."

"My dear, the pleasure is all mine," Ley said. And he took her hand and made sure his brother was looking before he kissed it. "Not sure what you see in my brother exactly, but what you got going on is most certainly not lost on me. So if you're ever in need of a real man in your life, I am at your disposal."

Bohicket rolled his eyes. "Nice try, little brother. But you'll have to do better than that, I'm afraid. Guess the little youngster here is getting hungry, or is it past your bedtime?

You're hungry; is that it? You're hungry? I think you can scrape some barnacles off the docks, if ya are. You'd like that, wouldn't ya, little guy? Well go on then. Go on, Fido, fetch. Leave the adults be. It's time we adults get down to brass tacks anyway."

"Brass tacks?" Aylin asked. "That serious, huh?"

"That's just it," Bohicket said. "It actually is."

"Then out with it already."

"Ya see, my idiot for a brother here has gone and got us into quite a bit of trouble, it seems," Bohicket explained.

"Oh?" Aylin said.

"And now he's decided it's time to apologize. Isn't that right, little brother?"

If only by his silence, Ley's answer was *right*.

"The trouble is," Bohicket continued, "we can't seem to find them."

"Who?"

"The Flying Men."

Bohicket went on to explain how they got in such a profoundly disastrous predicament, how they had discovered the Flying Men's island hideaway, confronted them about their part in Dew's death, and how the confrontation finally ended with Ley promising to give them away to the authorities. "And that is how it all started. The embargo of goods to and from the village. The cold shoulders. The suspicious glares. And now, I'm afraid, we've run out of choices. Ley here must amend what he said, or we will be forced to leave our home for good."

"I don't want to apologize, mind you," Ley interjected, crossing his arms.

"But you have to," Bohicket reminded him. "All the drinking water has dried up because the rain catchers need repair. To eat, we need new fishing line, and the roof needs patching, which takes a whole list of supplies that we don't have. We have tried to find them and apologize more times than I can count, but they are nowhere to be found. So I guess we are here to ask for your help in finding them."

Just hearing of the plan once again, Ley was in a huff. "They are nasty people, the lot of them," he said, unable still to swallow his pride. "They are, you know? They are nasty people. The worst kind of people because they killed our sister, and I hold them responsible. They are to blame."

"I'm not so sure you're right about that," said Aylin. "I happen to know better."

"Really?" Ley asked. "How so?"

"Because I know them. I've met them. And they are too kind to ever do that," she said.

"Still, we saw them do it, didn't we, brother?" Ley argued. "We did. We saw them."

Aylin shrugged. "I'm sure you saw what you saw. Can't argue with that. All I can say is what I know, and what I happen to know is quite a lot about them."

"Do you now?" Bohicket asked.

"I do. And I have to think your little sister Dew would also agree."

"My sister? What about my sister?" Ley said, clearly incited by the mere mention of her name. "On what grounds? On whose authority? Who are you to speak for her? I mean, how dare you? How dare you?"

"Now, now. I meant nothing by it," Aylin said to him calmly. "I loved your sister. Really and truly. We grew up together, played as girls together. And way back when, your sister and I would even go and play with them on occasion."

This, for Ley, was hard to believe. Was she lying? Was she right? How dare she?

"I can tell you don't believe a word I am saying," Aylin said. "And I can't say I blame you. But it's true, I'm afraid: your sister and I did play together as children. And at times we did play with them, right out there along the riverbank, where the water meets the sea. And yet I couldn't care less whether you believe me or not. Because I swear it is true."

"Then how do you explain what we saw them do?" Bohicket asked.

"I can't," she said. "All I know is they are good folks and act mostly with the best of intentions. I'd imagine that is why they were there in the first place the evening she died, since that is why they are always there: to rescue people from drowning and, if they fail, to help carry their souls up into the heavens, where all good souls go when they belong."

"Then your advice is to appeal to their decency?" Bohicket concluded.

"If they have any," Ley remarked.

"My advice?" she answered. "Is that what you want? My advice? Well then, this is my advice, take it or leave it. Or better still, just take it. I, sure as hell, don't need it. I never heed my own advice anyway. After all, I fell for you. So I say go to them and apologize. It's your last best chance to resolve the matter. I say they will hear you out, if you put it to them right. So try."

And though they both remained sufficiently wary of the outcome, the boys eventually agreed to her terms. They agreed to go and face them and make amends, so long as Aylin agreed to show them the way.

Chapter Twenty-One

"I'll take you," she said, **"as long as you both swear it stays** between us. Just us, and nobody else, you hear me?" And the way she warned them spoke to the risk she was taking in just guiding them there.

"Then why are you doing this?" Bohicket asked.

"I don't know. I'm an idiot or a glutton for punishment. I don't know . . . maybe just because. Plus, I admit, your brother is kinda cute, and I've always been a sap for cute boys," she said, winking at Bohicket. "Anyways, how much harder could they make my life? I mean, really? They've already shunned me for loving you. They already warn their children to keep away, like what I got might be contagious. I'm already a ghost in their eyes. So how much worse could it get? I mean, really?"

Until then Bohicket had barely considered what she had to face as a result of their actions. The pain of feeling ostracized in her own home, persecuted by the very same people she thought of as family. And it hurt him to think of her having to endure so harsh a punishment for his sake. "I'm sorry," he said, stopping in his tracks, "I cannot allow this. Not any longer. I've already asked too much of you already. I see that now. And I can't . . . I won't ask you for more. Just show us the way, and we'll take it from here. You go back. We'll take it from here."

Aylin stopped where she stood and looked his face over, until she could see how much it all pained him. "Bo, my dear, that's sweet of you to say. But I'm a big girl, and what I gave, you did not have to ask me for. Some things must be given freely, and my love is one of those things. So stop all that whimpering, and try and keep up, won't you?"

Together they circled back just beyond the village and, from there, headed south from one island to the next. They crossed a few creeks and a good many streams, before ending up a half-a-dozen islands away from where they'd started. And that was where Aylin finally stopped to tell them that rumor had it that the Flying Men had taken up residence in an old chapel of ease, until the threat blew over. The chapel was a few miles from where they were standing, and was built as a replacement for a praise house that once stood on the very same grounds. As Aylin explained it, the grounds were a hallowed place, where the enslaved people, who once worshipped in the praise house, were said to sing on the Sabbath and hold vigil over the disinterred bodies of their dead, before walking them out under the cover of night in a quiet parade. Then, according to their customs back home, they would make their way to the cemetery, where the dead would be buried a second time. "They did this because, as my mother would tell it, a Christian burial was what was expected of them," Aylin told them. "And so they buried their dead as such the first time. Burying them a second time was strictly forbidden and punishable by starvation or a hard lashing, and so it was of the utmost importance that the practice remain far from sight. They were courageous people. And nothing would deter them from observing their long-held traditions," she said with a certain pride spreading across her face. "Especially since nothing was more sacred to them than the ways of our ancestors."

Aylin said she knew a shortcut across the island. It took them through the cemetery, where before exiting the other side, she turned and cautioned them to do exactly as she did and walk out backwards. "A cemetery can be a terrible place, you know. Especially when it's haunted by the unsettled souls of people who were enslaved. The spirits of those who'd enjoy nothing more than to hitch a ride home with you when your back is turned."

"Spirits?" Ley said.

"That's what I said. I said spirits. See how they burnt all those trees? Turn around. Ya see? They do that to exorcise the spirits," she told them. "It's been said that, in life, trees and people can only survive in harmony with each other. What trees breathe out, we breathe in. Well, the same goes for death. In death, our spirits are said to return to the trees, and so burning them hollow is the only way of setting them free."

And hearing how serious she sounded when telling them this, the boys were careful to do exactly as she had suggested. They formed a single-file line and walked out backwards. And making it out safely, they headed out across the adjacent field, where they came upon the chapel of ease, which was nestled into an alcove of moss-covered branches.

It was just after midday, the sun was high in the sky, and all was quiet. Too quiet, in fact, for either of their liking. But wanting to impress Aylin with a show of his fearlessness, Bohicket swallowed back his trepidation and started in first. "Should we knock? No? Okay then," he said. Then he headed inside.

The chapel was small and cramped, with a dozen or so pews and a low ceiling. On the wall behind the altar was a cross. "That's why they built the praise house that once stood here," Aylin said, "The plantation owners, I mean. They built it, hoping that my people would come to Jesus. And my folks . . . well, they played along, so far as the plantation owners knew. And therein lies the joke," she said. "Let them think they are the only ones laughing."

Aylin appeared to be pleased with the stories she told them, so she told them some more. She told them tale after tale of all the many other ways in which the people who were enslaved there had revolted in quiet, so as not to alert the masters. "When really, they were their own masters," she said, "since they held fast to their traditions and, therein, uncovered their power."

"So where are they?" Ley asked, glancing around the room. "You said they'd be here."

"Give 'em time," she said. "Give 'em time, and they will come."

And so they each got comfortable on each their own pew, and they waited. They waited, and they waited. And to pass the time while they waited, Aylin shared a story she had heard from her mother, a story that had been passed down through the generations. And it turned out to be quite a long story. So long, in fact, that it was really more of a history than a story. It was a long and quiet history that served to illustrate the vital role the Flying Men played in ensuring the survival of those who ended up out there on the Sea Islands and, for nearly two whole centuries, worked those islands as enslaved people. "How, you ask? How did they help us? Well, we've got time, so I will tell you. First," she said, "they carried our messages for us. And by us, I mean all the many families who were forcibly separated and shipped away. By us, I mean all the babies who were taken from their mothers, all the boys who were taken from their fathers, and all the wives who were taken from their husbands." Aylin went on to explain that this is why the Flying Men came to see it as their job to bring tidings of good news and well wishes back and forth between families. And seeing as they themselves were never bound to work the rice fields, they saw it as the least they could do to courier love notes between lovers and spread word of another baby being born, and why, later on, they saw it as their solemn duty to spread the rumors they had heard of a man called Lincoln and a woman called Tubman, small reminders of the hope they knew as Moses. At some point or another, they took to playing the role of aerial scouts as well, she told them. And they made themselves useful by keeping a lookout for the bands upon bands of enslaved people they helped to run away. They developed a whole system of warnings they could share from the sky: three hoots of the owl if the plantation owner was spotted, four hawk calls to warn the runaways that the men with dogs and guns were nearly upon them. They also developed quite a number of carefully choreographed bird-like formations that could be seen from the ground and signal directions and danger to their friends below. When Bohicket heard this, he couldn't help but think of his little sister and how convinced she was that the formations of birds she saw in the sky were indeed telling her something. It is impossible to say for sure how many enslaved people the Flying Men helped escape to the North, how many safe havens they found for them to hide in along the way or how many rescues they coordinated all on their own, by the time they were done. Even after the war was fought and won and the Gullah people were freed, the Flying Men found other ways of helping them survive, such as scouting for wild boar and deer to hunt, by pointing them out from on high. They helped lug in drinking water until a well could be dug. They kept watch over the skies and sounded the warning when the seas were most ominous. And since the Gullah people were such excellent farmers and fishermen already, they were able to live out their days on those islands all on their own. Always, the Flying Men were dedicated to the survival of their friends. And always, they were there to look after them. "Why that is, I do not know," Aylin confessed. "They could've flown home. Sometimes I think maybe they should have. Yet they didn't; they stuck around, and they helped us out, maybe perhaps out of the goodness of their hearts, or maybe instead to atone for the guilt they felt for having been born freer than others."

Telling the rest of her story of the Flying Men and the Gullah people took up the remainder of their afternoon. And when at last the story was done, the sun had long since set and a quiet stillness had fallen over the world. The wind moved like water through a break in the trees, and it was then, at that moment, that they heard a sudden and distinguishable rustling in the sky outside.

"Hear that?" Ley whispered.

"Yeah," said Bohicket.

"They are coming," Aylin whispered. "They are here."

There came a torrent of wind that shook all the trees, as the entire host of winged men landed in one final flap of their gigantic wings. Then there were footsteps approaching the door, followed then by voices. Men's voices. Deep voices. Deeper still in how weary they sounded after a hard day's work.

Bohicket and his brother were on their feet now, and facing the door, they prepared themselves for whatever dangers they might encounter. They swallowed hard, balled up their fists and braced themselves against the loathsome prospects of finally having to face all of the Flying Men.

They heard the men huddling together at the steps, the doorknob turned, and the door creaked open. There, in the doorway, stood nine or ten men, each as tall as an evening shadow, their faces masked by night.

The first man inside felt for the light switch on the wall and flicked it on, revealing in a sudden flash of light, how surprised the men were to stumble upon these intruders. "What's all this? What . . . who are you? What do you think you're doing in our home?"

Bohicket recognized this man right away. He realized this was the very same man Aylin had arranged a rendezvous with, the very same man who had shook his hand, who'd looked him square in the eyes and introduced himself as one of God's holy angels. It was Piedmont Black. Bohicket was not upset about their deception. No, not in the least. He was more relieved to see for himself how deeply she had loved him, how willing she was to risk so much for him and his mother. First that, and now this.

"Hey, Sackren," Aylin said and stepped forward to greet the man. "It's me. Bea."

"Sackren?" Bohicket said. "Oh. Oh, now I get it. You were even good enough to lie about your name . . . Pete."

"Good God, girl," said Sackren. "Geez, it's alright, fellas. It's just Bea."

"Hi, Bea," the next man through the door said.

"Hi," she said. "Hi, Dumah. Hi, Raguel. Hi there, Maalik."

"Hi. Hello there, Bea," they all said, as they each filed in through the door.

The last man to enter was as thick as an oak tree, and equally as tall. He had to duck his head and shimmy in sideways to fit through the door, and once inside, he had to crouch down in a low stoop to keep from bumping his head on the ceiling. In a manner of speaking, he looked like an elephant trying to squeeze itself into a birdcage. He introduced himself as Abaddon, and it was clear, by the grayness of his beard, the crow's feet at his eyes and the stoic way he carried himself, that he was older and perhaps a bit wiser than the others in his company, which must've been what made him their de facto leader.

Only after the boys got a good look at his face did they realize that this man, Abaddon, was no stranger. Only then did they realize they had met him before. That he was, in fact, the very same man they had confronted and whose home they had attacked. And once the horror of this fact finally dawned on them, it was all Ley could do to keep from making a run for it. And he certainly would have, had there been a way out. There was not. And so Ley was left glancing around frantically like a cornered rabbit.

"It's you," said Abaddon, instantly recognizing them as well. "What's all this, Bea? What are you thinking bringing them here? Surely, these aren't the sort of boys you make friends with? Surely not. You're a good girl, Bea, and a good girl can't afford to keep such bad company."

"That's just it," Aylin replied. "They are my friends, and despite what you may think of them, they are good people. Not always good company, I'll admit," she added, shooting Bohicket a half-serious, half-playful look that said she wasn't quite over how he had wronged her. "But they are good people."

"That's not what we hear," Raguel chimed in.

"Quite the opposite," Sackren added.

"Well y'all should know, better than anyone by now, that what gets heard is rarely the truth," Aylin responded. "Otherwise, you've got a helluva lot of dead bodies to account for, and the authorities would be right to come looking for you."

The men laughed.

All of them, that is, except Abaddon.

"You have a point there, little one," Abaddon admitted. "Still, they were the ones who came knocking on my door, looking for trouble. And it's been my experience—and that's a good many years now—that, when you go looking for trouble, you can always find it. So far as I can tell, these two are nothing but."

Bohicket had had enough time, by then, to gather the courage he needed to step up and say what he had come there to say. "It's true," he admitted. "You're right; my brother and I have quite a nasty habit of finding trouble, and as of late, it seems to be following us wherever we go. But then, that's also why we're here. Forgive us for intruding like this, but we've come here to apologize. Isn't that right, little brother? We're sorry for what we said . . . or rather for what he said. But I assure you he didn't mean it. His anger got the best of him is all. Can you blame him? She was our sister. We loved her. And we were forced to watch her drown."

There was a sort of softening to Abaddon's face right then, a sort of yielding at the brow.

"And we are," Bohicket continued, "We're sorry. Tell them, Ley. Tell them we're sorry."

"I'm sorry," said Ley. "I was angry. I didn't mean what I said. I'm sorry."

"I mean, think about it," Aylin interjected. "If he actually meant what he said, wouldn't he have informed the authorities by now? I mean, he sure had enough time to. Am I right? But he didn't. He hasn't. So call it off, won't you? They aren't a threat to you. Certainly, you can see that, can't you? Haven't they suffered enough already . . . between losing their sister as well as their father, to say nothing of what the grief has done to their mother? Y'all are good men. I know that. You know that. So please, I beg of you, find it in your hearts to forgive them, to accept their apology and call it off."

Now, Abaddon had been alive on this earth long enough to recognize love when he heard it spoken. The tone in her voice had all the tell-tale signs of a young person in love acting out of utter desperation, as if a plea so small was not small at all.

"I see," Abaddon said, stroking his beard and considering her request. He looked the two boys over, almost to gauge their sincerity, and then he spoke for the group without conferring with a one of them. "We accept your apology," he said. "And we forgive you. Maalik here will go and speak with the villagers tomorrow. He will tell them we've reached an understanding, and it's time to call the embargo off."

And the boys felt they could finally breathe again, like they themselves had been drowning underwater and had only just resurfaced. And it seemed too that the world outside let out a heavy sigh right on cue, relieved that it was now permitted to keep on spinning.

"But before we agree to anything, you must make me a promise," Abaddon said. "And in return, we will promise to hold up our end of the bargain. I'm afraid we need assurances is all, and the only way this will work is if you swear to keep your mouths shut, now and forever, about us. You must swear to say nothing to no one. Not now, not ever. You must swear that our little secret is now your little secret, and you will keep it that way, like your lives depend on it."

"We swear," the boys agreed. "Cross our hearts. We swear, we swear."

"Because they do, ya know? Your lives, they do depend on it."

"We swear," said Bohicket.

"We swear, we swear," echoed Ley.

"Swear on your mother," said Abaddon. "Your word alone is not so good these days."

"We swear."

"On your mother."

"On our mother," they said. "We swear."

Chapter Twenty-Two

ABADDON DID AS HE PROMISED HE WOULD DO; HE FORGAVE them. And with the trade lines reopened, everyday life for Bohicket and his family got back to normal. Or as normal a life as they could hope for, while tending to their mother's ever-growing grief, which was, by anyone else's standards, far from normal.

But it would only take one vindictive person to out his mother for her part in her husband's transgressions. Bohicket knew the risks he was taking, and he knew them well. But having successfully mended his relationship with Aylin after what he had done to her, and realizing what losing her again could mean to his heart, he ignored the consequences of his actions and went to visit Aylin each and every day.

Strangely enough, it was his mother who had given him the final nudge he needed to go about braving the dangers. Hearing how he talked about Aylin, and seeing the love he tried so desperately to mask from his face was all it took for a rare softness to settle onto her face, and his mother set about fashioning a crown of flowers and marsh grass and seashells for Bohicket to give to her.

"What woman wouldn't want to be royalty? Give her this," his mother told him. "Do what is right. Make her your queen." And realizing the time had finally come for her to address the whole matter of courtship with her son, she proceeded to detail all the daily ways that a good man pays homage to his queen.

It had been quite a while since last he brought Aylin gifts, and she was so delighted by her crown that she always wore it when they rendezvoused at the beach. Over time, he came to know her more deeply than he ever had. He decided he would. And over time, he discovered new aspects of her that he did not know before: tiny secrets, disquieting fears and the profound love that she professed for the sound of certain words.

"I like debauchery because it sounds just as immoral as it is exciting," she told him. "And any of the good ooooo-sounding words like doodle and doozy and festooned." She also liked the words, hodgepodge and hogwash and hullaballoo because they sounded so messy. "And who doesn't enjoy the thrill of youthful shenanigans? I sure do. Especially when the time comes to skedaddle so you don't get caught. That's another fun word: skedaddle. Oh, and there's cattywampus and collywobbles too! Collywobbles: that's what I get after eating too much of Mama's gumbo."

It became clear, after discussing all the words on her list for hours and hours that Aylin had spent an unreasonable amount of time judiciously considering each word. Unreasonable perhaps. Maybe even ridiculous. But to Bohicket, the fact that she had put so much time into culling together such a list was nothing short of endearing.

"I'm just glad liquidious is not a word. Or is it? Who knows? Is it? Never mind, who cares. Either way, that word's just gross. Liquidious. Sounds like a festering wound full of pus or a bad case of the runs. Curdle," she said. "That's another one. Gross, right? The word itself sort of curdles in your mouth. Go on, try to say it without gagging. Bet ya can't. You can't, can you? Told ya."

And once she was through reciting her list several days in, Bohicket smiled a big happy smile. And almost to confess his fondness for her and her eccentricities, he suggested they let the world sound out the words as well. "I bet they sound different that way," he said. Then he set about showing her what he meant by this. He spent the majority of the daylight the rest of that week, carving each of her favorite words in the highest branches of the highest trees he could find. "There," he said while climbing down. "Now the wind can enjoy sounding them out, just like you. All you have to do now is listen. Listen and enjoy."

She did listen, and she did enjoy. So much so, in fact, that it gave him yet another bright idea. He escorted her down to the beach and, there, began writing out all her favorite words in the sand. "High tide isn't going to erase them, like you might think," he told her. "Don't you worry about that. Instead, the tides will come to carry them away across the sea, like messages in a bottle. Just imagine somebody somewhere—in Europe or Africa—finding them and reading them."

"So we're sharing," she said, delighted by the idea. "I like that. We are. We're sharing."

"Sure are," he said, nodding in agreement. "We are sharing. And what's more, it's entirely possible that maybe, just maybe, another girl, as lovely and strange as you are, will stumble upon them washed up on a beach, and learn to love them the way you do."

The very idea made Aylin beam. She would like that too.

From time to time, for a good many weeks, they would repeat those words to themselves, spelling them out letter-by-letter wherever they were, wherever they went, in order to taste the flavor the words left on their tongues. Aylin especially. Though on occasion, Bohicket would join in too, if only to show her how much he loved her. And in a way, they became linguists together.

The following days were good days in most respects. Far better, at least, than those to come. Bohicket enjoyed nothing more than to be in her company, and Aylin enjoyed having him around just as much. They were in love, and they could feel it, like one might feel the cool breeze on a hot summer day. And they were hot with it. So hot, in fact, that a cool dip in the ocean could not cure them of the heat.

Bohicket could not recall a time when he was happier or more at peace with his place in this world.

Some people would call it bad luck that saw to it that a boat full of people, who were enjoying a vacation on the water, capsized off the coast of a neighboring island. Every last person onboard drowned—a mother and a father, together with their two young children, their lush of an aunt and her intoxicated boyfriend, who just so happened to be driving the boat that day. Chalk it up to bad luck or a cruel twist of fate, call it irony or the saddest of coincidences, call it whatever you want to call it, but in the end, that is how the times changed for the worse. That is how the mysterious appearance of all those dead bodies that had come washing ashore up and down the Carolina coast in recent months brought the investigation finally to their doorstep.

The ongoing investigation would remain ongoing, but now it would continue on their islands. In a matter of days, detectives from the city police department and a rash of eager reporters from all the local TV stations and newspapers descended on their tiny islands, interviewing all the fishermen they could find and asking everyone else the most pointed of questions as to the possible whereabouts of these mysterious Flying Men everyone was talking about and seemed so decidedly ready to blame.

The result was an entire people thrown into a panic, a whole village straining under the weight of what should and should not be shared. The villagers were, in the end, a people with a secret. And as people with a secret go, especially when that secret is under threat of the light, they began to glance warily over their shoulders, seeing dangers at every turn and enemies lurking in the shadows. In time, this made them all the more suspicious of any and every one. Even their neighbors and their neighbor's dog. Even members of their own family.

And thinking it best to head off the inevitable direction

of their suspicions before it was too late, Bohicket decided to pay Mama Hawa a visit and assure her of their innocence in the matter. She said she believed him and thanked him for his candor, but warned him that even she would be powerless to put a stop to any such rumor. "If there's one thing I know about people, it's that people will think what they think," she said. "My best advice, for the time being, is to keep your head down. It's a dangerous thing: suspicion. But rest assured, this too shall pass. That said," Mama Hawa amended, "the only way to be completely certain that no one blames you is to get all the reporters off our backs once and for all. If that is even possible."

At Mama Hawa's suggestion, Bohicket did keep his head down. He knew he could at least do that. So he met up with Aylin only in secrecy and often by cover of night, which Aylin agreed was for the best, after seeing for herself how frantic her neighbors were growing, which was wholly understandable, as she saw it, given the nature of people so unaccustomed to prying eyes. "We were left so long to our own devices out here," she told him, "that it's hard to accept it when that changes. We don't trust outsiders. Never have."

Yes, keeping his head down was something he knew he could do. Convincing all those reporters that their search was in vain would be another matter entirely. It took him a few days to believe such a feat was even possible, and a few more days to formulate his plan. He managed to convince Ley to help him and then sent a letter to the Post and Courier, requesting an audience with one of their reporters and enticing them with a quite adamant claim that he knew the truth about these Flying Men they were after, along with a promise of proof so undeniable that the whole matter would be laid to rest immediately.

He and his brother set about gathering feathers and driftwood and fallen branches. And with the supplies they collected, they culled together two large kites shaped like two enormous birds, each with a wingspan of a good four to five feet. And to ensure the birds could fly, they cut ribbons of fabric from old bedsheets and then raided their father's stash of supplies for enough twine to send those birds high into the sky. And exactly as Bohicket had hoped, a local newspaper sent a reporter out to look into the validity of his claims the very day his letter arrived.

The reporter they sent was a sickly thinning man with bad breath and bad teeth, a man who behaved as if he was already out of time. It was nearly evening when the reporter arrived. He asked every question he'd prepared, but approached the whole assignment as if it were beneath him. It seemed he had his doubts all right and had made up his mind already. *Flying Men? Phooey! Children's stories, that's all. The stuff of the ignorant and superstitious. I'm an adult. Even I know better. Curse it all, I should have taken the legal beat when I had the chance.*

And so feeling a bit rushed, Bohicket answered all of the man's questions in turn. "Yes, I've seen them. I know who they are. No, I don't do drugs. Where would I even get them? Wanna see proof? Come on then, I'll show you." And with that, Bohicket walked the reporter out to the far side of the island.

"Well?" the reporter said upon reaching the beach.

"Just wait," said Bohicket.

"On what? What am I waiting for? You said you had proof. So where is it?"

"Sir, despite what you might think of bumpkins like me, I'm not some kook looking for his moment in the sun. Nor am I in the habit of lying to people and wasting their time. My mama raised me better than that."

"Okay then. Let's see it. You say you have it. Let's see it already."

"Patience," Bohicket said. "They say it's a virtue."

And right on cue, Ley came rounding the river bend and

racing his little johnboat out towards the sea. And there, coming into sight for the very first time, the reporter came to see for himself what at first appeared to be two flying men dipping and swooping high above the boat.

"See?" said Bohicket.

"Is that? No. Is that?" the reporter stuttered, swiping at his eyes in disbelief.

"Don't worry," Bohicket said. "You're not crazy. It's not what you think."

"It's not?"

"It's not."

The reporter was not wrong to be baffled by what he saw with his own two eyes. You see, in the half-light of dusk, the kites that trailed by two invisible strings behind that boat did appear, to the naked eye, like two men carried aloft by enormous wings.

"It's just a trick of the eye," Bohicket told him. "Dusk can be deceptive that way." And he went on to explain that what so many eyewitnesses had claimed to see were, in truth, merely the kites his little brother would sail from the stern of that boat. He told him that his little brother had taken up the odd practice the day their sister went missing. "He usually sets off around supper time, after his chores are all done, and roams the coastline in search of dead bodies."

"What . . . I mean, why?"

"Finality, they say, is the first step on a long, long road," was Bohicket's reply. "He's been out there every evening since the day she vanished, looking for answers, searching up and down the coastline for another dead body, hoping beyond hope to count our baby sister among them. I think it's the permission it might grant him to move on and, at long last, heal."

Ley continued to circle the boat up and down the coastline, those two giant birds hoisted high into the sky. "Giant," Bohicket explained, "so that she can see them from far away."

Seeing the confusion that still lingered on the reporter's face, Bohicket went on to tell him that, growing up in a place as strange as theirs meant wings in flight had long signaled their way back home. He told him, heck, he couldn't remember a time when they didn't. He told him that, come supper time most every day when he and his brother were typically still out fishing on the boat, their father would have strewn their yard with enough fish guts to see the skies over their house fill with flocks and flocks of birds. "It was a sight to be seen," he said. "A real ruckus. Wings, to us, have always been the signal to make our way home. And this, I guess, is just his way of calling out to her in much the same way. This is just him telling her it is time to come home."

By nearly all indications, Bohicket's plan appeared to have worked. The reporter left that night in a fog of sorts, a daze he was only just coming to terms with. The reporter left that night after taking down his name for his records. Bohicket Walpole was the answer he got. That's Walpole. Never June. And perhaps more importantly, the reporter left that night wholly satisfied, convinced that he had come to see the truth for himself.

Word of what the reporter had seen soon began to spread. And so it was that, day by day over the course of that week, the number of reporters and investigators snooping around those parts for a story dwindled slowly to none. Whether it was because his charade had been so convincing or because all their leads had finally dried up, Bohicket was just glad to be done with them. He was glad for the part he might have played in such an enormous feat.

Even with all the reporters gone, visiting Aylin remained a risk. But that would not stop him. Nothing would. He knew Mama Hawa was correct in suggesting he keep his head down for a while, and so he did just that and only ventured off to see her under the concealments of dusk. And if having to brave those risks evening after evening wasn't bad enough, the following days would see things get worse, as the actual reality of what fate had befallen their sister finally made itself clear to them, and the cruelty of an ocean current saw to it that one of Dew's favorite shoes came washing ashore on their island.

It was Ley who first discovered the shoe on the beach one morning. He just stood there aghast, quietly staring down at the question-mark shape of this last and final answer. And for a good long while, he studied every inch of that shoe from its muddy soles to its frayed but still sparkling red laces. He hoped if he stared at it long enough that all the many colors the ocean had sewn into its seams would spell out hints of a better outcome. The inside was full of tiny seashells and sand. Dew would have liked that. She loved seashells. And Ley found himself longing for its tongue to speak, to tell him the story of how the sea had unclothed her, exposing her legs, her arms and even her breasts: the considerable shape of a girl as yet unconcerned with the suggestions of a woman.

He took the shoe home with him that day, as if carefully bearing something sacred, something in the way of completion, in the way of peace. The sight of it struck them all the same way. It was not simply a shoe—a shoe is a shoe is a shoe—it was the closure in him finding the shoe, the truth they knew already in their hearts. And so right before nightfall, Bohicket, Ley and their mother carried Dew's shoe out into the woods and there dug the hole it would be buried in.

The sun was gingerly easing its fiery person down into the ocean, giving way gradually to an army of tall shadows. And that evening their mother sent the boys off to collect six conch shells each. And when they returned, having done as she asked, their mother carefully placed the twelve conch shells they had collected in an evenly spaced circle atop Dew's grave.

"But why?" they asked her. "Why the conch shells? Why

twelve?"

She appeared to be searching for something along the face of the ocean, like the ocean itself was yet another vision she was cursed with. Maybe she could envision the ceremonial raft set adrift, the boatman at the oars shepherding the bodiless soul of her one and only daughter, with such grace, such ease, out across the politically contentious borders between here and the hereafter. "To ensure her safe passage," she told them, "across the River Jordan. We come first from the water," she said, "only to someday return there. Water," she told them, "Water is a rite of passage."

Their mother gave the eulogy and prayed peace over Dew's soul. Ley read aloud a few verses from the Psalms and said amen, while Bohicket knelt at the base of a nearby tree, retrieved his pocket knife and carved an inscription in its trunk. It read: *Take her, oh Lord, with the morning dew.*

Concerns of the heart are a hard sell, it is said. Perhaps the hardest sell of all. And some things only get paid off in time. So it was in their mother's case. She went home that night and cried so long and so hard that they began to fear they'd soon be carried off on a tide of her tears.

Otherwise, nothing about their mother's behavior the next week was a cause for concern, until some days later, when Bohicket stopped by her room to ask about dinner.

All the lights were off, and all the curtains closed, leaving only hints of the outside world nearing dusk. She was an outline of herself in that darkness, and Bohicket could barely make out her faint silhouette sitting in a chair at the center of the room. He could tell she was cradling something in her arms and cooing playfully at whatever it was, while she rocked herself back and forth and back and forth in such a way it gave him pause. Bohicket could only stand there frozen in her doorway, until he finally worked up the nerve to enter the room.

Only by squinting his way through the darkness could

he tell what his mother had cradled in her arms. Even then, he could hardly believe it. Must be a trick of the light. It must be. But it wasn't. What he discovered, that evening in her room, was the urgency with which his mother was cradling his sister's shoe while softly humming a lullaby.

"Mama?" said Bohicket cautiously.

"Shhh," she whispered. "Shhh."

What Bohicket heard in her voice defied all logic. Her *shhh* was overcome with a strange and almost arresting need to never let go, to never surrender up what she loved. It was too dark to make out her expression. Too dark really to see anything. But in that singular moment, Bohicket was sure he was looking upon the face of love. And unsure how to address it, he just whispered, "Mama?" He whispered, "Mama? Is she sleeping?"

"Yes, dear," she replied. "She is sleeping. So hush, okay? Let's not wake her."

"Is she cold?" he asked.

"Yes. Yes I suppose she is."

And out of respect or empathy or something akin to both, Bohicket would wait for her to fall fast asleep in that chair before quietly removing the shoe from his mother's arms and venturing out into the rain-soaked woods to return it to the ground.

He assumed, since she never once brought it up again, that that would be the end of it. He assumed she was as happy as he was to leave the whole matter alone. He assumed that the act of finally laying her daughter to rest, having said her goodbyes, would bring with it the kind of finality his mother needed to heal and to move on. And he assumed that that night marked the beginning of that process and that it would only be a matter of time before the healing was complete. He was wrong. Though just how wrong he actually was wouldn't make itself apparent until the day he returned home, after a morning on the boat, to find his mother burying herself among the pylons beneath their house, in the exact same place that his sister used to spend all of her days playing.

Until that point, the visions, which his mother still claimed to have, had remained innocent enough. At times, Bohicket would catch her shaking the hand of an armchair as if, after some heated negotiations, her and that chair had finally struck a deal. She would twitter up at the birds in the trees and call down to the crabs hiding in their holes. She would host dinner parties and argue passionately with a ring of empty chairs over one topic or another. It was all odd and mildly disconcerting to be sure, but still innocent enough, until the day he found her there, beneath their house, burying herself in the ground like the flower she would claim to be.

By the time he reached her, she was mumbling incoherently and attempting to cover herself over in a blanket of dirt. Both her legs and one of her arms had already vanished into the earth. And seeing how busily she went about burying the rest of herself, Bohicket had a sneaking suspicion that somehow it was all related: the panic in the village, the men who came there armed with their leading questions, the tenuous feeling he got from being around to see it all. He felt as if there was something strange and unsightly connecting everything. Something shared in the land perhaps? The undercurrents of ocean running through all of their veins? The now broken rhythm to their lives lived out there? Perhaps yes. Perhaps no. Perhaps all of it at once, and none of it at all.

Bohicket got down on his hands and knees and crawled in close, and there, lying beside her, he asked her how her day was going. But she did not appear to notice him at all. She just kept shoveling handful after handful of dirt over her body and saying to herself, "I'm withering. I feel as if I'm a flower, and I am withering."

It wasn't the withering that worried him so much as the idea that she would refer to herself as a flower. His father had called her that, for as long as he could remember: Flower. His flower. He had plenty of other pet names for her as well, but he was most fond of that one. "G'morning, Flower," he would say in greeting her, every morning. "Beautiful day today, isn't it? Sun is shining; sea is calm. Made you a cup of orange juice. Want some breakfast? Can't say no to salmon and eggs. So how about it, my Flower, want some breakfast?"

"But Mama, you're not a flower," Bohicket protested. "You're a person. See? This is your hand, your arm, and that there is your head."

"Yes, but where are my legs? A person has to have legs to be a person. But not a flower."

"You buried them, Mama. Don't you remember? They are there. Just buried. Wiggle your toes, and you will see. They are there."

"I need water," she said. "I am a flower, and a flower needs water."

"Then here, Mama, follow me." And he unburied her, took her by the hand and walked her out to the edge of the ocean. "See there, Mama? Look around you. There's more water out here than you or any flower could ever need."

And without a word, she sprinted out head-long into the surf.

Bohicket knew better than to leave her be, so he stood watch from the waterline for nearly an hour, as she went under and came back up again and again, reaching her leaves into the air and letting the water rain down on her head. It was as if, for a moment, she became that flower, lost in a garden of fading sunlight and waves. Lost, or better yet: unfound.

Bohicket told Aylin all about it when he went to see her that night. And though he still could not bring himself to share what he found his mother cradling a few nights back,

Aylin got a sense of the defeat in his voice, the resignation he was gradually succumbing to, the realization that his mother's cause might as well be a lost one. "First, she's a bird," he told her. "Then she's a flower. And now she's a fish at home in the ocean." He concluded his story with a heavy sigh. "She will go by air. She will go by land. Or else, now it seems, she could go by sea." In his mind, his mother had become strangely elemental in the ways of her grief. "I'm afraid she is going, by one means or another. I'm afraid I'm losing her."

"Don't say that. There's still hope," Aylin protested. "We'll figure it out. We will fix her."

Bohicket was not so sure.

"Yeah but how? When I've tried everything? Everything, I tell you. I've tried everything."

"Not everything," said Aylin, as if struck suddenly by yet another idea. "It seems to me that, if flying is what she's after, why not let her be a bird? If she wants to be a fish, then by God, let her go swimming. And if she happens to be a flower, then let her bury herself feet-first and face the sky. Maybe the question is not what does she need? Maybe the question is what is she after? Maybe that is the question. And maybe that is your answer. Is she a bird, or is she a fish? Which one is she? Answer that. Is she a flower? Maybe then you'll find a solution."

What she was proposing, while admittedly strange, did have an odd kind of logic to it.

"Is she a fish?" she asked.

"No," Bohicket answered. "She's not a fish."

"Then she must be a bird. Tell me; is your mother a bird?"

"Yes," he said. "Chances are, my mother's a bird."

"Well then, why not give her wings?"

Bohicket could not help but laugh at how funny this sounded when he considered the sheer impossibility of what she was proposing he do. "Give her wings? Easier said than done, I'm afraid. Granted, it must be hard for you to believe, seeing as I kiss like a god and all. But despite all the physical evidence here before you, unfortunately, I am not God."

"Ya don't have to be," Aylin replied.

"And then she went and lost me," Bohicket said, lending their conversation a sort of narrative summary. "I mean, I was pickin' up what you were puttin' down, right up to your whole me-playing-God-and-giving-people-wings business. I mean, where do you suppose a guy like me comes across a spare pair of wings? Is there a store I don't know about? Is it called Wings 'n' Things? Or perhaps a farmer that grows a special crop of them? Is there a tree somewhere with feathery fruit? Tell me, love, I want to know. Where would a guy, such as myself, go and find himself a pair of wings?"

"The Flying Men," Aylin said. "Why not them? They have wings."

Chapter Twenty-Three

GOING TO ASK THE FLYING MEN AGAIN FOR THEIR HELP FELT A lot like pressing his luck. And really, it was. That is, what right did Bohicket have to ask any more of them, and what reason would the Flying Men have to help him, seeing as he and his brother had already sent them into hiding once before? So why would they? Why on earth would they agree to help him? Still, absolute necessity can defer the use men have for logic, and a man will try just about anything when he's pushed to the brink. Bohicket was pushed to the brink.

So having already tried anything and everything he could think of to cure his mother over the past few months, Bohicket decided to take Aylin's suggestion and go see them that very night. They rode together in his little johnboat out across the moon-plaid seascape en route to the Flying Men's island home, where he anchored on the beach and then led the way into the heart of the trees.

It was nearing midnight when they finally reached their homes, tucked high away into the trees above. Bohicket offered her a boost. She refused. And together they scaled the trunk of one tree and nearly lost their balance twice, before coming to stand outside Abaddon's door.

Bohicket knocked, no longer afraid of who would greet him.

(Or no longer *as* afraid.)

Abaddon answered after the second knock and swung open the door. A flash of light came from behind him. And judging by the expression on his face, he was just as surprised to see them as they were to be there. "Bea, my dear!" he said. "Always great to see a friendly face! But oh. Oh," he said when he noticed Bohicket beside her. "You again.

Your brother's not here to punch me again, is he? Tell me if he is, so I can be ready. Who the hell goes around punching a defenseless old man anyway? Has he no decorum? Surely your mama brought y'all up better than that."

"Not this time. This time, I come in peace," Bohicket replied with a deliberate smile. "See?" he said and locked both hands behind his back in a gesture of surrender. "See?"

"Come on in then. Come on," Abaddon said. "Come inside." And with that, he led his guests into his living room and, there, offered them a seat. "Want some tea? Coffee? Pick your poison. I got it all, and enough to kill ya."

"I'm good," Aylin said.

"I'm good too," said Bohicket.

"Good is not how I would describe you, young man. And anyways, that wasn't the question. Do you or don't you want something to drink? I'm up, and once an old man is down, he is down. Seems my old bones don't exactly agree with me as much as they used to, these days. So last and final offer. Do you, or don't you?"

Both Aylin and Bohicket said no. And so their host took a seat across from them in his chair, appearing a little suspicious of their motives for being there.

"I have to admit, I'm quite surprised to see the two of you again," the old man started. "We've held up our end of the bargain and called off the dogs. Way I hear it, things have returned to normal. Am I wrong? Don't tell me you've come to apologize again? We men are only as good as our word, you know? Don't tell me you've gone and broken yours already. Don't tell me you've gone and blabbed to those miscreant reporters about us."

Bohicket was clearly restless, which didn't help matters. "No sir. Nothing like that."

"No? Like what then?"

Suddenly desperate, Bohicket struggled to compose himself. He swallowed hard. "It's my mama," he began. And for a while, Abaddon calmly listened to the story Bohicket had to tell, of what had befallen his father and his sister, of the sadness that had engulfed his mother, along with all the various ways he had tried to fix her. "I'm at a loss now," he explained. "I've got nowhere else to turn."

"I see," said Abaddon, stroking his beard.

"We need your help," Aylin added.

"I see," said Abaddon.

Aylin went on to explain the logic in her plan. "This is all my idea," she said. "Way I got it figured, if his mama wants to be a bird, let her be a bird. Sounds silly, I know, but trust me, it has come to that. It has come to silly. Silly me and silly us. Silly plans and silly us."

Abaddon chuckled a little to himself. "I have to agree with you there, my dear. The whole thing does sound a bit silly. And trust me, I've heard my fair share of silly plans. Still," he added, "it appears you might be right. It appears the troubles you got might just call for a silly solution."

Bohicket chuckled then too, but more out of relief than over anything funny. "You mean you'll help us? You mean you will? Oh bless you, bless you! You can't possibly know how much that means to me and my brother. Oh bless you, bless you!"

"Hold on. Now hold your horses," Abaddon replied. "Let's not get ahead of ourselves. Take a breath. Wait one moment. All I've agreed to so far is that your situation sounds a bit silly . . . to say nothing of your plan to solve it. As for me helping you? That's another matter. Come to think of it, I'm not even sure how I can be of any help to you or your mother."

"Birds," Aylin said. "Don't ya see? Birds."

"Yes, my dear, I've heard of them before. I've heard of birds, even seen a few of them flying about, here and there, from time to time," he said. "Yet the question remains: what's that got to do with me?"

"But it's got everything to do with you. Don't ya see?" said Bohicket, clearly growing more and more impatient. "The way I . . . er, we . . . got it figured, the pain of it all has got her all topsy-turvy these days. Up is down, right is left, and the only way Mama has seen clear to dealing with it is reverting to the past, to a younger, simpler time. In her mind, all time is relative. And to deal with the whole wide and terrible thing she's got to deal with, Mama's simply reverted to her childhood, back to a time when, as a child, she had herself convinced that she could fly."

Abaddon considered this for a moment, before responding. "That does sound strange. Just strange enough, I'd say, to be true. I mean, if I know anything about life, it's that life is strange more often than it's not. The stranger things get, in fact, the more likely they are to be true. Just look at me. Take me, for instance. I'm a man, and I've got wings."

"So you understand?"

"Not quite. Ya still haven't told me where I come in."

"The wings," Aylin said. "We need your wings."

"We need you to be her wings."

"I see," said Abaddon.

The seconds that followed next felt to Bohicket like the tick-tock of eternity across the face of a clock. He felt himself growing older with each passing moment. He felt the slow turn of the earth under his feet take shape and give chase. He could've very well lived out his entire life right then and there in that very moment, only to then be reincarnated and live out the dozen or so lifetimes that followed in that same spot. He could feel his heart arresting in his chest, his lungs holed up within his body, just waiting to be freed of the paralysis that accompanies such dreadful anticipation. And he felt, right then, for the first time in his life, what it means to be held so wholly and completely at the discretion of another person's decency.

Abaddon did agree to help them in the end, thinking it

better to have a few more friends in this life than a few more enemies. He agreed to help them because, as he pointed out, Bohicket and his brother had done more than hold up their end of the bargain; they had singlehandedly distracted the prying eyes of the outside world at least for a time. "I will come," he agreed, "and soon. Just make sure she is outside and we can find her."

Bohicket thanked him incessantly, before he left. "Thank you," he said. "Thank you, thank you. From the bottom of my heart, I thank you. I am forever in your debt, good sir. Hand to God, from this day forward, now and forever, I swear, before God Himself, I am in your debt."

And when he dropped Aylin off on the shoreline just beyond the village, later on that night, he thanked her too. He thanked her by kissing her square on the lips so hard and so passionately that he got a sense of her gums pressed into his. Then he returned home that very night, thanking his lucky stars for this one last chance to save his mother.

Now, HIS MOTHER HAD ALWAYS BEEN AN OBSTINATE WOMAN with a certain kind of mean to her stubbornness. Or perhaps she was just downright mean. Not immovable so much, just mean, perhaps because it took a special kind of meanness to survive the life she had chosen. Which, of course, made coaxing her outside a whole ordeal.

At first, he tried to appeal to her admitted fondness for a beautiful day in the great outdoors, and he mentioned, in passing, that the fresh air might do her some good. When that didn't work, he tried inviting her on a walk, an outing on the boat, a day on the beach basking in the sun. "I didn't want to say anything before because I wanted to spare you your feelings. But, Mama, you're looking a bit pale these days. Hey, hey, don't blame me. Don't you go shooting the messenger. This is on you, not me. See here, you're the one who's always sayin' that a Southern girl can be forgiven a lot of things, just not her pale skin. 'Too much sun 'round here for all that nonsense,' says you. 'Too beautiful outside not to take advantage of a dose of Vitamin D. You say that. Not me."

He only managed to get her outside, in the end, by appealing to the mother in her, the mean sort of stubbornness that made her a good and decent mother. "I got a thing that needs fixin'," he told her. "And I won't lie to ya. It's a project. But some things just need a mother's touch. I'm not asking you, Mama. I'm beggin' you. Won't ya help me, Mama; won't ya please?" And when he had her attention, he went on to explain that the storm had left the graves in terrible shape and "it'd be a real shame to leave 'em that way." He told her, "They deserve better," knowing even she could see the sense in that. And later that morning, he walked her out into the heart of the island and, there at the grave site, left her to her devices.

She would need no convincing after that.

Every day over the days that followed, his mother got up at the crack of dawn and headed out into the woods, where she would use up every last glimmer of sunlight, leveling out the earth atop the graves and covering them over with seashells and flowers wrapped in marsh reeds. She then set about carving new headstones and planting flowers at their feet. In no time at all, that plot of land began to resemble a beautiful garden, complete with a winding walkway and a driftwood bench to sit on and gaze up into the wide and ever-expanding canopy of leaves overhead. In no time at all, what she created was her very own chapel of ease, a hallowed place, where she could go to pray over the souls of her husband and her daughter and be reminded always of what she had and what she had lost.

Bohicket spent those days awaiting Abaddon's promised arrival. He took up a perch atop his roof, and there he searched the skies over their house for any sign of the Flying

Men coming. For five whole days, he waited up there. He waited, and he waited, until one bright and sunny afternoon, it happened that Abaddon appeared as promised, and came careening in from down the coast with one of his winged friends by his side.

They did not need Bohicket to point the way to her. Evolution and decades of tried-and-true practice saw to gifting them with a pair of eagle-sharp eyes. Bohicket did not need to point the way to her because they had already spotted his mother from a good mile or so away, and they came swooping down from on high, snatched her up and flew her away into the sky.

Bohicket imagined the delight on her face, the moment she realized what was happening, the stunned expression of sheer terror turned instantaneously to surprise, the moment she discovered she was indeed flying like she'd always wanted to. And he found he couldn't help but cheer them on, as they cleared the tree-line and then carried her out and over the ocean. "Hurrah!" he cried. "That-a-way, boys! Hurrah!" And sitting atop the roof that day, it occurred to him to take a picture, same as he always had, to frame it out with care and craft, consider the angles, measure his approach, no camera, just his thumb and just his finger, eyelids for shutters. And once the timing felt right, he snapped that photo, where it would gradually develop in the darkroom of his mind. He took that picture to remember that moment, that day, the way her wings looked against that afternoon of sun. It was the details that he wanted to remember most: the composition of her body shadowed in light, the specifications of her person being extracted into the sky.

They vanished for a while, out over the horizon line, only to then come racing back in to shore. They circled up and down the length of the coastline, dipping and diving and looping and spinning and, all in all, mimicking the acrobatics of the wind. They were down at the water and then up again. And she let out the most animalistic scream that resounded in his ears like the call of someone in the throes of both some deep apprehension and that frightful ecstasy that comes in discovering any one true thing.

"Ley!" he yelled. "Get your lazy ass out here! This, you've got to see to believe!"

And fearing the worst, Ley came crashing through the screen door and out into the yard in what could only be described as sheer and utter panic. "What?! Jesus Christ. Bo. What is it?! Is it Mama?! Tell me it's not Mama! Is she okay? Tell me she's okay! Is it Mama?!"

"Oh it's Mama alright," Bohicket said and then directed his brother's gaze to the sky.

Seeing his mother being carried aloft like that by two winged men was far worse than he had imagined. "No!" Ley cried out in horror. "What are they doing to her?! Dear God, please put her down! Put her down! Put her down please! Put her down this instant!"

It was all Bohicket could do to keep from laughing at the terror on his brother's face. "Relax, little brother. She's doing just fine. Just look at her. Look. She's up there flapping her wings like she's finally found them!"

It took Ley a moment to take in the whole wild scene, but when he heard his mother giggling like a little girl as she swooped by again, he couldn't help but let out a loud cry of his own.

Inspired by the excitement of it all, Bohicket was down off the roof in a flash. He joined his brother out on the beach, and the two boys went chasing his mother up and down the shoreline together, pitching their hands wildly in the air and cheering them on.

It all made for quite the spectacle, and that's putting it mildly. The boys were just glad to have been there to see it. Imagine, if you will, the whole wide immensity in the heavens right then. Just you try, try to imagine it. Imagine the evening gathering in to occupy her body with more, more, more and more sky. Imagine the celebration the sight of her up there must have ignited in the clouds and the dumbstruck expressions on all those birds that just happened on by. Imagine what it was to bear witness yourself, so decidedly in the grip of gravity, that this strangely winged and misshapen thing, gliding mere inches above your head, could well be another angel taking up residence in the ceiling of your sky.

"She's flying!" Ley yelled. "Good God in heaven, look. Look! She's flying!"

"Would ya look at me now!" their mother cried, as she came skimming down across the surface of the waves. "I told ya I could do it! I told ya I could! Well look at your mother now, boys! She's really doing it! I really am! I'm flying!"

Chapter Twenty-Four

WHEN IT WAS ALL SAID AND DONE, THE VILLAGE HAD SURVIVED the inquest, as had its secrets. The villagers' resolve saw them through, same as it had now for centuries. All the journalists and the detectives and the investigators had given up and returned home, soundly defeated by all the answers they did not find there. And so those islands would return to a kind of normalcy again. And by year's end, the final toll of dead bodies that the sea regurgitated onto those shores would reach seventeen. But the reason this was, the reasons they died and then returned would remain a mystery even to this day.

It would take him some time, but before his eighteenth birthday, Ley would bid the island farewell and never look back. It would take him some time to come to this decision. But once he was positive his ailing mother was well looked after, Ley would set off decidedly to pursue his dream of becoming a pilot, like his father before him.

As for Bohicket, he would not part ways with his home so easily. He had always felt a special kinship with this place. And yet it was not simply his admitted fondness for those islands and their people. Nor was it simply his eternal fascination with their ever-winding waterways that would go emptying out into the oceanic currents and finally over the curve of the earth. Nor was it the honest lies or the falsifiable facts inherent in all those islands' many tales, both tall and true, that kept him there in the end. No, what kept him there really had a first and a last name, the name of a girl who went by Aylin, the girl he would eventually marry, despite the many troubles it would cause them. And though, a few years later, a bridge and a highway would be built, and their island home would be polluted with all the toxicity of developments and cars and the general endangerments of civilized man, Bohicket and Aylin would make his family's house their home and live there together to a ripe old age, seeing to all the needs of the island, out of some sense of allegiance that Bohicket felt to finish what his mother and his father had started. Yes, in time, Aylin would be his and he would be hers. All his. And all hers.

Still, Bohicket would never truly forget his first love, his childhood crush, and would find himself from time to time retrieving that same *National Geographic* from a box just to see the picture of the girl. Only to then be mystified all over again by the baffling nature of requited love, of Aylin's love, which was something he first learned about when gazing upon the young girl's face on the cover. While he understood how strange it was that he could never let this go, Bohicket would always find a reason to return to that photo every so often, as a sort of necessary reminder, not of the girl he once loved, but of how impossibly unattainable that love or any love had once seemed to him. And so he returned to the girl on the cover of that magazine year after year, if only to remind himself of how lonely and isolating it is when love is but a prospect. And before closing the magazine once more, he would take care to mark in his mind the date and the year that love became more than a prospect for him. He would remember the surprising tilt of the earth that day, as if the whole wide sky were nothing more than a ship capsizing in the ocean. He would take care to remember every last detail of the instant he stumbled finally upon it: her sitting all pretty and alone out there on that beach, carving another animal out of driftwood and smiling her way into his life. And so it happened that the girl on that cover of his magazine acted as a kind of continuous reminder to be thankful for the love he had found in Aylin because he was lucky. Damn lucky. You see, very few things on this planet are as rare and precious as the love that the two of them shared. You might even say that, if every great love story is all about yearning, then every great love story and their own love story were really one and the same. And their yearning was so deep for one another that it would never wane. Not once. Not ever. And if what they yearned for was a love so inconceivably lost in one another that it was completely unaware or unashamed of itself, then Bohicket and Aylin got exactly what they asked for. And their love for one another would only grow richer and fuller as the years wound on, until the night Bohicket kissed his wife, told her goodnight and never woke up again. She would bury him the next day beside his sister and his father and his mother, in the same plot of land where he was born and where, to this day, some have it rumored that he goes on yearning for her still, even from the grave.

What's more, a strange twist of fate would see to it that Abaddon and Bohicket would become the dearest of friends. For the remainder of their stead on God's green earth, the two of them would enjoy the kind of friendship that only comes around once, and so by right, should last forever. As for when this peculiar friendship of theirs began exactly, one might say it began that very day, when Abaddon made good on his word and appeared in the skies over their house, only to then dip down and take their mother flying. And one might say it all began when he found the time later to join Bohicket and Ley on the beach as well as the necessary patience to answer all of their questions.

And as it goes, Abaddon sat with them for a while, after returning their mother safely to shore, and there, he took the time to talk with them, even while their mother went skipping off down the coastline, lost in the throes of her own delight. "Sure you can," he told Bohicket. "Sure. Go on. Ask me anything. Can't say I'll have an answer, but you can ask."

So Bohicket asked him the one pressing question that

had been torturing him now for far too long. He asked him whether or not he'd happened upon their father the day he'd drowned and whether or not their father was in any condition to be saved. He asked him if he had said anything worth repeating before he gasped last and died.

Now, if their father was known for anything, it was his penchant for weaving the most outlandish tales, the kind of big-fish stories that no one in their right mind would ever have believed. Still, even though most of his claims were largely unfounded, if not out-and-out absurd, he did have a way of telling them like they were as honest-to-God real as those big and universal truths only experience can teach you. It was perhaps how he'd told them, so assured and confident with an air of authority, or else it was how often he would follow up his claims with some humorous anecdote or another. Take, for example, the time he'd claimed to have hitched a ride on the back of a whale for the better part of a mile out to sea, before the whale wised up, realized he wasn't a barnacle and shook him loose. "It's a whale of a tale, I know," he'd said to them. "But then, what's a whale without a tail? Or a man, for that matter?"

And yet as far-fetched as all of their father's stories seemed to be (particularly now that they were older and a bit wiser), something about the certainty with which Abaddon responded to the question suggested that their father was not the only one given to the curious habit of embellishing the truth. Really though, it was the cool and collected way with which he retold the whole tale that started the boys thinking that their father, when it was all said and done, might've very well been onto something. If not truth, then something in the way of truth and how a lie gets truer the more it's told.

Because, you see, what Abaddon told them was a whale of a tale, by even their father's standards. It too was equal parts true and equal parts false. Where that line was drawn, however, was anybody's guess. Because what Abaddon told them was that he had indeed come across their father that day on the beach, and their father by then was nearly dead. "If I could have saved him, I would have," Abaddon told them. "If I could have, trust me, I would have. Sadly though," he said, "already, your father was as good as gone."

What made his whole story far stranger was how he surmised that their father's body came to rest on that beach at all. "It was the strangest thing, I tell you," Abaddon admitted. "The strangest, most damnedest thing. I mean, heck, if I hadn't arrived in time to see it happen with my own two eyes, I wouldn't have believed it myself. There were fish, you see. A whole school of them. Thousands, perhaps even millions and millions, of them. Minnows and sea bass, tarpon and the like. There was a sea turtle too, if I'm not mistaken. They had formed one giant swirling mass beneath his body, which then formed a current. That, I suppose, is how they managed to carry his body up from the ocean depths and onto dry land. I know, I know," he said, "I know what you're thinking, and I can't say I blame you. You're thinking: this old man is bat-shit crazy or in desperate need of some glasses. And while you might be right—I might be crazy—let me assure you, my sight is as good as it ever was."

"You can tell us the truth, you know," Bohicket said.

"I am."

"We're not children, you know."

"Yes, I know."

"We can handle the truth, you know."

"Yes," Abaddon said. "I know."

Ley was busy burying both of his palms in the sand. His mind had drifted to some far-off place, even perhaps to a place in time, to some place in the past, or else to an image he got of his father's limp body being exhumed from the water and carried onto the beach. Wherever his thoughts might've gone was of little matter when his words became a presence. "I believe you," he told Abaddon without looking up at him. "A man, who respects the ocean, deserves the ocean's respect."

"I agree," said Abaddon.

There was this strange sort of silence that settled in right then, as if to join them in honoring the memory of the dead. It gathered in close and peopled the empty spaces around and between them. It stayed there a while, longer than they wanted or expected it to. But even that did not last long. In no time at all, a loud gust of wind swept in from off the ocean and tousled the heads of the trees above them and briefly played with their hair, before continuing on its way, fragmenting the sunlight atop the water in its wake, and elongating the great distance between them and the horizon.

Bohicket longed to hear the tall-tales of his father once more, to think of the seagulls overhead as doing more than just squawking, to think of them as echoing back one of his father's stories, as voices atop voices repeating the stories back so many times over that they were, at last, made true. He imagined it was so. That the gulls were voices. He breathed it all in, then let it all out, as if relinquishing his grasp on something he'd never quite grasped. "That's about right," he said.

"What is?" Abaddon asked.

"A proper end to his story."

Abaddon nodded in a way that suggested he believed he had done them some good. "Good then. Right," he said. And with that, he started to his feet and opened his wings as wide as they'd go. He flapped them twice and began to ascend.

Looking back on the time Bohicket and Ley spent just sitting there under the closure of that sky, nestling in close to the silence as if together waiting for something to come of it, no longer dreading the silence but allowing a little room for it to take up residence in their lives, perhaps that was when Ley had first made up his mind to just up and leave home someday. And perhaps that was when, at the same exact time, Bohicket realized that he never could. Maybe so. Maybe not. But whatever decisions they did or did not come to that day on the beach, one thing did eventually make itself abundantly clear: something about their mother was different when she returned from her walk. Something about her had changed. For the better, they hoped.

A little later, she would reappear from down the beach. And from the start, it would be clear that the real change in her came by way of how her body appeared to have awakened at the shoulders and how her eyelids seemed to gather in calmly at the corners, as she squinted off into the sun, like a woman who was finally afforded the time to stare directly into it, to pause for a moment and enjoy the setting of her life.

Was their mother ever really healed? In some ways, no. In some ways, yes.

Yes, Bohicket believed. He believed yes, simply because he had to. What choice does a man have, really, but to keep on believing? So, in the end, Bohicket had only to do just that. He had only to keep on believing, if only to endure the gravity of his life. And so that is precisely what he did; he went on believing, Yes and yes, yes and yes. Because the way he saw it, a story like theirs simply must have wings. And in a world like this, where indeed certain men were granted wings, it seemed only fair that women were too. And having been alive long enough by then to see such impossible things made real, the only cost to Bohicket really was the high price of believing his own story was true.

And so Bohicket and Ley remained where they were for a while after that, sitting so perfectly still and looking on, while the dark silhouette of their new friend got smaller and smaller, as he vanished into the distance and, before long, was nothing but a dot, a speck pixelating the horizon, a period to end one sentence and begin another.

For more information on the Gullah/Geechee Nation
and how you can show your support:

Gullah/Geechee Sea Island Coalition
P.O. Box 1207
St. Helena Island, SC 29920
GullGeeCo@aol.com
gullahgeechee.net

Acknowledgments

I would like to first thank my three favorite people this whole world over, my wife Tiffany (truly a woman with wings) and my children Carver Blake and Anilena Pevensie. No one—and I mean no one—deserves the kind of love, inspiration and support that I get from you every single day. My one wish is that all the magic and beauty this world has to offer will be yours someday.

Growing up in a family of ten, stories of family have always been a sort of habitual return for me. And so I would be remiss if I did not thank my mother Ruth-Anne, my father Burke, and all of my siblings, Michel, John David, Andrew, Roman, Claire, Dayne, Abram and Drayton, as well as my Grammie, my Aunt Lynda and Aunt Lydia. You are solely responsible for me falling in love with folklore and magic as a child, whether it was my mother reading us Tolkien, L'Engle and C.S. Lewis, my father making up his "Morpoise and Porpoise" stories or my Grammie recounting the ghost stories and the old Gullah tales she'd heard firsthand living on the Charleston Sea Islands.

To the whole Ciccarelli/Clementi family, my other-mother Deborah Clementi and my other-father Lou Clementi as well as my brothers-in-law and my sisters-in-law, Cary, Louie, Jackie, Jenny and Brandon, your love and support through it all has meant the world. With a special thanks to Courtney Curatolo for saving my eyes and my appendages from certain doom.

I'd like to also thank the SOR crew, Andrew Hammes,

Andrew Svoboda, Willie Cornaz, Ben White, Luis Jackson, Will Deem and Andrew Jones, for being such incredible friends and for always keeping me grounded.

Teachers are the quiet juggernauts in our society, their tireless work too often going overlooked and unappreciated. So I want to also say thank you to Carol Dickerson, Dixie Thompson, Carolyn Deem, Jeanne Leiby, Sheri Reynolds, Janet Peery, Tim Seibles, Michael Pearson and Phil Raisor. People, who do not understand that teachers mean everything, understand nothing. You are all saints in my book. And as a teacher myself, I want to also thank all of my amazing writing students over the years, and the always supportive Creative Writing family I have at the Charleston County School of the Arts.

I'd also like to thank my writer and artist friends, all of whom have been so integral, in every single possible way, to who I am today: Sean Scapellato, Seth Sawyers, Beth Webb Hart, Rene Miles, Anne Cimballa, Justin Baker, Megan Link, Danielle DeTiberus, Marjory Wentworth, Sam Rogers, Mike Rogers, Cat Ellis and Dave Ellis, without whom this whole endeavor (and my sanity in general) would have been abandoned long ago. All writers need an edifying community of artists around them, and I could not ask for a better one. I will never play the lottery because the fortuity that led me to each of you is already luck enough.

Among the predominant themes in this novel is that of rural black and white Southerners surviving on the same plot of land, together with all the stunning horror and breathtaking beauty that has and does comes with that. Someone far wiser than I once said, "the South is the live-wire of the American experiment," and so I would like to thank all of my Southern brothers and sisters who continue to fight the good fight every day.

When it is all said and done, I want nothing more from this novel than to honor the Gullah/Geechee people and their unparalleled storytelling tradition that has been such a large part of my life and such a large part of the fabric of America and Charleston itself. And perhaps then, hopefully, it can help my readers realize the vast importance of helping to protect Gullah/Geechee land and culture. So finally, I'd like to thank Queen Quet and the entire Gullah/Geechee Nation for all the breathtaking beauty you have exacted from your struggles and song.

About the Author

As the oldest in a family of ten, stories of family come naturally to F. Rutledge Hammes. His grandparents moved out to the Sea Islands early in their marriage and made friends in the Gullah community, and he grew up enamored by all the stories and folklore he was told as a child. It wasn't until he was a junior in college that Rutledge decided to try his hand at writing fiction; a proud and pledged poet, he became inspired by the minimalist style of Raymond Carver, Pat Conroy's sense of character and place, and the hard-hitting subject matter of Dorothy Allison. He has long believed that magic is at the heart of Charleston, SC, and so magic must be at the heart of the Charleston novel. Through *A Curious Matter of Men with Wings*, Rutledge hopes readers will see the redemption that comes to people who keep their promises to one another and stand together regardless of ethnicity, culture and class. He earned his MFA in fiction from Old Dominion University, has had numerous short stories, essays and poems published in various journals and magazines around the country, and is a contributing writer in several books. He is presently Director of the Creative Writing program at the Charleston County School of the Arts, the most awarded middle- and high-school writing program in the nation, and is the 2019 South Carolina Arts Commission Prose Fellow.

Share Your Thoughts

Want to help spread the word about *A Curious Matter of Men with Wings*? Consider leaving an honest review on Goodreads. It is our priority at SFK Press to publish books for readers to enjoy, and our authors would love to hear from you!